More praise for
FORMOSA STRAITS

"Rich in atmosphere, the film-noirish *Formosa Straits* works as more than just a page-turner. There are history lessons, speculations about China's national character, and canny references to old movies."

—*People*

"Sweetly sinister . . . A fine chase thriller [with] a cinematic flavor."
—*The Charlotte News and Observer*

"[Hyde] reveals a grit and craftsmanship that are hard not to admire."
—*The Washington Post Book World*

"Hyde writes with brisk, narrative skill."
—*St. Louis Post-Dispatch*

"A ripping tale . . . [that] plunges into intrigue . . . An expert craftsman, [Hyde] makes every word count, carefully constructing memorable characters and, here, a Chinese puzzle box whose innermost chamber holds a politically explosive secret. . . . [An] intelligent and finely wrought thriller . . . This novel soars."
—*Publishers Weekly*

By Anthony Hyde
Published by The Ballantine Publishing Group:

THE RED FOX
CHINA LAKE
FORMOSA STRAITS

FORMOSA STRAITS

Anthony Hyde

FAWCETT CREST • NEW YORK

A Fawcett Crest Book
Published by Ballantine Books
Copyright © 1995 by Tusitala Inc.

Excerpt from *The Red Fox* copyright © 1985 by Tusitala Inc.

http://www.randomhouse.com

Library of Congress Catalog Card Number: 96-96928

ISBN 0-449-22576-3

This edition published by arrangement with Alfred A. Knopf, Inc.

Manufactured in the United States of America

First Ballantine Books Edition: January 1997

10 9 8 7 6 5 4 3 2 1

For my brother, Chris, with love

I want to thank Heather Jon Maroney and Andrew Wernick
for some vital intelligence,
and Phil Tilney for his crucial words.

I can't make head or tail out of you, Mr. Chang. Are you Chinese or are you white, or what are you?

My mother was Chinese; my father was white.

You look more like a white man to me.

I'm not proud of my white blood.

Oh you're not, are you?

No, I'm not.

Rather be a Chinaman, uh?

Yes.

What future is there being a Chinaman? You're born, eat your way through a handful of rice, and you die. What a country! Let's have a drink.

—dialogue, Josef von Sternberg's *Shanghai Express*, 1932

1

I EASED THE DOOR SHUT BEHIND ME AND STEPPED ONTO the porch, but that was as far as I could get. I couldn't move, I couldn't breathe, I couldn't feel my heart. Shock, I thought, that's all it is, just shock. Numb with shock. That was the cliché. But I felt dead inside—as dead as Cao Dai on the other side of the door.

So I waited.

What was I going to do? Somewhere, my mind was deciding, but for a moment all I could do was hang on. Why tonight? *Why had this happened to me?* I felt sick and closed my eyes, concentrating, holding it back. I squeezed them tight shut; as a kid, that had got me through everything, pain, humiliation, everything, just get down into yourself and wait. So that's what I did. I waited. I wasn't sure how long. But then, slowly, my senses came back to me. I opened my eyes; I could feel the rain prickling against my cheek and the Pacific wind cold on my neck, and there was a patch of sweat in the small of my back. Finally, carefully, I managed a breath. My lungs filled with cold, damp air and I could smell the oil smells blowing up from the refineries along the Tan-shui River. I listened; I thought I could hear something near, soft as a whisper, chink, chink, chink, and then, far-ther off, the comfortable rumble of traffic. . . .

But no, that was still shock. My mind was jumping around, filling in the silence where the beating of my heart should have been. *Chink, chink, chink*—I was remembering that from years ago and the comfortable rumble of traffic was straight from a book, yes, the real traffic was hissing by on the Kangting Road just beyond the whispering rain, but I was remembering Los Angeles, some old detective story from the forties, movie stars and private eyes, half a century before homeless people and guns. What a catastrophe L.A. had become. Except I'd give anything to be there now. But I wasn't there, I was here. I told myself that. And now I was thinking again and I could hear my heart and I knew I was all right. *What was I going to do?* Because I had to do something. I had to decide. . . . I was still holding the door, and I looked down at my hand. I was wearing a glove. I'd been wearing a glove the whole time. . . . Did the glove tip the balance? Maybe. But it was more than that. Taiwan, R.O.C., is a reformed police state but it is still a police state, and in a police state, my friend, you learn to steer clear of the cops. Actually, the cops wouldn't even be the worst of it: the General Police Bureau is bad, but behind them is the Taiwan Garrison General Headquarters, the military unit that has long been the real authority on the island—and they'd definitely be involved in any investi-gation of Cao's murder; Cao was easily that big, that important. I didn't want to be "interrogated" by them—if it suited their convenience, God knows what I'd "confess" to. So . . . stay out of it. Don't get involved. Could I? No one had known I was coming. No one had seen me arrive. The door had been ajar, I'd just pushed it open, and then, inside . . . had I taken my gloves off, even for an instant? I was sure I hadn't. Yes, I guess the gloves did tip the balance, for my wrist gave a little twitch and the bolt snapped back in the lock like a bomb in my hand and I jerked away. I stepped back. One step. Listening, I again stood perfectly still in the dark, wet, Taiwan night.

No one had heard me, but I knew I had to get the hell out; to be seen leaving now would look like a confession of guilt. I peered down the stairway. It was wood, shiny with the rain. At the bottom was a small asphalt courtyard, dark and wet, gleaming; everywhere I looked I could see wet dark eyes shining back at my eyes from the night. But I told myself that was just nerves, and I made my legs work, taking a step, then another, growing a little easier for soon I was in the shadow of the building, and at the bottom of the stairs a dripping lilac bush leaned an even darker patch of shadow across my way. I waited there a moment, looking behind me. The narrowing rise of the staircase was like an image in a nightmare; at the top was the door, as black as a cave. But at least I wasn't up there now. And there was no one else in sight, no one at all. The back of the building was dark—as the rain kept falling, I could see the glint of glass in a window, but no light. And there was a door—a moldering spill of trash, then a door—but it was a metal door, like the door of an industrial building. Which was probably what it was, of course, one more part of Cao Dai's empire. And there was no car parked there, nor a scooter, not even a bicycle propped against the wall. How had Cao come? I wondered. Had anything been parked there when I arrived? I didn't think so. No, I was certain no one had seen me, but anyway it was too late for doubts, I just had to get clear. That was it; all I had to do was walk away. But, believe me, that was easier said than done. As I stepped out of the shadow of the bush, into the open, the back of my neck prickled no less than if I'd been in Sarajevo or Belfast or Beirut. But there were no shots, no cries, no sudden lights. I walked across the yard to a break in the wall, then out, keeping my face pressed down into my coat, the heat of my breath pressed back into my mouth, and headed for the shadow of the next building. *Don't run.* It took all my strength, but I didn't. And finally I looked up and saw no one, nothing except the wet halos of the lights on Wuchang Street, shadows of people hurrying along through this wet winter night.

No one had seen me. I could breathe again. It was a miracle; in this vast, crowded city, no one had seen me. No one could possibly have seen me until I came up to the corner. And then I was one wet face in five thousand, or even ten, for the sidewalk was jammed with people, workers, shoppers, tourists, kids—from the offices around Chunghsiao road, or heading toward Snake Alley or movies or restaurants—each hidden from the other in the rain and the dark, and disguised in the flashing neon on the stores, huge banks of neon images and Chinese characters that turned your face red, green, and yellow by turns so you could have been anyone, any race, from any country. Coming out of the alley into those bright flashing lights, I drew a good long breath. Yes, anyone could see me now and it made no difference. I was lost in the crowds and the din: the cars, the taxis, the buses, the vendors shouting their wares even now in the rain. So no matter what I did—even if I ran screaming down this street like a madman—no one would notice me. I'd made it. I was absolutely innocent, but I suppose murder and death touch everything with guilt, and so that was the feeling: *I'd got away with it.* Looking up at last, the rain sprinkling my face, I felt a tremendous rush of relief, and remembered how I'd felt as a kid getting out of the house and into the streets, wandering all by myself, lost in the crowds. That was a kind of freedom and I felt it again now, I could have whooped for joy. Looking up ahead of me, I saw a white face, presumably an American face, and I ducked away instinctively, but then thought, no, no, I was safe, no one knew me, no one would recognize me—especially not him, especially not an American—and I remembered another time, the first time I'd seen a black-and-white movie. I was fifteen, and a bunch of us had gone downtown to an old dingy moviehouse and seen an old dingy movie, something great, I think it was *Wages of Fear.* But now, as that white face passed me by, I don't believe it was the horror or suspense of the film that brought back the memory, no, it was the peculiar pleasure of sitting in the black-and-white dark looking up at that black-and-white screen, for it had created a truly magical world in which everyone had an equal footing. Now, crazily, in this place—for it was as bright as a Kodachrome in *National Geographic*—I seemed to have joined it. I was as anonymous as Yves Montand's stand-in.

I kept walking, letting the relief work its way through me. But my heart was still racing and when I saw, up ahead, a pay phone, I stopped dead in my tracks. *You could still call.* I waited for a second. I worked it out. . . . I'd found the body, I'd panicked and run, now I was calling from a pay phone—it made a kind of sense, at least if you were in Amsterdam or London or Vancouver. But this was Taipei. *Don't take any risks. Don't be a fool.* And so I went on again. But only a block farther along—I was beyond the Chunghsing Bridge now, angling away from the river—I began to feel in my pocket for a coin as I came up to another phone. I wasn't exactly sure what I was doing, I was still getting over the shock—the way the door had swung open under my hand, the strange room, Cao's body, the blood—and maybe, as much as anything, I simply wanted to hear the sound of my own voice, as a kind of proof of my existence . . . I was still that far gone. In any case, I had three dollar coins. In Taiwan, that's enough for three local calls. I picked up the receiver, though I still hadn't really thought who I would call, even made the decision that I would call. The police? "Emergency" is 110. But I wouldn't dial that anyway, I'd phone the Foreign Affairs Department in the police force. It deals with all foreign nationals because of the language problem, and even though that didn't apply in my case, Charlie Li, my father's old lawyer, had drilled it into me as a kid: "You have passport. You take advantage. Take advantage. Understand son Nick?" And that was the smart thing to do, take advantage every way I knew how, and the number was right there on the first page of my book, but it wasn't the number I dialed—it would have been mad to call the police, I knew that, the logic of what I had done still seemed irrefutable, and so without thinking my fingers picked out another number, the number of Laurie's apartment. Laurie runs the office; even though I'd been in Taipei a lot this past year, she was Westcoast Trading ninety percent of the time. She's American, but in some ways is more Chinese than the Chinese. Her Mandarin and Cantonese are as good as mine, her Fukienese is better—when we really get going, switching around, we're rather impressive. Was she in love with me? Maybe I asked the question of her so I didn't have to answer myself, but now all I wanted was to hear her voice, hear my own. The phone started ringing. Laurie's about the only person I know who plays fair with her answering machine. If she's at home, she always picks up, so she must have been out, for in a second her message came on, played through, and I said, "Hi. Me. Nick. Ah, listen, call me. . . . Well actually I'm going to shower now and then I want to go out and pick up a few things . . . but give me a call. Love."

I set the phone down, sweating a little. But it had been my voice, my true self, I'd even sounded calm. And my little mind game had worked. I could feel the anxiety recede, like a wave, and relief came in, another wave. I took a long, deep breath, and really now began to feel like myself again, Nick Lamp, junior dealmaker, all decked out in my navy wool topcoat and my new black gloves, feeling just a touch too elegant in my smooth, gray sharkskin suit—but I'd thought, Look a little like a crook, that's what Cao wants, that's what he expects. I walked on. I walked just to walk—to find my own stride. But then I looked around me, and up ahead, spilling a yellow patch of light across the sidewalk, was a tiny restaurant, the kind you'll find all over Taipei, a street vendor who's rented out a cubbyhole and moved inside. Seeing it, I was suddenly famished. I went in. There were three tables with chairs, two others with benches set up as booths. I sat at one of these, looking out at the street. And only then, as I slid into my place—bending at the waist to fit around the table—did I become aware that there was something in my pocket, a magazine, rolled up tight as a stick, a club. I took it out; it seemed to burn in my hand like a torch. For the magazine had been lying beside Cao's body, an inch from his outstretched hand as he lay on his gorgeous Chien-lung carpet, with his blood flowing like a red river among its scrolls and symbols, its leaves and fruits and flowers, toward the medallion of blossoms at its center. A trickle of blood had been about to touch the magazine, I remembered, and some uncon-scious, fastidious instinct must have caused me to pick it up. Now I unrolled it like a morbid scroll. But it was just a copy of *Asiaweek*, articles about the Singapore stock exchange and Korean steel, a cover story on Qian

Yizhang, the Hong Kong industrialist. He'd been one of Cao's rivals. So rich, in fact, he made Cao seem poor. Had Cao died in a spasm of jealousy? But then I felt a spasm myself, of fear—the magazine was evidence, proof that I'd been in that room—and I pushed it away, pressing it down between the bench and the wall. And then I thought it all through again, what had happened, what I'd done. But it was all right, I thought. I made myself tick off the points, one by one. No one had seen me arrive or leave. A lot of people knew that I'd been trying to do a deal with Cao, but so were a hundred other people. I'd never met him. I'd never seen him, except from a distance. And his call this afternoon, right out of the blue, had been made personally, almost secretly; not by an aide, not from his office. I was sure of that— because I hadn't believed it was him. He'd insisted, irritated, his old man's voice caught up in the phlegm in his throat, spitting his anger down the line, "Cao, Cao, you want see me don't you? I knew your father eh? Okay. I see you then." My father had known him years ago, before the war. . . . How old was Cao? My father had been dead for six years now. Cao was a little younger, and from what I could gather he was still going strong. But that's why he'd agreed to see me—my father—but I was sure it had all happened on the spur of the moment. That had been borne out by the time he'd appointed and the address he'd given me—at night, and not at any of his offices or his home or a restaurant, but in that apartment which you could only describe as a "love nest," everything Chinese red and peacock blue, lacquered as bright as a whore's face. His dragon room. He was known for that; he was in his seventies at least but he had a relatively young wife, an actress, and bought women by the score. Presumably that was where he took them. And where he'd asked me to come. Confidentially. In secret . . . Yes, the more I thought about it, the more certain I was. No one had known I was going there and no one had seen me, and I'd left nothing behind. Routine police investigation would never discover the slight personal connection between us, so all I had to do was walk away. I was home free. Did I feel a reflex of guilt at my failure to do my civic duty? Maybe. But I kept it under control. This wasn't my town. Besides, it was a different kind of society with different duties. *Don't get involved.* That notion didn't originate in a New York tenement but a Chinese village. The Chinese are great mothers and fathers, wonderful uncles and aunts, marvelous grandmothers and grandfathers, but lousy citizens. Citizens of what? China has meant too many different things over too many centuries, and all the Emperor brings is pain and death and taxes. I was out of it—I was *well* out of it.

Right then, that was what I decided, and so I ordered a bowl of *niu-rou-mien*, sucking down every last noodle and tipping up the bowl to sip the last drop of broth. And that was so good I ordered another, and then I had some tea. I drank that more slowly; its warmth ran through me, the taste cleaned the other tastes out of my mouth. I sat quietly, feeling better now. Outside, the world moved on. That seemed incredible; I got up. I told myself all I had to do was pay the bill and find a cab. Tomorrow I'd read the headlines, "Cao Dai, Billionaire, Murdered!" "Taiwan Industrialist Shot!" I'd go to work as usual, pretend nothing had happened. A few days would pass. One deal had fallen apart, but there are always more deals. And then a week would be gone. Would I dream? Would I have a nightmare, a haunting of dark alleys running with blood? I doubted it; I don't dream much and anyway dreams always come to an end. I could hardly feel guilt for Cao Dai—I remembered what my father had told me about him, murders, drugs, gambling, whores, treason, extortion, every kind of fix; if I lived a thousand years, I would never see the evil he had seen, do the evil he had done. In ten days I was heading for Hong Kong and by the time I returned the police, the newspapers, and myself would have gone on to other things.

Yet—this was the strange thing—it wouldn't let me go. All I had to do was walk away, go home, forget about it. But I couldn't. Not quite. You just can't forget murder that easily. And there was something else. As I stood outside that little restaurant, I sniffed the air and smelled the damp, sour stench of the city, the rain, the cars, a million Orientals, and—now that my fear had passed—a whiff of excitement too. That came off myself, I caught the scent of my own skin, my fresh-shaved face, the starch in my collar, some lingering richness in the silk of my suit. I was *up*. And as I walked down the Kangting Road with ten thousand other people, possibilities seemed to open in the darkness ahead of me, questions kept asking themselves. Most of these were obvious, such as who had

killed Cao, and why. But that wasn't quite it, something
else was afoot. Cao's death, I was certain, had nothing to
do with me. I'd gone there hoping to do a deal with
him—the old man's family was one of the most powerful
in Taiwan, maybe all of Asia—but from his point of view
I was at the level of a kid peddling lemonade from a
stand. So I couldn't be involved. Yet something was happening, conceivably something huge, and I was at the
edge of it. What was going on? For me, in every way,
tonight had been a disaster. Cao had been my trump card;
or, to shift the metaphor, I'd been cashing in a huge
chip—his friendship with my father in prewar Shanghai.
Now all that was lost, but the funny thing was I didn't
feel anger and disappointment so much as excitement. I
was on the edge of something big, some vast opportunity.
I had no idea what this could be—there was nothing specific in my mind—and maybe it was only the adrenaline
that was still racing through my veins, but I couldn't
stop, I couldn't just leave it. I had to do . . . what did I
have to do? It was still a question, apparently. But for a
time I didn't know the answer and just kept walking
through the black slick streets. Then, turning the corner
at the Kangting Road, I realized I was heading back
toward Cao's alley. I stopped. Was I crazy? But looking
around I saw a phone booth, and that gave me the idea,
which I suppose should have been obvious enough, and I
picked up the receiver, dialed the police—the regular
police—and with an accent that could have come out of
the toothless mouth of an old lady in Chungshan Market I
told them the old man was dead in his whorehouse, told

them where, and then hung up. I was quite calm. Well ...
I'd done something. For someone, somewhere, I'd set the
cat amongst the pigeons. I'd played out my bit part in the
drama, even if I didn't understand the plot. Slowly, I
walked away from the phone. There was no one around. I
turned into Cao's alley. It was dark, the rain still hissing
down. I looked at my watch and saw it was now five
minutes to eight. I was astonished; my original meeting
with Cao had been set for seven o'clock, so almost
exactly an hour had passed. I cocked my ear, listening for
sirens in the distance, but for the moment the only living thing I heard was a cat. Then I was up to Cao's building, looming in the night, and I stepped back into a
shadow across the road from his wall. I kept listening,
but after a few moments, when I still didn't hear anything, I began to get a bit antsy. There was no sense
being stupid about this; I'd done what I could, now I
should get the hell out of here. And I began to turn away,
but just then, at the top of his stairs, I caught a slight
displacement of the night. A movement. And as the
sounds of the city died for an instant, I heard two quick
hard taps on the wood of the steps. I held my breath. I
was paralyzed. I stared. But I remembered the shadows
that fell across the stairway and my eyes moved, as if
on their own, and focused on the gap in the wall just
as a figure appeared there. A woman. Somehow, I was
certain of that. Then I heard a snap, which I knew was
the catch of a purse. A light flared. Her hand was trembling, but she was lighting a cigarette and in its glow I
saw the frightened face of a young, very beautiful

Japanese woman—who, I suddenly realized, must have been in the apartment just as I'd been standing above Cao's bloody corpse.

2

WAITING FOR THE SOUND OF SIRENS, I FOLLOWED HER through the night.

That was instinct, a reflex. Everything depended on no one's having seen me—if she had ... My head began spinning with the implications. I'd been so sure. But she must have been hiding. That was all I could think—she must have been hiding in the back, then she'd started to leave and heard me come up and ... But it didn't make any difference how it had happened; it had. *She'd seen me.* And then, in the distance, I did hear the sound of sirens wailing in the night—but were they coming here?—and for a moment I came close to panic. Emerging on the Chunghsiao Road, I was overwhelmed by the lights, the crowds, the traffic. What an irony. Only an hour earlier the busy streets had seemed a sanctuary, but now everything was reversed and negative, the film was frozen. Then my desperation deepened—I lost sight of her. But she'd only stepped off the curb to flag a cab. I just had enough wit to raise my own arm and grab the one after hers.

In the cab, however, I began to get myself together: I suppose the terror of a cab ride in Taipei will submerge any other fear. My driver was the usual maniac, crazed with culture shock; he wore a John Deere cap, the seats were boudoir pink, and Michael Jackson whined from the tape deck. Chen Chung-kuang, he was called, which translated into something like "the Always Brilliant Chen." And he was, in his own mad way, cutting off buses, running a red light, and almost taking out a whole family—mother, father, three kids hanging on like possums—on a motor scooter.

"Don't lose it," I said, pointing to the cab.

He laughed. "Like in the movies."

"That's it." Then, in English, I muttered: "Follow that cab."

He laughed again. "Hey, man, I speak English too."

"But keep your eyes on the road," I said in Cantonese.

"No, no, speak in English. I like to practice. Soon I'm going to head for the States. I have a game plan, all worked out. I will start in the East. Graceland. Then the West. And then California."

Graceland. Well, why not? "Hollywood," I said. "You like Bruce Lee."

"Okay, but not just Hollywood. Pebble Beach too."

He chattered on and I leaned back, deciding I couldn't keep up with him—although, despite everything, he was keeping up with the Japanese girl's cab. I became a little calmer. I now realized how lucky I'd been. If I hadn't finally called the cops and gone back to Cao's alley, I would never have known about the girl at all. Then, as we skidded through the night, it also occurred to me that maybe I'd been jumping to conclusions. The girl had obviously been coming from the apartment and she'd been trembling, fearful; she must know Cao was dead. But wasn't it possible that she'd arrived after I'd left, and hadn't seen me at all? That gave me a kind of hope, but as we headed north up the Chengte Road, I couldn't make up my mind. Cao certainly had women in that apartment—that was the point; but somehow I doubted that he'd arrange a meeting with me while he was entertaining. On the other hand, if she'd come after I left that meant she had a key, and would a man like Cao ever grant such a privilege? No, not with his suspicious mind—the carpet he'd died on had been worth a fortune by itself. . . . She'd seen me. She'd seen me not. Like a screwball parody of a lover I went back and forth as we kept on, north, then farther north till we left the city proper and entered the suburbs, lights sparkling like stars in mean, ugly galaxies. Finally we turned into a concrete maze which I actually recognized, Tienmu. The girl's cab slowed, then stopped at the corner of a short, dark street with five low-rise apartment buildings. She paid off her driver and went into the third of them.

I handed Chen the money showing on his meter and told him, "Wait."

"Stand by," he said, "right here," then he opened the door—his cab had one of those levers that the driver works, like a bus.

I stepped onto the curb. I waited a second. Now that we'd arrived, I had no idea what to do. That was a different panic again. So she'd seen me, or maybe she hadn't, but what was I going to do about it? I thought, To hell with this. Just get to the airport. Get out. For a second, I was close to that. My life seemed to be fleeing me, rewinding into the night; Miss Smith in the second grade—the only teacher I ever liked—a trip to Hawaii we'd all made when my parents got settled, various girls, various drunks, a square in São Paulo, that whole incredible stretch in South America looking for oil . . . I was more or less the black sheep of the family, the only one of us who didn't go to college, but South America had given me the best education anyone could have. Now it made no difference. Nothing did. Everything was being swallowed up by one question, *Had she seen me?* I had to find out. I didn't know how, but I had to, and I went up to her building. The security was simple, no doorman, barely a lobby; just a speaker and buzzer system. The girl was in 436, she had to be, for there was only one Japanese name on the directory: Yuki Yamoto. I reached my thumb out toward the button . . . but then stepped back. Because now I thought of something else. *She hadn't called the police either.* Which meant . . . that she hadn't seen me? Possibly. So all I would do by going up to her place was reveal myself to her. At which point I realized what I actually had to do was more complicated: I had to discover whether she'd seen me without letting on that I knew who she was, that I knew she'd been in Cao's apartment. Which made me back off. Through the door. Until I was on the street. Then down the street, heading back to Chen. But a moment later I turned around and saw the girl coming out of the building. She'd come home—but now she was leaving again.

She turned the other way, which was lucky, because I was close enough to catch the tapping of her high-heel shoes and glimpse her small, smooth profile above the turned-up collar of her raincoat. And it was also lucky that she didn't see Chen—for it quickly emerged that she was looking for a cab herself. . . . I wondered why she hadn't kept the one she'd come in. In any case, when I waved Chen up, and we followed her along, she led us about three blocks over to a little shopping area with a cabstand. She got right into a car; everything about her said she was in a hurry. We started off again. But backward. South, down to the city. And I had the feeling I was descending, moving off an orbit down to some strange planet; there was a science-fiction feel to the way the traffic moved, the way the lights streamed past. Taipei, Taiwan. On pink satin sheets I was entering a dream world. A never-never world. Or at least part of the place is like that, one aspect of it, a world between the West and the East, the world of sex and vice, movies and advertising, music, neon, drugs, fantasy, and it is only in this world that the West still has any influence at all. The Chinese love playing the roles in our old movies, speaking our old lines. Our clothes. Our styles. Hey, man. Okay. Whiskey and tweeds are still British, even here, in a way the steam turbine has long since ceased to be, and a Chinese girl's tits, somehow, know about Marilyn and Madonna and even the porn girls, yes they acknowledge them, even though electrons moving down a wire are as Chinese now as chopsticks. In any case, as the streets went by, that's the world we went into, Sugar Daddy Row, the area around Shuang Cheng Street near the President Hotel—an old R&R area from the Vietnam War, the equivalent of Bangkok's Patpong District or Manila's Ermita or Seoul's Itaewon. Yuki. Yuki Yamoto. I remembered the girl's name from the apartment as the car rocked me back and forth in that seat, as Eric Clapton rocked out of the tape deck. She belonged here. Of course she did. She was one of Cao's whores—no wonder she hadn't called the cops. And when her cab finally stopped we were up a narrow street of bars and restaurants. As she got out and paid the driver, I caught a flash of silver sequins under her raincoat, and then she disappeared down a lane beside one of the bars. It was called the Lucky Lotus and was a kind of Taiwanese nightclub, a wine house or *jiou-jia*, which meant she was a *jiou-nyu*, for which "hostess" will do as a translation. She'd come to your table and drink and laugh, drink and laugh—and then, if you paid enough, you could take her out to drink and laugh some more.

I paid off Chen and stood a moment on the sidewalk. It was raining very slightly, just enough to put a slick, coated-paper gloss on the night, the sidewalk, the neon, the reflections in the windows, Chen's cab as it disappeared around the corner. I thought about Chen. He'd remember me, and remember the girl's address. But so what? How could he identify me? Not easily. And there was no connection to Cao. So that was all right. But the girl, definitely, was not all right. Whoever she was—

whatever category of "domestic help" she fell into—the police would find her; she was too beautiful a woman to go unremembered. And if my presence came out then . . . almost anything was better than that. I was better off going to the police even now, in fact I even had a little card to play. I knew about Yuki Yamoto. Maybe she'd called someone from her apartment—for some reason, the fact that she hadn't kept the cab seemed funny to me—but she certainly hadn't called the police, and I could tell them that, tell them she'd been there. I actually considered this seriously for a second, but just then I had an odd piece of luck, a small coincidence. Not that it meant anything; all it did was make things a little easier: I could have gone in by myself—there would be a bar where "loners" could drink—but a *jiou-jia* is really set up for groups, six, eight, ten. It's that kind of experience, Oriental macho in the worst way, boys with fat bellies and fat wallets pretending to be men; the whole bunch of you pile into a private room, with a big table, and then the booze and the girls are brought in. But now, as I was standing there deliberating, with the neon and the rain flickering over my face, listening to the sad sounds of loud music leaking around the doors of the bars—what is grimmer than vice once the tourists get hold of it?— another cab pulled up and four Americans got out, one of them bawling, "Harry, how in hell do we get back to the hotel?" and then stood on the sidewalk looking lost and a little foolish. I went right up to them—now I didn't hesitate—and said, "Hi, how's it going?"

They looked startled—at hearing intelligible English, I

suppose, or perhaps fearing some kind of con—but then one of them laughed. "Well we're not exactly sure. . . ."

I said, "One of you gentlemen's Jack Carson? Chase Manhattan?"

Then I began to wing it, making up a story played off the doubt in their faces. I gave them a name, said I worked for Chase Manhattan and was supposed to meet some clients for a little wining and dining but it looked like I was being stood up. And then I capped it off by pulling out a card, which a kid from Chase had given me the week before, and they all laughed, "Hey we can play this game too," and began pressing their own cards on me, everything spelled out in characters . . . because that's one of the points Americans are always briefed on when they come to Taiwan, the way Chinese swap their business cards around. I only had the one, of course, but they hardly noticed; in fact it all worked out. Harry or Jack or Ken, one of them, said, "Look, you give us the tour, we pick up the tab—how about it?" and so we went in together, conducted by the liveried footman through embossed brass doors into a big gaudy room with a red lacquered ceiling, green dragons, and golden lotus blossoms everywhere. The entrance hall was as noisy as a market, and once they got into a private room my companions began adding to it, hoots, hollers, rebel yells— one of them, I think, was from Alabama or wherever the "Razorbacks" play. I'm certain they were drunk before they sat down, but I quickly made sure of it. Shao-Hsing. Kaoliang. Bai-Gar—which is 150 proof; they were game for anything. Even the food . . . I got into the mood and fed them snake soup, turtle stew, sautéed eel, black-fleshed chicken. Supposedly, they're all aphrodisiacs. "You eat that stuff you'll sure get it up, but I don't know that it'll ever come *down*." They laughed at that. They laughed at everything. They loved me—whoever the hell I was, because after the first half hour I forgot the name I'd given them. Not that it made any difference. Because, by then, we were ready for the girls, the *jiou-nyu*. You pay a set fee for each one who comes to your table, and they spend about twenty minutes and then move on. They were gorgeous, as whores can be; when the first batch came in, there was actually a hush among my mob. Small, superbly coiffed, dressed all in silk and satin and with makeup as hard and smooth as *chaussée-poignée*, they had the smell of pussy you can buy but will really have to pay for. The first group was all Chinese and I was soon busy translating. All they do is talk, in fact—they don't strip; it's not like table dancing; and you keep your hands off them. Instead they tell jokes and little stories, a few even sing: however remotely, they're the descendants of concubines. We had great fun with the first lot, and then a second; soon my new friends became even more boisterous and found they could get along without me. So they weren't noticing me as the third group paraded in—with Yuki second through the door.

I suppose places like the Lucky Lotus have it all worked out; after a couple rounds of Chinese girls, a bunch of Americans might get a little bored. Accordingly, the third batch was exotic, a Thai, an Indonesian, a Filipino with Spanish blood still showing in her high,

slanting cheeks—and Yuki, the Japanese. She was
lovely, despite her getup: a high-necked red satin dress
splashed with sequins that was sheer from her throat to
her navel, too much makeup, too much perfume; Cao Dai
had chosen well, or, more likely, someone had chosen
well for him. She was the color of champagne, immaculate, graceful, but with enough pout in her face to make
her sexy as hell. Her eyes, even without the black false
lashes and green shadowing, were huge. I watched them.
Her gaze, a hint more aloof than that of the other girls,
moved easily around the table, over our faces, came to
me and . . . I'd been wondering about that moment. If she
recognized me, what would she do? But now I met her
eyes and there wasn't the slightest flicker of recognition.
I was sure of it. . . . True, she was a bar girl, a working
girl, she saw a hundred faces a night, the sweaty sheen on
their skins a glare that burned her eyes, their hot liquored
breaths suffocating the air she breathed. When she
looked at me, all she expected to see was another customer. But that's all she *did* see. I caught her eye and
stared. All she did was smile. I was absolutely certain.
She'd never seen me before in her life.

Relief washed over me; I could feel myself go limp,
sweat flushed from my skin. I could have whooped for
joy and in fact it seemed I suddenly couldn't stop
laughing—I'm surprised no one noticed the change in
me. I was even so bold as to put my arm around the Thai
girl, but turn to Yuki and say, "All Americans here. A
good Japanese can get all their money." At which she
laughed, and replied, "You must be polite"—I wasn't

sure whether she meant this as an admonishment to me or
a clue to her own strategy. And as the tension flowed out
of me, I could even feel the liquor start to work. I'd been
doing a little drinking; there was no way to avoid it. As
the local man, I was pushing the more exotic concoctions
like Chu Yeh-Ching—light green, a hint of bamboo—
and Wu Jia-Pi, dark and sticky, full of medicinal herbs
and yang. Now, in a nice sort of way, it got to me; for a
time I didn't have a care in the world, and some time
went by, a little time, the girls moving around the room,
the men laughing and yelling and drinking, but then I can
remember one of the Americans saying, "Christ, I
wonder if you could take one home?" He wasn't speaking to me but to one of his friends, whose reply—an
emphatic, negative motion with his hand; a hard rasp in
his voice—got through to me: "Don't even think about
it." But of course you could think about it and that was
the moment the idea came into my head, or at least the
moment when I began to think about what happened
next. Nothing had to happen. No, no—I was out of it. I
was home free now. And yet . . . was I?

The liquor now worked to give my mind an edge. I
watched Yuki. Watched her face. What did she know?
Those big questions I'd thought of earlier came back to
me again. Something big was going on; it touched me, it
touched her—but what was it? The question drew me on;
I couldn't quite leave it. I wanted to walk away . . . in fact
I got up, left the room, I did walk away, but I went down
to the toilets. The room echoed with laughter, the inane
hee-haw laughter of Chinese men on their own, shaking

their pricks out of gray silk suits but backslapping each other like hillbilly drunks. Leaning forward, I pressed my forehead against the cold tiles above the pipe and told myself to get out, now, they wouldn't even know I was gone. It was all over. There was nothing to fear. But as my piss splashed into the bowl I could see Cao Dai's red blood flowing across that glorious carpet, that Oriental landscape of totems and omens, symbols and spells. *I'd picked up that magazine and not even known it.* What else didn't I know? Something. Everything. And there was a lot *to* know. So I went out, and upstairs; at the top of the stairs the rug was so thick I seemed to be floating. And maybe the liquor had something to do with all this, but really I was intoxicated in a different way, I felt heady with something else. All the same, I had no fixed plan but then I saw a page—that's what they usually call them, and he was gussied up like some fool of a flunky in front of a British hotel—and I called him over. Because, you see, you can take those girls home. You pay off the management—a "takeout" fee, a kind of corkage charge—and after that it's between you and the lady. It was still early in the evening; that put the fee up—two hundred U.S. I gave him. Then I made my way back to the room. The girls were just switching over, Yuki was coming out. I told her what I'd done and she gave me a look, because you're supposed to do it the other way: get the girl to agree, then pay off the boss. But I already had money in my hand—too much—but enough too much to make it all right. She nodded. "Outside?"

I waited in the drizzle, blinking in the same wet dark

that had met me at the top of Cao Dai's stairs. The same night. The same rain. Nothing had changed. . . . Then she was standing beside me, holding her raincoat closed at the throat. "You have a place?" she asked.

I shook my head. "Your place."

We got into a cab and she gave the driver an address, though not the place I'd followed her to.

"Those Americans—your friends?"

"Not really."

"I like Americans."

"Yes."

"But they can be dangerous. They never know what they are doing so you never know what to expect."

"But you always know what they want."

She laughed. "Me? Yes, I always know what they want." Then she laughed again. "Sometimes, though, I'm surprised that they want it."

Her Chinese was okay, but she hadn't been born to it. We rode on in silence. I looked out the window and the night worked through me, everything that had happened, the wet city shiny with its lights, the liquor, the fear. But it was a different city and I was a different man. The car drew up. Yuki got out. And I was conscious, as I paid the driver, of her standing on the sidewalk in the rain with her body and head turned away, waiting, that this was a professional posture assumed a thousand times before. She was there; she was not there. And as I came up to her, at the precise moment when we might have been together, she turned away: she was with me, she was not with me. Her high heels tapped on the cement walk, grit grated beneath the sole of her shoe as she stopped at the door. Did I have my head down? Rain prickled the back of my neck. She had a key. We entered a dark, sour lobby. There were three doors and she went up to the middle one. She had another key.

"Where is this place?"

"A friend's. It's all right. A friend from the club."

I wondered if she was suspicious. But more likely it was convenience, a regular swap; or the girlfriend might get a cut. She flicked on a light but was already moving, "In here," across a small hall into a dark, cramped living room. I could see the bright light from the hall through the doorway, but here she only turned on a table lamp, which filled the room with shadow. A couch. A coffee table of metal and glass. "You can sit down." A wall unit with a bar, shelves, slots for the stereo. She switched on the television. A man was reading the news; a map of Korea, then footage of Kowloon. Shadows flickered in color. But there was no sound. Sitting, I felt my body, stiff with tension. A muscle in my thigh began trembling, twanging like a string. She had her back to me and I heard a VCR sucking up a tape, the television went to snow, and then there were images of Americans fucking. "Okay? I'll be back in a minute."

She went out of the room and I relaxed, letting my head loll back, my eyes lazily turning all on their own to the screen. A blond California kid, all oiled muscle and tan, slipped his cock into the smooth red mouth of a blond California girl. In Taipei, Taiwan, R.O.C., I could hear water running. Then I thought I heard her brushing her teeth and I thought how extraordinary that was, but my attention drifted and I watched the screen until Yuki came back. Yuki Yamoto. She'd changed her clothes. Now she was wearing a wrap, a purple kimono with a pattern of white Japanese characters, hard to see, wound around her body, but I think they meant "peace and prosperity." She sat down beside me—but a little away from me.

"It is best if we decide the money first."

"Of course."

I got out my wallet. I gave her some bills. "How much do you want."

"Everything."

"Then a little more."

When there were no bills in my hand she nodded and turned away—I suppose she put the money some-where—and then leaned toward me, and down, so she was so close to me her hair brushed my shirt; but I couldn't see her face. She opened my belt. She pulled down my zipper. But as she bent her head lower I said, "Not like that."

She leaned back and looked at me with an appraising glance. What was she thinking? What did she know? What did she expect? I was sure now that she didn't know me, that she truly had never seen me before. But that didn't make any difference now—I'd seen her and I had to know, I had to know it all.

Reaching behind her, she found a cushion and tossed it to the floor by my feet. And that was a temptation, God knows, in every way. To have her kneeling there—she would have been all in my power. But I'm not like that, I never have been—worse luck. With beautiful girls, I either love them or admire them from afar; and so, as she made a little move to go down, I reached out and seized hold of her arm so tight that she grimaced with pain.

"I want to know everything," I said. "I want to know everything about Cao Dai."

3

CAO DAI.

Christ I must have looked fierce. I was going to kill her. I could see it in her eyes. She was going to die, she knew it, she was looking into my eyes and seeing the eyes of her killer and she looked away. Any lingering doubts now vanished; she had no idea who I was, she was even too frightened to figure it out, to figure out what it meant that I'd seen *her*, and I rammed it home. Before she could think. "Tell me. Now. I know you were there. I saw you come out."

"I didn't."

I shook her—"Yes."

"I didn't."

"Yes you did. I saw you. I followed you. Number 436. You live in number 436. Tell me. You have to tell me. Did you call the police?"

She shook her head. "I called Ito."

That's why she'd gone back to the apartment, to call Ito. . . . But who the hell was Ito? Except I didn't want to ask questions. I didn't want her to doubt me. I knew

31

everything, I was in total control—that's the way it had to be. And so I said: "Never mind Ito. Tell *me*. You have to tell me everything. When did you go there?"

"Early. Ito came and got me early."

"And he took you there?"

"Yes."

"Why early?"

"I don't know. Because someone was coming. Cao wanted . . . to do it. We were in the bedroom. But then someone came up, before we started."

"Who came?"

She was almost in tears. She shook her head. "I don't know."

"You do."

"No. I never saw him. I don't know who it was. I stayed in the bedroom."

"But you heard them talking."

"Only a little. I was watching the television."

Now, on the television, the boy had the girl on her side, almost turned onto her belly, with her leg folded back, California Dreaming, I thought, and I remembered someone calling this position the Mongol rape, I couldn't think why. But he leaned forward and I could feel myself lean forward with him, pressing it home. "What were they speaking?"

"Cantonese."

"So you heard them. You see? What did they say?"

She was shaking her head, desperate. Her face was wet. She was so frightened she could barely think. I tried to calm her a little and lowered my voice. "It's all right.

Just tell me what you heard—as much as you heard. That's all."

She turned away from me, looked at the television; even now she couldn't stop watching it, I couldn't stop watching it, the face of the girl on the screen registering the boy's movements inside her. She was rapt. Her eyes closed. It was bliss. And it was real enough to hold Yuki's attention and she worked to get hold of herself. She grew calm, she swallowed, and then she said, "They were just talking, I think. But then arguing. They were talking about a man from Shanghai, a long time ago."

"How long ago?"

"From the time of Mingxing, he said. I don't know what he meant. And Tian Han. He said other names too. . . . I think Butterfly Wu, something crazy like that. But I couldn't hear."

"But Mingxing was the man from Shanghai?"

"No, no—I don't know. I don't think so. Cao Dai said he had known someone a long time ago, in Shanghai, and now he was seeing his son. His son could be useful. But I'm not sure who it was—it wasn't important—"

"All right." I hesitated. The man Cao had known in Shanghai, the son who could be useful—that had to be my father and me. But how could I be useful to Cao? "What did he say about this man from Shanghai?"

"Nothing. I swear it."

"But what was his name?"

"Cao didn't say. I didn't hear. I don't know."

"The other man, though . . . the man Cao was talking to—who was he?"

"I didn't see. I don't know."

"But you heard his voice? Had you heard it before?"

"Maybe. It might have been a man . . . I don't know his name. They were arguing. Cao was angry—I could hear his voice. Cao said he didn't want to, but he had no choice."

"He didn't want to do what?"

"I don't know. How could I know? The other man tried to calm him. He said they could do it. There was no need to worry."

"But this man . . . he must have killed Cao?"

"Yes . . . I'm not sure. I said I didn't see. I didn't see anything. Another man came—"

"Another man?"

"Yes. I'm almost certain. They stopped talking. I had the TV on, but I thought I heard a noise, a gun. . . . Then I couldn't hear anything and I almost called to Cao, but finally I waited. I was going to come out. But then I heard someone else, very quiet, coming up the stairs. I was frightened then. I thought they were coming to look for me, I thought they knew I was there. So I hid in the bathroom. I stayed there. Finally I came out when I couldn't hear anything and I found Cao, lying on the floor. I didn't know what to do. So I ran—I just ran. And then I went home and called Ito and he told me to say nothing had happened."

She stopped. She was out of breath, as if she'd lived it all through again. I looked at her carefully. Her face didn't give much away. All I could see was her fear, her fear of me, and of all that had happened this night. Of course she was lying. Dogs bark, snakes bite, whores and cops lie. "I ran—I just ran." No; I'd seen her lighting that cigarette—she'd been afraid, but also cooler than she was pretending now. Still, I was sure, in a general way, that she was telling the truth. She'd gone to the apartment so she could call Ito—that's why she'd let her cab go— and then he'd told her to carry on as usual, so she'd gone to her job at the club. Of course, being a whore, she'd also called Ito because Ito, somehow, meant money to her. But that had nothing to do with me. She clearly had no idea that I was the man who'd come up the stairs, who'd frightened her into the bathroom, and she had no idea that I was the son who might be useful. How? Why? But those weren't questions for her. I leaned toward her and took her arm again. "And that's what you did? What Ito told you?"

"Yes."

I leaned back. "Good. That's exactly what you should have done. It's all right, you see. There's nothing to worry about. Forget everything. Forget Cao. Forget me. Forget everything. You understand?"

She nodded. I stood up. Behind her head, the tape had run out, the TV flashed a random, hissing pattern of static. I went out the door and didn't look back. And I never saw her again.

4

IT WAS OVER.

I leaned back against the seat of the cab.

And then everything let go; the tension broke and fatigue rolled in, like a wave over a dam. It was incredible. I suppose, these past few hours, I'd been running on pure adrenaline. And the booze, at least a little. Now I felt close to passing out and I turned, pressing my forehead against the cold glass of the window. For a second I just held on, leaning there. Outside, the city went by, yellow lights and darkness, then more lights. Finally my head began to hurt where it was pressed to the window, and I leaned back against the seat again. But I still felt awful; and then the motion of the car began to make me feel sick, and eventually it got to be too much and I told the driver to stop. I stepped out of the cab into a dark, ugly industrial neighborhood. I wasn't sure where I was. It must have been someplace on the other side of the river beyond San Chung City, though it made no difference; I just walked around aimlessly, trying not to think. The rain cooled me down. I trudged up a long hill, my wet pants clinging to my thighs, and at the top I looked back toward the city, and as I watched the lights dancing in the black waves on the river, I began remembering South America, the way the burning gas from the wells reflected in the lakes, as though the lakes were on fire in the night. And I remembered the sound of the camps, the hard laughter of the men in the dark, the radio that was always playing too loud, the endless chug of generators, the soft hiss of the water leaking around couplings in the pipes, trickling and pooling in the mud. What a time that had been. Years ago. But it made a certain sense that I should remember it, for it had been a time of exile—I'd felt as lonely then as I did now. It had also been a great gamble—I wasn't coming back unless I made it—and I thought, not for the first time, that what I'd learned there, more than anything else, was how to gamble and win. Well, I was gambling now. Back then, I'd won with a mixture of luck and nerve, picking up some oil rights in a deal that was just this side of legal. *Just this side of legal.* But that's all you need, isn't it? I'd done it neatly. Remembering it never did my ego any harm. And now, as I walked out my exhaustion, I also recalled how the story had made my father laugh, launched him on stories of his own. Of course, that had been a major part of it, as important as the money; I'd been proving something to him. I still was. I always would be. What the hell—that's what sons do—and it occurred to me that my father had understood this perfectly, had known it all along. "Someday," he'd said to me then, "you'll go back to Shanghai."

"You've never left," I'd told him.

He'd smiled in a hard, rueful way he had—the smile of a gambler toting up his losses. "Aren't we all sons of the Yellow Emperor? And you know what they say . . . our souls live in our villages."

It was true—my father's village was Shanghai—and maybe, if tonight had worked out, I'd have taken a step in that direction. But tonight hadn't worked out. Still, walking, I was calming down, and then the rain began falling harder, so I found another cab—in Taipei, there are so many cabs you can even get one in the rain. I still felt lousy, though. Everything was catching up to me. I wasn't drunk, but I could feel the liquor rolling over in my gut. And now that the night was passing, I remembered how it had started, with the horror of Cao's bloody body in the middle of that carpet; I admitted to myself how horrified I'd been—I'm not squeamish, but dead bodies are not a regular part of my evenings. But I tried not to think about it, rolled the window down, kept my mind on the city passing by, the lights and the dark. And I kept telling myself I was safe. I went over it again and again, like a priest saying his beads. No one knew that I'd seen Cao. *That* was my luck this time. No one. Laurie knew that I was trying to, that I *wanted* to—but she didn't know that he'd called because Cao had phoned me at home, at my hotel. And no one had seen me at Cao's apartment. If she thought about it, maybe Yuki could work out that I'd been there, but she wasn't going to think about it, she was going to keep her head down. Just like me. Yes, absolutely, I was safe, I had to be, and if I could get through the next hour, even the next twenty minutes, it would be over.

Or that's how it seemed. So I watched the city. And I felt I could have been watching a movie, it was so remote, unreal. But then Taipei is like that even if you're not half-dead with the exhaustions of murder; it always looks like a photograph of some other place, Tucson, Tokyo, Toronto. Any twentieth-century town will do. Nothing grows old here, things just wear out and get replaced with something new all over again—you never look at a building and see the past, a hint of a movie theater in the facade of a restaurant, old warehouses done over into lofts, old signs showing through the paint. No character, people say . . . actually that's not true, it never is, you just have to know where to look. In Taipei, you look up the lanes, along the riverbank, under the loading ramps. Where, God knows, I'd found it tonight. But now I just kept staring at the darkness and worked at not being sick, and finally we were back in West Taipei—downtown, more or less—and then we came up to the bus terminal, which was where I'd told the driver to take me. People rushed around, and no one noticed anyone, let alone me. I got out. A ten-minute walk. Then it's over. I steadied myself. I was still feeling bad, but the cold, sharp rain kept me going until I reached my hotel.

My hotel is nothing, just an eight-story office building with beds instead of desks in the rooms; there are a thousand like it in Taipei. But it's cheap, central, and—by now—an old habit.

I crossed the lobby. Longchen, the deskman, gave me

a nod, then went back to his girlie magazine. That was par for the course. I spend about six months a year here and they hardly notice me now. The elevator came. Upstairs, there was no one in the corridor. So, despite everything, I'd made it. I almost collapsed as I stepped into my room, but I kept going and hung up my clothes. And there was still some hot water left, so I stood under the shower until it ran out.

But I knew the day wasn't over. I was exhausted. But something was running inside of me and it still hadn't stopped. I knew I wouldn't sleep; there was no point trying. So I put on my bathrobe and went over to the window. I was surprised, somehow, but really it wasn't that late and the city was still on the move, cars tracing out the wet streets, lights in buildings drifting high above the misty dark. I tried to relax. Say this was a film, I thought. Nick Lamp, businessman, stumbles into Taiwanese murder. . . . I could see how the scene would play. The camera would move slowly through the reflection of my face in the window, dissolve into the mysterious night, and the music would come up. This was the moment when I was supposed to think about the meaning of life, wonder why all this had happened to me. That was certainly a question to ask. But I didn't really fit the part. I've always been prepared to let the meaning of life take care of itself, since the answer doesn't make any practical difference. Or not usually. The only trouble was, I kept thinking of those moments, which had drawn me along, when I'd sensed larger forces at work, the sense that I was at the periphery of something much bigger than I could imagine. And my instinct hadn't been wrong. I knew nothing about Cao's death, yet somehow it touched me—in some obscure way, which I didn't understand, I'd been important. It all did have greater meaning. Yuki had been confused and not entirely believable, but at one point I was sure she'd been telling the truth. *Cao Dai said he had known someone a long time ago, in Shanghai, and now he was seeing his son. His son could be useful.* Well, I was the son. How in hell could I be useful?

It was a curious question, no matter which way you looked at it. Something must have changed, something must have *happened*, to make me useful *now*. Because there was a little history to all this. Until a year ago, my company had been largely a trading operation, but I'd wanted to go beyond that and, after a lot of looking, had bought the North American rights to a special kind of tire. It's designed for construction equipment, Bob-Cats, graders, front-end loaders, and so forth. It's solid rubber—actually a synthetic composite—and comes in pieces which bolt onto a special rim. So you can't have a flat; even if part of the tire is damaged, you simply bolt on a replacement section. That can be a tremendous advantage. With a conventional tire, a flat puts your machine out of action—but you still pay the operator—and you generally have to go miles to find a new one, which then takes special equipment to put on. Since a lot of construction equipment is rented, this can be a nightmare. So, it seemed to me, I had a better mousetrap, but of course there was a competitor, an Australian company with a similar product. To beat them I had to keep my costs down, and that's where Cao Dai came in; he had tire-manufacturing plants all over Asia. I'd worked out a careful deal, a generous deal; but it was no deal—I couldn't get any response. I'd thrown in a kicker, the sole license for the entire Canadian market—which I was sure would appeal to him since, through a front, he owned the biggest chain of heavy-equipment dealerships in British Columbia. In any event, I'd worked up both the offer and my approach very carefully, using contacts here in Taipei, but also in San Francisco, Vancouver, Singapore, and Colombo. And certainly I had used my father's name, because he'd known Cao, even if I wasn't certain how well. Despite all this—here was the point—I'd made absolutely no progress. Letters received noncommittal replies, telephone calls weren't answered. Until tonight, that is. And the call had come from Cao himself. Why? What had changed? What had happened? Why had I suddenly become so useful? Out there, in the city, I'd been right; something very big was going on and it touched me—even if I didn't understand why, or how.

Five minutes later, I was no closer to understanding—and then the phone rang. I hesitated a moment, but why shouldn't I pick it up? I had nothing to fear. Still, my voice came out as a croak. "Hello?"

"Hello? Nick?" It was a woman. She must have sensed my uncertainty. "It's me. I'm downstairs. I got your message."

Laurie. It took me that long to recognize her. Had I left her a message? But of course I had, I'd phoned from the street after walking away from Cao's place . . . but she'd been out. Where had she been? The question was somewhere in the back of my mind, but I could only stammer, "I just got in." I sounded inane. I couldn't seem to help it. "I just got out of the shower."

"I called a while back, but I had to come over this way so I thought . . . why don't we go have a drink."

I felt a rush of queasy panic, though whether that was from the prospect of more liquor or seeing her, I wasn't sure. But I knew I didn't want to go out. I couldn't face that. At the same time, I couldn't turn her away. "Why not come up?"

"Sure."

Laurie Stadler was thirty-two, which made her younger than me, but not too much younger. I'd met her two years ago in Hong Kong. Something very nice had almost happened between us, but we hadn't been able to do much about it because she was traveling with her mother. She'd spent most of her life in the Far East. Her father had been a U.S.A.F. colonel attached to the Nationalist Chinese Air Force, and a personal friend of Chiang Kai-shek's; after he'd retired from the military he'd become some sort of adviser and stayed in Taipei. So had the mother, when he'd died; in fact, she'd only gone back to San Diego, very reluctantly, about eighteen months ago, because of a heart condition. Laurie had returned with her, but once the old lady was settled she'd come straight back here and shown up at my office, looking for a job. It was ridiculous, really; I couldn't pay her half what she was worth—she knew Taiwan, China, the whole Far East, infinitely better than I ever would: law, languages, customs, the works. But she liked the freedom, she said; most of the time, she ran the whole show. And of course there was the personal side. But that was interesting—I was no longer quite sure what it meant. In Hong Kong, if conditions had been different, we could have had a very good time, an old-fashioned fling. But we hadn't; and now—my latest theory—we were either going to have something more or nothing at all.

I opened the door to her, and she came in, a little damp from the rain.

"I listened to your message," she said, "and I called, and there was no answer, but I had to go out, and I just kept walking . . . and look where I walked *to*."

It was obvious that something had happened. Some crisis. She was all on edge. Of course it had to do with me; it must. But, God knows, I wasn't in any condition to deal with it. I took her coat. "Really want a drink?"

"Yessir. I *really* want a drink."

I didn't. I couldn't face it. I poured her a whiskey in the kitchenette and called behind me, "I'm going to have a vodka tonic," which was actually all Schweppes. I came back into the room. She was perched on the arm of my chair and I handed her the whiskey; she took a sip, then a slug. It obviously wasn't her first tonight.

She smiled.

"You okay?" I said.

"No. I called my mother."

So that was it. "Trouble?"

She shook her head. "Not really. No more than usual." She shrugged. "She was drinking. She started *me* drinking."

"Okay," I said, pointing. "That one, plus one more. Then you're done."

"You're the boss. . . ." She took a quick sip of her drink and slid off the arm of the chair. "She should never have gone back."

"I was never sure why she did. The doctors are just as good here, and a hell of a lot cheaper."

"I know. I suppose she didn't really understand how completely she'd settled here, how much she loved it. She'd never been here, you know, until she married my father, but at the end I think she loved it as much as he did." She took a couple of steps and had another sip of her drink. "They both loved this place. It was part of what kept them together, even though they didn't exactly love each other."

"It's a lot to have in common. Maybe you shouldn't be so sure that they weren't in love."

"Don't worry, I'm sure." She lifted her glass and her forefinger made a quick, negative motion. "But that wasn't necessarily, *directly* the issue . . . if you know what I mean. I mean, they were married. He was in the air force and they were married. . . . It was like that."

"Right."

She was standing in front of the mirror. Turning her head, she looked at herself and now she was speaking to her own reflection. "I always understood why she married him, but I've never been sure what he wanted. It was always so hard to tell what he felt, under that uniform."

"Uniforms are like that."

"Yes. Like those guys at the Shrine. Do they feel anything at all? No. No one standing that stiffly at attention could feel a thing. . . . Uniforms. That's it. They're *uniform*, aren't they."

"Yes."

She nodded. "I'm like that, too, in a way."

"I don't understand."

"I mean . . . I'm beautiful, aren't I?"

"Yes."

She was still looking into the mirror, and now her hand, holding the glass, pushed at her hair.

She went on, "I'm beautiful, I know it, but the trouble is I have that very *American* beauty. It's too regular. Too uniform. Like a model or one of those women on morning television. They're all the same. Nordic blonds. Thirty-five . . . not to be *too* vulgar . . . twenty-eight, thirty-five, not to be too vulgar again. Perfect. But all exactly the same. I can never tell them apart. I can never remember them. You know what they say about blacks—?"

"Yes. Or Chinese."

She turned back toward me finally, and smiled. "Exactly. That's me. People see me and they think, She's gorgeous, but the next day they can't remember my name." She finished off her drink. "Hear anything from Cao?"

"No."

It was that abrupt, the switch. And I'd lied. And Laurie knew I'd lied. There was one beat of silence in which we both knew it; I could see it in her eyes and she could see it in mine. But isn't that one way it can start? We had a secret. I knew I had to seal it, before she could say anything, before I could say anything. And she must have known what was happening because she dropped her glass, just dropped it right on the floor as I stood in front of her and caught her hands at her hips and held her. I leaned down and kissed her. She was right there, all ready. When I took my mouth away, she pressed herself against my shoulder and whispered, "I guess that's what I came for."

But I still didn't say anything. This was something that had to be *done*; it was the doing that meant everything now. I had to possess her. To betray me, she'd have to betray herself. That was the idea. Or that's how it started. But then it was more, I was saving myself from this night, the horror of it, the blood, the fear, the sex in that bar, Yuki—the fear in her eyes as she'd looked up at mine. What had I looked like? I was saving myself from that, I felt love again, and it was like some memory, terribly lost, that you've found again. She was beautiful, whatever she said, I would never forget her, not her breasts, full and perfect, soft and white; I could never forget them because they were the breasts I'd been searching for all my life. I loved her breasts and she knew it, and began moaning with the pleasure of it. She was reaching down stroking me and moaning . . . but not so far gone, as I spread her legs, that she couldn't murmur, "Nick, it's been months, months and months . . . I'm not using anything. . . . You wouldn't have . . . ?" I had a safe in the drawer of the bedside table. She was sweet. She put it on. And maybe I was surprised at that, but I believed her, she hadn't had a man in a very long time. Her hips were frantic; she moved like a woman who's desperate to feel, but afraid to feel, hysterical, frightened—just a touch of that—but I slowed her down and then it was fine. She moved with me. She moved all on her own. And when she kissed me, for one sweet moment I forgot it all, there was only her, and when I remembered again I was at least able to lose my panic in her. It was lovely. Crazy, but it was about as good as it can be, and at the end I swear I almost passed out with my arms around her.

She was right there with me, kissing me, holding me.

We lay together for a moment.

I felt I was in love with her but my heart was beating at the bottom of some terrible well. And I couldn't speak.

And then she whispered, "You're coming out," and her hand slipped down between us and kept the safe from coming off inside her. Then she eased it off, and began kissing me, and her fingers were playing with me. She whispered again, "I love it, I love it." She meant my foreskin, I think; she was playing with it, sliding it back and forth over the head. . . . She came up and kissed me but she kept my cock in her hand. "I love it," she said again. She kissed my face, traced her tongue along my cheekbone. "You're so handsome. I love your eyes." And then, whispering now in Cantonese, she said, "I love you."

I held her. Then I fell asleep. I thought Laurie did too. I slept for about twenty minutes, so deeply I might have been dead. When I awoke the lights were off, except for a yellow glare coming out of the bathroom; and I'd been asleep long enough that I shielded my eyes. Laurie came out, turning, seeing me; and then seeing I was awake.

"Hi. I've got to go."

"No. Don't be crazy."

She came over and sat on the edge of the bed and kissed me. "Really, I have to. I wish I didn't—" She bent down and kissed me again. I could smell her wet raincoat. I tried to hold her, but she patted my arm. "No, tomorrow," she said. She got up and blew me a kiss. "It was wonderful, absolutely wonderful." And then she disappeared in the dark and was gone.

I sat up, confused—why had she left?—with sleep still clouding my mind. Then I felt uneasy. I didn't like it. . . . I wasn't sure what I didn't like, but I didn't like something, not at all. Something was going on. Something was going on all around me which I didn't understand. But all at once I didn't have the strength to understand, even to try. It was too much. It was all too much, this night, and suddenly I could taste the liquor working at the back of my throat, I could smell it, and I staggered up, stumbled into the bathroom, ducking my head against the brightness, reached out blindly for the basin, and then sagged to my knees in front of the toilet. I closed my eyes. But it was no good, I could see the blood spreading across the carpet and I could smell the oily stink of the river as I'd stood in the rain, and it was all coming up, all of it, the broth and the noodles of the *niu-rou-mien*, the liquor from the club, the yang, the Chu Yeh-Ching as green as bamboo . . . I puked it all up like a dog or a drunk in a doorway and leaned there, gasping, almost wishing I was dead.

For a couple of minutes, I stayed there. But I felt better, the way you always do. Getting up, I leaned over the basin, turned on the taps; and as I ducked my head down to the water, I caught a glimpse of myself in the mirror. But I couldn't bear to look at myself. And after I'd washed my face and rinsed my mouth, I leaned back against the wall, knowing that if I just turned my head, I'd see myself, but I couldn't bear to look. What was going on? *You're so handsome. I love your eyes.* My eyes and my face, which were so much like my father's. *The man from Shanghai.* Whose son I was. *How could I be useful?* But those questions were all too much, at least for now, and my mind eased away, and a memory came drifting back to me. I'd been thinking of my father so much tonight, and now I did again. I must have been very young. Because this was in San Francisco, where I was born, where we'd lived before they headed north. My father was going out; he was standing in front of the mirror, adjusting his tie, his dinner jacket—"tuxedo" was a word he did not allow—and I'd been watching, thinking he didn't see me. But of course he did. And staring at the image of his face, which was now so much my face, he'd said, "Always remember, you are Han Chinese, but not *just* Han Chinese." Then he'd turned, and bent down, and pointed to his eyes, my eyes. "Always remember, our eyes go back to Genghis Khan. Never forget it, little Nick—we are part of the Mongol Hordes." He was looking very serious, but in that way I already knew meant that he was telling me a joke. So I'd laughed, and he'd laughed; then, tux or no tux, he'd scooped me up, set me on his shoulder, and carried me off to bed.

5

THE NEXT MORNING, WAKING UP, I FELT BETTER THAN you might have expected, probably better than I deserved. Which is to say, I felt only half-dead. It wasn't exactly like a hangover, more the way you feel after a week when you've been steadily drinking too much. I was exhausted. Flat. Like a cartoon character who's been run over by a steamroller. But it wasn't that bad; I knew I was going to survive. It was just that I still didn't want to look in the mirror, I didn't want to look at my face. *Losing face.* Chinese are obsessed by that, and maybe I'd lost some face with myself. So I showered, passed on a shave, pulled on my clothes, and went out. There's no restaurant in my hotel. And I guess it says something about my state of mind that I walked down to the Chunghsiao Road and went into the Hilton—which has the best orange juice, the best scrambled eggs, and the best American-style coffee in Taipei. What I wanted that morning was to start all over again with something I understood.

But I didn't understand much.

Of course, in a sense, that was question number one. Did I want to understand anything at all? Sipping my coffee, I watched a group of Australian businessmen trying to be polite to their Chinese counterparts—anxious bewilderment among the Aussies, determined patience on the part of the Taiwanese—and worked it out. Cao had been murdered. That was the central fact. Despite my blundering, I was now confident that I couldn't be tied to the scene of the crime, but—subsidiary fact—I was nonetheless involved. There was no other way to interpret what Yuki had overheard. Cao had reversed himself, and agreed to see me, because I might be "useful" to him. But how? Something occurred to me now which I'd overlooked before. Yuki had overheard Cao talking about me to his visitor, the same man, presumably, who'd killed him. Could that have been the reason for the murder—to prevent Cao from seeing me? It was hard to believe but it almost looked that way—though it all depended on who Cao's visitor was. I tried to remember everything Yuki had said, wishing I'd asked her a lot more questions. All I really knew was that the visitor had been Chinese, or at least they'd been speaking Chinese— but then if you overheard me speaking English, you'd assume I was white. Presumably, he was also someone Cao knew, since he'd been welcomed into the apartment and he and Cao had apparently been talking amicably for quite a while. Then—*after I'd been mentioned*—the visitor had turned into a murderer. Could you draw a conclusion from that? Maybe. But only maybe. I hadn't been mentioned by name, for one thing, and how could I be so important without knowing what that importance was myself? There were too many blanks. And there was a fair chance, I decided, that none of the blanks would ever be filled in. I'd picked up the papers on the way over—the *China Post*, the *China News*—and there wasn't a line about Cao, or any other murder. Of course you could explain that because of the time; I'd called from the pay phone sometime around eight, and by the time the police arrived it could have been too late to make these early editions. But it was probably more complicated. Cao was very, very important; the police would naturally proceed cautiously. There'd be political checks; the police at the scene would do very little until they had clearance from higher up. And certainly nothing would happen until Cao's family was consulted—and they would already have been alerted, you could bet, because Yuki had called Ito, Cao's pimp. I could just imagine the phone calls, conferences, meetings. And everyone's first instinct would be to play it down. The rich, everywhere, hate scandal, and maybe rich Chinese hate scandal more than most. I certainly would have bet a lot of money—regardless of what finally came out—that the public would never get a real description of that apartment, and they might not hear how the old man had died at all. Which, all in all, was okay with me. But not *entirely* okay. It was crazy . . . last night, all I'd wanted was to be clear of the whole mess. Now that I was, I kept feeling a tug—what was going on? how was I connected? What "use" could I have been? But I told myself those questions were both dangerous and unanswerable; I was out of it, and should stay out of it. I'd had my share of breaks; what I needed now was to use my common sense.

With that in my mind, I left the Hilton and took a cab to my office, which is a little north, not far from the airport (Sungshan, the domestic airport). It's a mixed area, with a lot of light industrial and service companies; I like it because it's cheap and an easy walk over to the bars and restaurants along the Chungshan North Road. But this is the old Taipei, 1950s ugly—like Frankfurt, say—and my building is a seven-story Kleenex box. I'm on the fourth floor: reception, two offices, decent teak furniture, and the pine scent of Glade air freshener—Miss Ping Ong insists. But that is her only failing. That morning, as every morning, she greeted me with her usual rosy countenance and happy smile. She's a joy; one of those Chinese women who's never quite lost the round, happy face of a child. Her life revolves around her family, working for me, getting rid of her acne, and the lurid love life of her friends. She was now in seventh heaven, the new lotion had eliminated all but three spots on her chin; and Laurie still hadn't come in.

"She's having her hair done, I think."

"Great."

"Guess why!"

"I couldn't, Ong."

"I think a new boyfriend, Mr. Lamp!"

"And who would that be?"

Ong giggled. "I won't say! You won't hear it from me!" She giggled again. It was an astonishing sound; you almost thought it was a put-on, playing up to some sort of image, a stereotype of the Oriental she felt she ought to fulfill—like a black kid grinning for the white folk. But it wasn't that. Chinese kids still have real childhoods, they actually get to be children, and learn to be polite, adult, which means they also learn to be embarrassed and ashamed and curious . . . and giggle, a pleasure Ping Ong still indulges in.

She followed me into my office.

"There was a fax from your brother, Mr. Lamp."

Since this concerned "family," Ong had separated it from the business correspondence, though it was actually routine: my older brother's monthly communication from Los Angeles. He's a lawyer, Arthur. Then comes Alistair, a chemical engineer in Houston. Denise, a nurse, hasn't worked since she moved to London—her husband is a financial journalist. Barrington is an accountant in Kamloops, B.C., which was where my parents retired. I'm the youngest. As usual, Arthur was worrying about my mother, who lives in a retirement home in Vancouver and refuses to move to Los Angeles and stay with him. I've long held that Arthur protests too much and would panic if she ever did head south, but then, as the youngest, I'm likely prey to evil thoughts. In any event, I dealt with all this, moved Ong along, and then got on the computer.

We keep the machines running all the time, but there's a password; I logged on, and began checking through all our files on Cao.

Of course there was no point pretending that we—I— had had no contact with him; there was too much evidence at the other end, faxes, letters, phone messages, two detailed business proposals. But I decided to err on the side of caution and began to check whether any of this might excite police interest if they came across it. To begin, I found a whole subdirectory of correspondence. Some of this was recent, but most was addressed to an executive named Lin Mao-sheng at Cao's corporate headquarters, head of their planning group. I couldn't see why anyone would notice them; they probably got dozens of similar items a day. But I'd sent four letters to Cao personally, two within the past six weeks, and since both mentioned his connection to my father, they stood out as a little odd—especially, I had to admit, because I couldn't be clear about what the connection was. That was a saga on its own—how well had my father known Cao?—and led me to three faxes I'd exchanged with my brother Arthur, who's now more or less the family historian. They didn't seem particularly incriminating. Yes, he vaguely remembered Cao's name coming up, a minor figure in stories about Father's life in Shanghai during the thirties, before the Japanese came. Cao, he thought, had been wild, a playboy, a financier—how Father always described himself—but also a gambler. "Of course, he always told those stories to shock us, and tease Mother." Right; in my father's accounts, Shanghai was a cross between Dodge City and Paris, with a touch of Weimar Berlin thrown in. He concluded by saying that I shouldn't trouble Mother about it, but that's just what I'd done—"remembering" is never any trouble for her at all—and I still had her letter in a file. I dug it out. She'd written, for some reason, in English, an English that was all her own, touched by the accents of missionaries' sermons, servants' gossip, the offerings of colonial thespians. She had never met Cao. She reminded me that she and Father had only met in Hong Kong, after he'd left Shanghai, "and right away, you know, he began working to get us to India, thank God for that." Yes, or I probably wouldn't be here—my parents would have died in a Japanese camp. But then my father was always politically astute, he could always see what was coming, and having seen the Japanese march into Shanghai, he didn't want to see it again. By December 19, 1941—when they indeed marched into Hong Kong—he was happily settled with my mother in Bombay, where he spent the war as a translator for the British navy. Still, he went back to Shanghai in 1946—he'd made a lot of money there—and that's where Arthur was born. "Your father was always very careful though—he was such a naughty man!—never to introduce me to friends from his bachelor days. So I only ever heard a few stories about Cao, how he loved gambling and also actresses. I will speak ill of the dead: some people said that he seduced Patty Rhodes, who was in the Dramatic Society, and that she had a child. Who knows? You say he is in Taiwan and I'm not sure, but perhaps your father helped him. We had no fear of the Communists of course, they wouldn't hurt a British subject, but for a man like Cao, it was quite different. (Perhaps I am mistaken, but I think he was under a cloud because he'd gotten on well with the Japanese in the war.) Anyway, I vaguely remember that your father helped a number of friends get into Chiang Kai-shek's army, which meant they were taken off in boats at the very end, or at least that's what people told us—we were already back in Hong Kong by then, because I was having Alistair and then Denise. Really, I don't know much more than that—I'm afraid I can't be much help at all." She was right, it wasn't much; and on the basis of what she'd told me, it certainly hadn't been easy to work up a nice, diplomatic, ingratiating introduction to Cao. *Dear Cao Dai, My dad knew you back in the good old days in Shanghai, you know, when you were a bit of a crook and a cocksman. . . .*

Other members of the family had been rather more helpful. Gus, my sister Denise's husband, had spent two years in Hong Kong with the *Financial Times*. He'd sent me a long analysis of Cao Dai's business empire, and I'd scanned it in. He didn't pull any punches. Cao, in fact, was a crook. "You remember that line of Balzac's, *behind every great fortune there is a crime*? In Cao's case, there must be a dozen of them. I expect the biggest took place when the Japanese were in Shanghai, 1937–45, when some people say he helped the Japs push heroin (as opposed to opium) as a way of weakening and demoralizing people. I've checked around, and the Japanese certainly did this, but they generally used Koreans. Anyway, he apparently got on well with the Japs and a lot of those tire plants you're interested in were originally taken over from Japanese owners just after the war. Some people (again!) say that he got them cheap on the understanding that they'd later be able to buy back in; I don't know about that. But there's no doubt that the huge development he's putting together in Shanghai has Japanese money in it, just a minority interest, but he still has those contacts. . . . My advice: be very, very careful." Gus had also turned up the fact that Cao owned a number of Canadian heavy-equipment dealerships, and I'd asked Barrington to check it out. He had; he'd even made a special trip into Vancouver; and a lot of faxes had gone back and forth. At the time, I'd thought it was quite a coup, and eventually I'd worked it into my offer. Now, reading everything over, I wasn't so sure; it all seemed less than discreet. So I tagged every one of those files—and every other file with personal stuff on Cao, especially the material my family had given me—and erased it. And I mean "erase": even Peter Norton wouldn't get it back.

For a moment, I sat back, trying to remember the name the Japanese had given their empire during the thirties and forties. Then Laurie opened the door. Always, before, she would have knocked. She'd had her hair cut—incredibly short.

"It's beautiful. You look gorgeous."

"You're sure?"

"Absolutely. Totally. You're the most beautiful woman in Taipei. Formosa. China!"

That earned me a kiss. Then she whispered, "I wanted everyone to know, without actually saying anything."

"Miss Ping Ong knows."

"Well of course she does. But that's okay. Next week, she'll be on to something else."

"Maybe even business."

"Speaking of which . . . just now . . . when I came in. You were thinking something."

"I was trying to remember that name . . . what the Japanese called their empire, during the war."

"The Greater East Asia Co-Prosperity Zone . . . no, Sphere."

"Right."

She cocked her lovely, new, glossy head. "What's going on?"

"Nothing."

She was looking at the computer. "Are you in some kind of trouble?"

"Am I?"

She came closer. "Bigger than you know."

We kissed and then she dabbed my mouth with a Kleenex. But I decided I wanted more and I was kissing her again, but very softly, and through her blouse I could find the soft shallow mark of her spine. I pressed myself against her and she pressed her cheek into my shoulder. She was wonderful; I realized—I suppose it's what you always realize—that I'd never been in love before. Then, after a moment, she murmured, "Mary Williams."

"Mmh." Mary Williams was a friend of hers; she taught at the Taipei American School.

"We're supposed to have dinner tonight."

"Okay. . . . But give me a key. And I'll be at your place when you get back."

She pushed away from me and kissed my nose just as

Ping Ong knocked at the door—and called out, "Come in, Ong," which was definitely my line.

Ong came in, her round face set to register any emotion at all, as long as it was extreme; and we all ended up laughing, and when Ong blushed Laurie began blushing too. Finally, thank God, the phone rang, and Westcoast Trading began operations for the day.

Everything went smoothly until about twenty past ten, when I went around the corner to a newsstand.

I wanted to see if there was anything about Cao in later editions of the papers. There wasn't, not a word. But as I turned away, a magazine caught my eye. It was *Asiaweek*. It took an instant to make the connection, but then I remembered that this was the magazine I'd taken out of Cao's hand as he lay dead on the floor and hidden in the restaurant.

I bought a copy. There was something funny about it. This was *Asiaweek*, and the magazine I'd taken from Cao had been *Asiaweek*, but they weren't the same—different editions? Probably. Cao's was an old one; this was the latest. But it made me think—I told myself to forget it, but then I wasn't so sure. Do fingerprints stick to newsprint? Probably not. Except this was fairly glossy paper. . . . And maybe it had an address label on it. Say it was found in the restaurant. Then the police would try to work out how it got there, which would lead them . . .

I still hadn't made up my mind what to do—if I should do anything at all—but I hopped a 502 bus and rode it downtown. By the time I got to the station, I was feeling edgy. Maybe I wasn't sure of my own motives, whether I should really be worried or if I was just indulging my curiosity. But I was supercautious. I walked through Wuchang Street, past all the cram schools, then headed over to the river, then south again; a very roundabout way to get to that restaurant. By the time I reached it, I was sweating a little—last night was coming back, the taste of the noodles, the wet city streaming past outside the window—but I went in anyway. Brown, impassive Chinese faces looked up at me. I sat down. There was a smell of steam and soy. The faces turned away, but I could feel them watching me as I sipped my tea. I could feel them watching me as I slid my hand into the crack between the seat and the wall. . . . But of course they weren't watching me, what did they care? And I found the magazine without any trouble. It was all rolled up, tighter than a Brit can roll an umbrella, but I smoothed it out—as though I'd taken it out of my pocket—and I began to read.

Right away, I knew something was wrong.

It was weird. I compared it with the copy I'd just bought, and they had the same date but were completely different. I began reading an article; all the photos and captions were about new steel technology, electric furnaces, minismelters . . . but the text of the article was all about cellular phones. It was so weird, because really there wasn't anything sinister about this, but I knew—

What did I know? I knew something very strange was going on, that's what I knew, and that this magazine—however remotely—was a connection between Cao and myself. So I got out of there fast. Two blocks away, they were digging up the road, and the workmen had built a fire for themselves in an old oil drum. I didn't hesitate; I threw the magazine in and watched it burn, a piece of ash fluttering up in the breeze. Then I found a cab. As I sank back into the seat, I realized my shirt was damp with sweat. I thought about the magazine. I didn't like it; I didn't understand it, but something was going on, and it was way over my head. And when I got back to my hotel, the waters closed in. For the first time ever there was a man sitting in that chair in the lobby—and Chou Li, the day man, had a funny look on his face.

"You are Mr. Nicholas Malcolm Lamp?"

"That's right."

He was tall, wearing a trench coat belted tightly at the waist, as if a typhoon might be blowing outside. He was civilian, he had credentials from the Foreign Affairs section of the police, with his name spelled out in English, Fung, Fung Ho, which was almost funny. Almost.

"You must come with me, please."

"What's this about?"

"It is serious, Mr. Lamp. It is about a murder. A young woman, Yuki Yamoto."

I was stunned. *Yuki* . . . I must have said it aloud, because Fung said, "You know her?"

"No. Of course I don't know her."

He nodded, as though that only made sense. Then he said: "She is Japanese."

Japanese. What a contemptuous twist he gave the word, though you had to know the language to catch it. But that's the truth. To the Japanese, Westerners are barbarians; but to the Chinese, the Japanese are infinitely contemptible, a race of dwarfs, deformed, wretched, beyond all redemption.

6

THERE WERE NO LIGHTS IN THE ROOM, NOT EVEN ON HIS desk, but every second panel in the ceiling was fluorescent. I thought of cheap soap, and cheap, rough, paper hand towels; the light was gray like that. Hospitals. Camps. I was remembering one summer at a camp I'd hated.

There was no air. There was something wrong with the air. We weren't underground. I wasn't exactly certain where we were. We'd come in through an underground garage, through heavy steel doors with panic bars, and down a linoleum corridor where the air hadn't moved in a year but someone had been sick last week. We must have walked for a block. Then there'd been an elevator, and that too-close-to-the-Chinese smell, all the rice and the soy on their breath. I hadn't noticed how many floors we'd come up. I'd followed him along another corridor, with offices. There weren't any windows. I'd thought we'd come in at the main police building, but this was probably an annex. If you looked out, if you could look out, maybe you'd see Hengyang Road. I tried to imagine what it looked like, but I couldn't.

He said, "You are very sure you haven't seen her, ever, very, very sure?"

In English, he could say his *r*s velly, velly well and was proud of it. I couldn't remember his name—Fung Ho was just an errand boy, he'd dropped me here, and this guy had rolled up his sleeves and started in to work. And I'd forgotten his name completely; but now, after three hours of his questions, was probably not a good time to ask. "Let me see the photograph again."

He pushed it across his desk.

I hadn't taken my raincoat off—I wasn't going to be here long, was I?—but I was uncomfortable, not hot, exactly, but heavy, weighted down. Now I wanted to take it off, but I knew that would be a bad idea, too. I stretched out my hand, feeling the weight of the sleeve of the coat, and picked up the photograph. It was a picture of Yuki Yamoto. Maybe she'd wanted to be an actress, or a singer; the photo was posed like that, three-quarter profile, leaning into the camera. If she'd been a star, it would have had her signature across the bottom. I said, "She was Japanese."

"Yes." He took it as an explanation. "To you, they all look the same?"

"No, no, that's not . . ."

"Cute." He leaned forward, looking at her face. "Like a little monkey." He leaned back. "They are a special taste, wouldn't you say, Mr. Lamp? The Japanese?"

"Sure."

"You wouldn't have that taste, Mr. Lamp? They say, down there—you know—that the hair is very thick and grows right up into the crack."

"I wouldn't know about that. Even if I did see her, it wasn't that close."

"But—you're saying?—maybe you did see her after all?"

"If I saw her, I don't remember. We've been over this a dozen times. Even if I saw her, I certainly didn't kill her."

"No, no, that is not the point now. But we have a witness, who says you were with her."

I looked at his face. He was lying. All of this, in some way I didn't understand, was a very big lie. A cover-up. A setup. Maybe both. I was still in shock—*Yuki* had been murdered, but Cao hadn't been mentioned. If I didn't know differently—because I'd made my anonymous phone call—I could almost believe that the police still didn't know what had happened in that apartment. But they did know. And they knew about me, but not much, not anything certain. They hadn't charged me, they weren't that close. They were feeling, feinting, sizing me up. I was more or less convinced they were looking for a patsy and I was trying to say, *Choose somebody else.*

I looked at him carefully and managed a smile. "Is this witness Japanese too?"

"Maybe."

"A girlfriend of this woman?"

He smiled, and leaned back, and folded his hands on his stomach. "Maybe that's a good guess, Mr. Lamp." He nodded. His chin touched his chest. "You are exactly right. Girlfriend of this woman, also Japanese, says she saw you together."

"When?"

"Around seven o'clock. Now you remember?" Yes, definitely he was lying. Because, at seven o'clock, I'd been leaving Cao's apartment, and Yuki, almost certainly, had been inside. No one had seen us together. But that's what they were interested in—seven o'clock, and Cao, not Yuki; after all, she'd been alive, and working in the club, not long after eight. But they weren't really interested in her at all. All they cared about was Cao, and seven o'clock, and I wondered now if I hadn't made some egregious blunder. A blotting pad, an appointment book, somewhere in the apartment—with my name penciled in for a meeting at seven. If that's all they had to place me there, it wasn't much, probably not enough . . . although, I suspected, if I gave them the least encouragement they could make me a murderer real quick. I said, "I can't remember seeing anyone around seven."

"Maybe you were going out to have dinner . . . why not?"

"Well, I was on my way to dinner—I was walking around, looking for a place—but not with her."

"But you don't say where you walked, or where you went?"

I was worried about the Lucky Lotus. If they worked at it, they could place me there, with Yuki—but not till much later, not till after Cao's death. But they weren't really interested in Yuki; I was more and more convinced of that. Even if they tied me to Yuki, the important point was not to be linked with Cao. I stuck to my guns and asked, "When was she killed?"

"That is being established. Don't worry. Don't worry at all, Mr. Lamp. We only want to know where she was, that is all. Very simple."

"I think you should find yourself a new witness."

Just then another man came over and bent down to whisper in the ear of this man whose name I couldn't remember. The new man was short and wore a white shirt all rucked up in the sleeves; I realized he was wearing expandable metal garters—I hadn't seen them in years. There was a certain amount of frowning, whispering back and forth, then the man who'd been interrogating me said: "Your lawyer is here, Mr. Lamp."

I must have looked very blank. I certainly felt very blank. I hadn't asked for a lawyer. I hadn't called anyone. Asking for the cop's name, taking off my raincoat, demanding a lawyer, they'd all seemed like bad ideas. But I nodded, as though it was what I'd been expecting all along.

He turned a card over in his fingers. "Robert Young. He'd like to see you—we would have no objection. You understand, we only want to ask you questions. That is all. It's very, very simple."

I played along. "I only wish I could be more helpful."

"No, no. Perfectly all right. Perfectly." He nodded toward the man with the garters. "You go with Mr. Wong Li, and he will take you to him."

Robert Young. I knew the name from somewhere, but

that was as close as I could get. Trailing along behind
Mr. Wong, I crossed the room, only now seeing how
large it was—a vista of desks, people, computer monitors, telephones—for I'd been all closed in by that lurid
light, the weight of my coat, my own fear. My neck
ached. I lifted it up—had it been bowed?—and pain
jabbed down into my shoulders. Weaving our way, we
reached the back of the room and a door, which Mr.
Wong held open for me, and then we headed down a
flight of bare concrete stairs, with a rail that had once
been painted blue, then yellow, and was now a chipped,
crusted amalgam of the two. At the bottom was a landing
with a small door at one side—though, it seemed to me,
we hadn't descended a full floor at all. But we passed
through all the same, and Mr. Wong led me along a
narrow passage, ending at a door, which opened into a
small, windowless room with green walls and worn gray
carpeting on the floor. It was like a vault, lit with the
same fluorescent tiles; they were like patches of radio-
active plastic. I looked around. We were between floors,
we had to be. And I thought, It has to be wired. There
were four chairs, with chrome legs and dark red plastic
seats, and a table with metal legs and a plastic wood-
grain top. Mr. Wong smiled. "Wait. He come on in a
minute."

He went out, and I sat down on one of the chairs, its
slippery seat. I stared at the door; then I took off my coat.
But I seemed to have no strength. It took all my effort to
keep my head up and stare at the door in front of me. And

a moment later a door behind me, in the back wall, opened; I jumped with surprise.

"Mr. Lamp? Robert Young. Good to see you again." A man came toward me with his hand outstretched and a smile on his face. He was big, broad-shouldered; he looked very American. He had blond, tightly waved hair, hard-looking, like the hair on a statue. "When was it? At the AIT, I think. You remember, we had that long argument about Henry Liu."

Yes, I had met him somewhere. And the AIT—the American Institute in Taiwan—was a likely place. And maybe I'd heard the name Henry Liu, but I wasn't sure who he was. I began to get up, taking Young's hand, but he held my arm and swung down into the chair beside me. He whispered quickly, "Look, I just saw you out there and wondered what was going on. So I asked a few questions and—given the answers—thought maybe you could do with a break. But if you want me to get lost, that's fine."

"No. Thank you."

"Is it serious?" Young was whispering too.

"I'm not sure. I don't know."

"I ask, you see, because Kang usually gets the big cases."

Kang . . . so that was his name.

I said, "A woman was murdered. A Japanese woman, a dancer or hooker—I'm not sure. Yuki Yamoto."

"Did you kill her? But don't answer. This place is bugged." He smiled. He had white, even teeth and good brown skin—yes, he looked very American. And the suit helped; single-breasted, soft-shouldered, a light brown with a tiny check.

"No," I said, "I didn't kill her."

"Do you think that *they* think you killed her?"

"I don't know. They say someone saw us together at seven o'clock."

"Last night?"

"Yes."

"Were you together?"

"No."

"Have they produced this witness?"

"No."

"Named him?"

"Her. No."

"Have they charged you? Arrested you?"

"No. They only say they want to ask me these questions."

"Do you have a lawyer?"

I let out a breath. Seeing him, hearing his voice, hearing his English, were letting me relax. "I guess I'd use Charlie Li."

Young laughed. "Good old Charlie. You know him? Wonderful man. Every Round Eye out here has learned something from Charlie. But I think he might be past it now. Harry would do you better."

"Yes." Harry was Charlie's son, one of them, number-one son.

"Do you want me to get him down here? It wouldn't be any trouble . . . for me. Or for Harry, I'm sure. Or

would you like me to help? If you want, I'd be happy
to—then you could see Harry later."

"I don't know. I'm not sure."

"At least let me get you out of here. You look pretty
beat."

Yes. Yes. Yes. "Yes, why not?"

"Okay. Give me a buck to make it official." He
grinned. "I love tangling with Kang. Even that name!
Gives me a hard-on."

I gave him N.T.$100 from my wallet and he stood up,
lightly slapping my shoulder. "This won't take long." He
strode over to the door, the one I'd come in, and disappeared. I settled my coat over my arm, then shifted it to
the chair beside me. I realized how tense I was and
stretched back, easing the ache in my shoulders. The
room was almost perfectly silent; I suppose soundproof.
But far off were vague sounds, scarcely identifiable—but
the world, going on. I looked around the room. It had the
dreadful, dreary quality of certain public spaces like
airport departure rooms. It made me think of JFK;
but this wasn't shabby—it didn't have that same third-
world quality, which actually gives JFK a certain seedy
character. I began thinking of airports generally,
which seemed a reasonable compromise, wish fulfill-
ment, maybe, but not straying too far from immediate
reality. CKS . . . CKS was a fitting memorial to a shrewd,
tough-minded megalomaniac, and a good reminder that
these people have something to fight for. La Guardia I
liked, you could feel the history, imagine prop planes
warming up on the tarmac, pilots searching for the wind

sock. Miami wasn't so bad, I didn't even mind the little railway with the cars that talked to you. And you could step outside and feel the soft, damp wind and watch the thunderstorms build up in the afternoon. LAX was the same, after you came up from the tunnels you had the palms and the warm wind, and stars against the black Pacific sky. Heathrow . . . well it gives a fair impression of what you're in for, crowds of rude people, dirt, lots of dirt, the place never finished. I liked Paris better. And Nice. More palms, and those French machines that give tickets for parking. Hong Kong was okay, the first time you barely noticed after the excitement of coming in through the hills, the plane seeming to drop into the sea. Berlin. Okay. Old-fashioned. Toronto was awful, exhausting, mindless. Vancouver you—then I tried to remember the codes, NRT for Tokyo, CMB for Colombo because it was called Bandaranaike Airport, SIN for Singapore, HLP for Jakarta, Calcutta Dum-Dum, CCU. . . . With only a little cheating, I figured, I could make it all around the world; but I hadn't got past Abu Dhabi when Mr. Wong returned and took me out of that room to another, upstairs, or at least higher up, where there actually was a window—though I didn't recognize the street outside.

"You smoke, Mr. Lamp?"

"No."

"Okay to smoke here."

"Thank you."

He went away. I checked my watch. And eighteen minutes later, Young came in.

"I'm not *completely* convinced that this room is bugged, but let's be careful anyway. Tell me—did they take a blood sample from you?"

"No. But they asked me my blood type."

"Really. And?"

"I told them. AB."

"You know what your blood type is?"

"My sister's a nurse. She used to practice on me."

Young grinned. "That sounds like fun, playing nurse with your sister." He gave my shoulder a little slap to show that this was a joke. He was an American lawyer, all right. Then his expression turned businesslike. "That explains a lot. You see, they found semen in Miss Yuki. And you can get a blood type from semen . . . and of course it was AB."

"Christ." Then I said: "I didn't have sex with her, and I didn't kill her."

"That's okay. Don't worry about it. I'm not a forensic expert, but I know it doesn't mean very much, not in paternity cases anyway. Blood types can exclude, eliminate, but they don't prove anything positively. Millions of people have that blood type . . . actually I think it may be especially common among Orientals. Anyway, just because they found it in her doesn't mean much. What's more interesting, really, is that they didn't ask you to take a test."

"What do you mean?"

"Well, it sort of shows that they're not that serious about you—yet. A test might narrow it down, you see, because they can find more stuff than just the blood type now, proteins, enzymes, God knows what else."

"I don't understand."

"I mean, they could exclude you easily enough if they wanted to—make it definite, one way or the other. But they don't seem to want to. They prefer to hold you for some reason."

"Did you find out when she was killed?"

He shook his head. "Kang is cagey about that. It would sure help, though, if you could prove where you were, and what you were doing, around seven last night."

I was trying to work this all out in my mind, trying to work out what was in *their* minds. Kang worked on big cases; that meant Cao, not Yuki. Which was confirmed by their interest in where I was at seven, the time of Cao's death—but a time, they must have known, when Yuki was still alive. I wondered if there might not be a terrible irony here. Once they were satisfied that I couldn't establish a firm alibi for seven o'clock, that left the way open to frame me, to concoct some story that put me with Cao—which was exactly where I'd been. I was trapped. And there was this business with the semen. And my intuition—which I now believed more than ever—that something very big was going on. Yes, I was being set up. Or—but there was no "or," no "on the other hand." There was only one side to this coin: I was being set up. But why? Why me? And why—Young's point— didn't they just go ahead and do it? Something was holding them back, somehow they were still uncertain. The police—power—were part of what was happening, I was sure of it, but power is never simple, and not necessarily united. I was one possibility, but there might be others; some final decision still hadn't been made. All I could do now was make that decision as difficult as possible, keep them off balance. Maybe, when I thought about it, I hadn't done such a bad job; at least I hadn't rolled over and played dead. But I was tired, exhausted. Looking at Young, I spoke the simple truth, "It's all hit me too suddenly. I need time to think."

"Well, exactly. That's just what you should do—go home and rest and think—"

"I can go home?"

"Sure. That's all fixed. They only wanted to ask questions—for the time being, anyway—and I told Kang he'd asked enough. And when he said he wanted to keep your passport, I told him to go to hell. Which gave me considerable pleasure, let me tell you." He grinned. "Want to ask for your money back? I'd probably give it to you."

I didn't want my money back; I just wanted to get out of there. But even Robert Young couldn't find his way, and we had to get Mr. Wong. He was, I supposed, inscrutable; or at least I couldn't be sure whether they were annoyed at Young for having organized my release, or merely indifferent. In any case, Wong took us all the way down to the parking garage, where Young said he would be happy to drive me home. On the way out, I noticed, he showed a pass. I wondered what kind it was. But out in traffic, his credentials were excellent; he had just enough nerve, but not too much. Maybe he was reading my mind, because he said, "Kill or be killed."

"Almost."

"Exactly." He smiled. "Look—I don't want you to think I'm some kind of ambulance chaser, but would you like me to go on with this? I think you *need* a lawyer—don't panic or anything, but I'd say it's that serious. So if you don't want me, you should get someone else. Like Harry. He'd be fine."

"What would you do?"

"Poke. For the time being. Poke Kang, to see what he's up to. And poke you to get some sort of evidence about where you were at seven o'clock . . . that seems to be the crucial time."

He was right about that, more right than he knew. Of course, it was the one time I couldn't account for; once I placed myself at Cao's apartment, I'd probably be finished—certainly I'd be fighting a rearguard action. But seven o'clock was crucial in another way; it was part of the puzzle . . . of why Cao had finally agreed to see me, of the other visitor, of what Yuki had actually seen, heard, done—which must have been why they'd killed her.

But I wasn't going to get into that with him and I just said, "Okay. You're on. Poke. It's good of you—thanks. I'm glad you showed up."

"Great. And don't worry, everything will work out. What we should do . . . tomorrow, I'll see what I can stir up. And you think things over tonight. Then maybe we can have lunch, compare notes."

I agreed; he scribbled the name of a restaurant on the

back of his business card and then dropped me at the
hotel.

Inside, Chou Li gave me that quick, look-away glance
which is reserved, in totalitarian countries, for people
who have fallen under the eye of the police. I didn't say
anything; just asked for my mail, then went up to my
room. I drank a glass of water, then sat on the bed, trying
to think. There were so many questions, all those questions about Cao and Yuki, but some others too. A couple
were nagging me more than the others. Laurie, for
example, the question of sex, semen, and condoms. . . .
But I couldn't get it clear in my mind, and there was no
use looking, the housekeeper had already been through
the room. . . . So I called the office. No answer; it was
already past five. But that was all right, too, and I began
moving now, I went straight out, taking the elevator all
the way down to the basement—once, by mistake, I'd
stumbled onto this: you made your way along a series of
corridors and then there was a small door into an alley. It
was already pretty dark; no one was going to see me. I
came back to the street and walked two blocks and found
a cab. There was a lot of traffic; it was getting on to six
by the time I reached the office. But the building stays
open late, and you don't have to start signing in until
eight o'clock—in Taiwan, people keep different hours,
given all the time zones Asians deal with. Ping Ong had
left a couple of notes on my desk, a few calls, but they
were nothing important. I ignored them and I began
poking at another question, going through my commercial and business directories. I was looking for Young,

Robert. But he wasn't in any of them, not as a lawyer, or even a "legal and commercial adviser"—which usually means a foreigner with an off-island law degree who can't practice in Taiwan but can help with customs, banks, bureaucrats, and so forth: they have deals with local firms if they have to appear in court. I thought a moment, and picked up the phone; but then I put the phone down, because Charlie Li would want to know why, and I wasn't sure I wanted to tell him. Then, while I let my mind keep working on Robert Young, I got on the computer and checked my diary. There it was, about three weeks back, an invitation from the AIT to a reception; so I could have met him there, just as he'd said. The AIT has been the U.S. pseudoembassy since 1979 when President Carter withdrew recognition of the Nationalist government and recognized the mainland Communist government instead. Most countries have equivalents—there's the Anglo-Taiwan Trade Committee, the Japanese Interchange Association, the Hellenic Organization for the Promotion of Exports, a dozen others—and I knew people in all of them. On the off chance, I dialed the AIT number. A man who works in the technological development section named Vern Geberth was working late—I'd spent a lot of time with him, talking about tire plants. We exchanged pleasantries and then I asked if he'd heard of Young.

"I think so—I guess I remember him because of the name."

"What do you mean?"

"You know, the actor. *Father Knows Best. Marcus Welby*."

"Of course. That's why it rings a bell."

"Yeah, but he worked here all right . . . just a second." I could hear him flipping pages. "There's no listing now, though . . . I could ask in the legal department. I'm sure that's where he was and there's always somebody there."

"That's okay. It's just that I ran into him, and he said he was working as a lawyer and I remembered him being at the AIT."

"I thought you used Charlie Li. Your old man knew him, or something."

"Well, Charlie's getting a little long in the tooth."

"Not Harry."

"I know but . . . well I was just curious—it was nothing really."

"How are things going with Cao Dai?"

"They aren't. I just don't get any response. They're barely polite."

"Hang on. I've heard that's how they play it. Then, bang bang, you get your deal."

We chatted a little longer, then I hung up. There was an envelope on my desk, with my name: Laurie's key. I switched off the light, locked up, then took the stairs instead of the elevator. The lobby was empty except for the security guard, but I wasn't taking any chances and there was an easy fire exit that opened on another alley. I was getting used to alleys. I walked into the darkness. The traffic swept past on Mintsu East Road, the car lights flashing in my eyes. It was cool . . . but not damp, so that

made it okay: now there was a nice, normal thought. . . .
Taking my life in my hands, I crossed the road, then
ducked into a side entrance of the President Hotel. I
walked right through it, a lot of American Chinese
looking lost, a few Japanese, a huddled clutch of Swedes
or Scandinavians, or so I guessed—anyway, a nice crowd
to lose yourself in. So I was sure there was no one behind
me, though I kept checking for another block. Now I was
in Shuang Cheng Street, not so far from the Lucky Lotus
in fact. Sugar Daddy Row, the marines called it, but that
was before my time and actually, in the winter rain, it
makes me think of Glasgow, for the cold has that same
stony feel, and the light spilling out from the windows
seems just so faint, the warmth within just so inviting. I
pushed into one of the pubs—a lot of bars here are set up
like pubs—I think the Hope & Anchor, and ordered a
hamburger, eating in a beery, misty fug. There was
music, Irish Rovers stuff, and students, jabbering away—
a lot of them American. But I hardly noticed. I was
thinking. I thought hard, and I was still thinking when I
walked over to Laurie's apartment, around eight o'clock.
It's on the edge of Dinghao, the newest fashionable area
in Taipei. I'd been there before; but now, as I used the
key and stepped inside, everything was different. I could
smell her; the smell of themselves women carry in their
hair. I could see her, the way she moved; for her body
defined the spaces between the chair and the coffee table,
the angle of the open door between the living room and
kitchen. And I could even hear her voice when I took
down one of her books and started to read, she had the

kind of voice that can slip away and hide inside itself, *I am always drawn back to places where I have lived, the houses and their neighborhoods. . . .*

I put the book down.

Who was she? Where did she come from?

Cao, Yuki, Laurie, Young. *Everything had happened so fast.*

It was barely nine when she came home. I'd found a bottle of chardonnay in the refrigerator with a note, "I'm not cool but this is—maybe happiness is a man to come home to," and I met her at the door with a glass in my hand. And as she smiled at me, her cheeks flushed gently. I held her. "Have a good time?"

"I didn't much notice."

I kissed her. "Last night . . ."

"It seems like a hundred years ago."

"Yes. I've been thinking . . . we're not exactly taking our time about this."

"Don't be frightened. Believe me. *Me*." She kissed my ear, my neck.

Oh I wanted to believe her and I said, "Okay, I believe. But last night, you know, afterward. . . . What did you do with the safe?"

"What? You mean . . . ?"

"Yes."

She nipped my neck. "What a crazy question." She nipped my neck again. "I flushed it down the toilet. I didn't want to embarrass your maid." She brought her face around and leaned her forehead against my forehead, kissed my nose. "Correction. *I* was embarrassed— that the maid would find it and then she'd know. . . ."

"You're sure?"

She looked at me. "Is something wrong?"

"Nothing's wrong," I lied.

She kissed me and whispered, "Don't worry about it, then. Anyway, that's one problem that's all taken care of." She clasped her hands behind my neck and stood on my toes, and rocked back and forth.

"What do you mean, it's all taken care of?"

"What I say, dummy. This afternoon, I got something." She rocked forward now and kissed me softly on the lips. "I've got it in me now."

7

No matter how you looked at it, I couldn't see the point of not telling her; so I did tell her.

Maybe I didn't say anything about semen and blood tests, and for some reason I passed over the magazine I'd taken from Cao's apartment—but everything else, I told her.

When I was finished, I watched her face; in fact, the whole time, I'd watched her face. And I said, "Somehow, you don't seem surprised." And I thought, watching her eyes, *You don't have any reason to be suspicious, not when she can look at you like that.*

She said, "I knew something was wrong."

"When?"

"That night. Then. It was all right with *us*, but something was wrong." She smiled. "When things are going right, something has to go wrong."

"No," I said. "Don't be frightened."

"No. I'll be angry—but *you* be frightened. Remember, Nick, this place is not exactly a democracy. There's *rule*

86

here, and there's *law*, but not necessarily the rule *of* law. If you know what I mean."

I did. I was having it proved to me. The next morning, drinking coffee, I looked out her window across the city. If Taipei ever becomes an Asian New York, maybe Dinghao will be its Upper West Side . . . even if it is on the east side of town. Already there were a lot of rich old people, rich young people, and very small dogs. From here, you could see all the way to the river and the bridges, a mile or so of high-rise towers, boulevards streaming with traffic, and banners of neon which, even now, were prepared to battle with the sun. It looked free and modern, and that's the way it wanted to look, that's how it wanted you to see it; but I knew Taipei still hadn't escaped its past. Chiang Kai-shek had built Taipei and he'd been an old-fashioned generalissimo, a dictator; and the city he'd modeled his new capital on was Shanghai, the Shanghai of the thirties and the forties: where law was power, and power was the law. Moreover, the very layout of the place expressed his political ambitions, for the streets are usually named after rivers and mountains and towns on the mainland so that the map of the town mimics the map of the country: you find Beijing Road in the north, Guangzhou Street in the south. Chiang had been dead for years, of course, but things hadn't changed that much. I watched a plane drift down toward the city, still so far out it was probably above the sea. Young had managed to get my passport for me; but what would happen if I tried to use it?

Laurie came back with all the papers. There was still not a word about Cao. "I don't understand it," I said.

"You should. You damn well better."

"What do you mean?"

"This is China, Nick. This is Taiwan. This is all about *li*."

Li is one of the more important Chinese words to know. It means something like "good manners" or "propriety," and it's also used for the rites and ceremonies that express such feelings, especially to your ancestors. But it means much more than that. *Li* is the honorable path; *li* is the highest standard, the highest court, to which you can appeal: *li* is the gentleman's code taken to the nth degree. As a practical matter, it often means putting your family first, and so I said, "You think the police are going to let the Cao family settle this on their own?"

"Possibly." She shrugged. "*Bao-jia* isn't just custom here. It's almost official."

There's another important word. *Bao-jia* is an old Chinese way of organizing responsibility, based on families. In the twelfth century the Duke of Chou divided the whole of society into units of ten, one hundred, one thousand, and ten thousand families. Each unit had a leader, responsible for all the families in his unit, every leader being responsible to the next higher in the chain. So, if someone in your family had a problem—committed a crime, for example—the head of the family was initially responsible; if he couldn't deal with it, he passed it on to the leader of the ten-family unit. And so on. Criminal matters, welfare problems, health problems, work problems—any sort of problem could be dealt with in this structure. In fact, *li* demanded it; taking a problem outside the family—to the courts, say—was a kind of humiliation. I knew all this, but . . . "I don't think so. This is the twentieth century. Cao's companies are quoted on the stock exchange. And we're talking about murder."

She gave me a look. "You *do* know what a banana is?" Yes, I knew; yellow on the outside, white on the inside. . . . "You're thinking like one," she said. "We're not talking about murder, we're talking about power and money. Cao's dead. A lot of things will change because of that, but do you think anyone cares who did it? The police will handle this exactly the way Cao's family wants them to—or if Cao's family's going down, they'll handle it the way their *enemies* think they should. But either way, no one's interested in justice."

"All right. I'm not arguing. Give me some credit— that's how I figured it from the beginning."

"I know. I just wish you hadn't called them in the first place . . . the police, I mean. At least they'd be a little less certain about the time."

"I'm not sure it makes any difference." I shrugged. "Besides, my father made me memorize the Magna Carta, age of ten."

She smiled. "He sounds like a remarkable man."

He had been, in a way. I wondered how he would have handled this situation. I knew one thing—he wouldn't have trusted anyone *because Nick my son the only person you can ever really trust is yourself.* . . . It was true, though, about the Magna Carta, and maybe some vestige of my father's notion of citizenship—not at all Chinese—had made me phone them. My father was an Anglophile, though actually not a sentimental one. He'd understood the British—or liked to think he did—precisely because he was Chinese. For example, it would never have occurred to him that his children should memorize the Declaration of Independence. The idea of revolution, of a new start in a new world—the attempt to make a new world—always struck him as silly, childish. (He thought Mao was a charlatan.) China is part of an old, old world and there's no way you can ever start over; so the British idea—you keep redefining the king—seemed a lot more sensible. But even more important, I think, was the language. My father loved the English language. He spoke it and wrote it easily, naturally, beautifully, which was another reason for the Magna Carta, because he always said you had to know a little Latin to really know English. English was his link to the modern world, the real key to the modern world, even more than science, and he was right about that; the British are long gone, the Americans are going, but not the language. He used to scold me: "To be Chinese and speak English—what more do you want?" Right now, what I wanted was five minutes of his advice. But I said to Laurie, "What I still don't understood is how I come into this at all."

"Well, you could be right. Cao made a note somewhere that he was meeting you at seven. Or it could be Yuki Yamoto. They'll know her connection to Cao by now and they could already have established that she was with you at that club. So, therefore, you're linked to Cao too."

"But why don't they just come out and ask me about this?"

"Because they haven't worked out how they want Cao's murder to play—they haven't even decided yet to release the fact that he *was* murdered. But I think you're missing the point. I'm sure, by now, the police are certain of at least one thing, namely that you didn't murder Cao. Even if they haven't made up their mind what they want to do about it, there's no way they would have let you go—no way they would have let that lawyer get your passport back—if they actually thought you'd killed Cao."

I said, "If you're right, then there's only one reason why they brought me into this at all . . . they're trying to frame me. Or at least they're working out whether they can."

"Yes. Don't you get the feeling . . . it's almost as though they're holding you in reserve . . . a solution if they need a solution . . . if you see what I mean."

I did. She was probably right. Laurie was born here; she knew how this place worked, she knew it in her bones. Now she leaned over and kissed me. "Be careful, Nick. Don't trust them, not for a minute. Don't trust anyone."

And I thought of the semen, which wasn't mine, and, according to Yuki, wasn't Cao's—and why would she have lied about that? So she must have seen someone after she'd seen me, or else. . . . *Don't trust anyone.*

I looked at Laurie.

What did I feel? What did I think? I loved her. I so wanted to love her. She was sitting on the couch, her legs tucked up beside her, so beautiful, so *white*, so American. But she was here, in Taiwan. Except what did that mean? What side could she be on? Behind her, on the bookshelf, in a dutiful line, stood framed photos of her parents. Her mother had been beautiful, too, in a lovely, clean, timeless American way, part of a long gallery of American beauty, so many in each generation, just as Laurie had said, so that finally something particular in their beauty was lost, and they all looked like one of those lovely, lost movie stars you don't quite remember—Debra Paget, say. The mother's name had even been Coralee. And next to her was Laurie's father, the Colonel, in gritty black-and-white, standing beside a Chinese flier and his plane, a Saber jet if I remembered my old war movies right; a John Wayne hero. All these people came from such a different world than me, but we'd all ended up in the strange world of Taiwan. I had to wonder where I fitted in. Maybe, in fact, I was a way out, a way of cashing in your chips and making your exit, one last big pot. Or was I the chance to stake a claim, to prove your loyalty, earn the favors that would get you through the rest of your life?

"All right," I said, "I won't trust anyone." I don't think my next thought even occurred to her. "And maybe the first person I won't trust is Robert Young."

No, it hadn't occurred to her, not for a second. She didn't even blink, just said, "Why not?"

"The way he turned up like that. The line he took. I'm not exactly certain who he's working for."

"But you said—"

"Yes, they know him at the AIT."

"Well who do you think he is—if he's not who he says he is?"

I shook my head. "No idea. He's probably on the level, but he could be a cop, some kind of informer. For the time being it doesn't necessarily make any difference. A lawyer's not going to do me any good one way or another . . . and I don't want to make Young suspicious. But I do want to know. So I want you to go into the office and fax my brother in L.A. Ask him—"

"Alistair—"

"Arthur. The lawyer. Alistair's the one in Houston, the chemist."

She was all attention. "Got you."

"Ask Arthur about Young. If Young really is a lawyer, he should be able to find out about him. Make sure he knows it's important, but don't tell him why."

"It's almost ten . . . they'll have left already."

In Los Angeles, it would be six o'clock, yesterday evening. "He has a fax machine at home. Send it there, too—the number's in my book."

"I'll go change."

She left the bedroom door open. I watched her slip off the cashmere sweater she'd been wearing, and the jeans, and change them for a plain white blouse, and a gray jacket and skirt that was technically a suit, but wasn't, not in my eyes, not the way the short jacket curved into her long smooth waist and the skirt clung to her hips.

When she emerged, she kissed me. I could smell the perfume between her breasts, I could smell her hair. I held her and said, "Don't worry, this will all work out."

"This?"

"Everything. You know what I mean." Did I believe this? *Yes of course I did. . . .*

She took her head off my shoulder. "Nick, you know what I'm like, I'm never going to say, 'We need to talk,' or 'I want to talk.' I'm not like that. I've never been like that."

"Yes. That's part of it, isn't it? Between us."

"Ever since Hong Kong . . . it was either going to happen or it wasn't."

"It's happening," I said.

"I just want it to be all straight. . . . The way it ended up, my working for you . . . that was all luck. I didn't plan anything. It just happened."

"I wanted it to happen. I'm glad it did."

She kissed me. "Okay. Just so you're sure."

"Don't worry."

We kissed again and then she leaned against me and said, "Last night, I was thinking . . . I don't belong here, but it's the only place I can ever be. And I thought maybe it was the same with you."

Was it? To tell the truth, I wasn't sure. Where did she belong, where did I belong? But I said, "You see? We've got a lot in common."

She smiled and gave a little laugh. "My God, I'm

having the most important conversation in my life, standing in the hall. Let me go. I've got to get out of here."

And a moment later she was gone.

She was very beautiful. I was sure I was in love with her. I told myself that what had happened really had nothing to do with it—there was only one reason why I wouldn't trust her, and it made me sick. So I thought about Young instead and decided to check a point. The AIT was only a ten-minute walk and I had a couple of hours to kill. I went over there. It is not an embassy; there's a flag, but no marine guards at the door, and although the people you talk to may look and sound like government officials, they've all officially resigned from the foreign service; they will happily answer your questions about visas and passports, but the paperwork is sent to Hong Kong. Still, there's lots of security and it took me a while to get in. I wanted the library. As Laurie had said, Taiwan is not a democracy. Things are a lot better now than they used to be—martial law was lifted in 1987—but even today the press is watched carefully and there's censorship; in the past, foreign papers and magazines could have whole pages cut out of them. But diplomacy has its privileges and the AIT's copies of the *New York Times* would be okay. And all I wanted to do was check a small point: Who was Henry Liu, and why would I have argued about him with Robert Young? I went through the *Index*. The first listings for Liu, Henry, came in 1984, and there were a lot more in 1985. Well, he existed; so maybe Robert Young and I had talked. Except

I didn't remember a thing. So, after a small negotiation, I settled myself in front of a microfilm reader with a dozen rolls of film and for the next couple of hours, item by item, watched a major political scandal unroll across the screen. It was fascinating, actually. At first the stories were small, written by anonymous correspondents for the wire services, AP, UPI. Then they were longer pieces, "special" to the *Times*; and finally the heavyweights moved in, articles by senior correspondents like Fox Butterfield, and eventually, on February 11, 1985, there was even an editorial, "The Long Arm of Taiwan." And all this was caused by the murder of a single man, an obscure journalist named Henry Liu.

To understand his story, you had to know a little Taiwanese history. Today, both the government on Taiwan—the Nationalists, the Kuomintang—and the mainland Communist government agree that the island is a part of China, a province; their quarrel is about who's the legitimate government of the country as a whole. But actually, if you look at history, this isn't so clear. Taiwan's original inhabitants were aborigines, probably from the Pacific islands, and no more Chinese than Dan Quayle. In fact, the Chinese didn't arrive in any significant numbers until the fifteenth century, and they pretty much stayed on the coast, with the aborigines controlling the interior. Then, in 1517, the Portuguese discovered the place. They called it Ilha Formosa, "Beautiful Island," and for the next hundred and fifty years Taiwan's history had more to do with Europe than China: the Dutch arrived and fought the Portuguese, and then the Spanish arrived and fought the Dutch. It really wasn't until a hundred years later that China entered the picture again, in a way that oddly paralleled the modern era. On the mainland, the Manchus were overthrowing the Ming dynasty, and ultimately the last great Ming general, Koxinga, was forced to flee to Taiwan—just as Chiang Kai-shek was forced to retreat here when Mao took over the mainland after the Second World War. In any case, Koxinga's army threw out the Dutch in 1661, and he managed to hang on—nursing ambitions of a return to the mainland, just like Chiang—for another twenty years; but finally, in 1682, the Manchus prevailed. It was only at this point that Taiwan truly became a part of China; even so, it was very much on the periphery and it didn't actually become a separate province until 1887. And that only lasted eight years; in 1895, Japan defeated China in the Sino-Japanese War and Taiwan became part of the Japanese Empire. This is the crucial fact of modern Taiwanese history: for the first half of this century—for the better part of the modern era—Taiwan was under Japanese rule. The Taiwanese were Chinese, yes; but their connection to the mainland, never very strong, was now weakened even more. They developed their own sense of identity; many learned to speak Japanese—many older Taiwanese still do—and watched Japanese movies, read Japanese books, and a few were even educated in Japan. They didn't love the Japanese, but there's no doubt that the Japanese made Taiwan a far better place to live, during most of this century, than the mainland. There was enough food, government services, a real economy—

under the Japanese, for example, Taiwan produced about as much electricity as the entire mainland. So when the Nationalists arrived and the Japanese left, the Taiwanese had both high standards and fairly high aspirations. They hoped, at long last, to take over the island and run it in their own interests. And of course that didn't happen. Chiang Kai-shek's mainlanders essentially took the place of the Japanese and when the Taiwanese rebelled perpetrated a massacre in which at least ten thousand Taiwanese were killed. Until 1987, Taiwan was under martial law—ostensibly because of the war with the mainland, in reality to keep the native Taiwanese under control.

This was the background to Henry Liu's story, and his life, as I went through it, was like a filter that threw the whole history into relief. Liu was not native Taiwanese; he had been born on the mainland and had come to Taiwan as a young man in 1949. His family had been landowners, so inevitably they'd supported Chiang Kai-shek and the Kuomintang—the KMT, the Nationalists. So had Henry, at least in the beginning; at a time when the government kept a tight lock on the press, he became a reporter for the *Taiwan Daily News* and eventually was made their correspondent in Washington, a fair sign of his loyalty to the Chiang Kai-shek regime. But the good old U.S.A. corrupted him; "freedom," when it's not just a word, can do that, and he finally fell out with his old employers. He stayed in the States, became a U.S. citizen, went into business with his wife, and, politically speaking, disappeared for a couple of years. But then he popped up again, writing anti-KMT articles in Hong Kong papers and in the Chinese American press—demonstrating a truly bad attitude so far as the KMT was concerned. Finally, bringing all this to a head, he started writing a biography of Chiang Ching-kuo (known to his friends as CCK), who had become president of Taiwan in 1978 on the death of his father, Chiang Kai-shek (known to his friends, supposing he had any, as CKS). This biography was journalistic, gossipy—the sort of thing that's usually called *yeshi*, wild history. There were a lot of juicy bits about the Chiang family, their marriages, sexual careers, feelings about each other, so forth. CKS, for example, had married several times. The first was arranged, traditional style—he was fourteen, the girl was seventeen—the second was to a high-class hooker from Shanghai, and the last, the most famous, was to May-ling Soong, one of the famous Soong sisters, who was friend to American presidents, Henry Luce, Bill Buckley, and all. Madame Chiang had supposedly converted the generalissimo to Christianity, but apparently that hadn't stopped him from taking a number of concubines, and in fact welcoming wife number two back to his bed. CCK, the product of the first marriage, evidently hated his famous stepmother—and hated his father for the way he'd treated his own mother, calling him a wife beater. All this, of course, was not the sort of thing you talked about in public . . . and then Liu had made things worse by going into CCK's political past as well. It was funny, in a way. CCK, who Richard Nixon would probably have considered one of the leaders of the Free World in the struggle against godless atheistic communism, had actually been a Commie himself. He'd gone to a university in Moscow where the Russians indoctrinated Asians and blacks, and joined the Komsomol, the Communist Youth League. And he was apparently a real believer, a man of true faith; in 1925, when his father had been shooting up the Communists in Shanghai, he'd issued a statement condemning CKS as a traitor and calling for his public execution. Worse, he'd then married a Russian woman—his kids were all half-Russian—and spent ten years or so running a hydroelectric project in the Urals. He became a regular commissar. Altogether, it certainly wasn't the past a leader of a "Little Dragon" was supposed to have. For raking it all up, Henry Liu clearly deserved punishment—an example had to be set—and in the fall of 1984 a couple of thugs beat him up and shot him. This was in Daly City, a suburb of San Francisco. I'd once thought of setting up an office in San Francisco and had lived there for a couple of months. Spinning my way through the microfilm, I knew just how the cops would have played it. These people were Chinese, therefore the murder had to be about (a) drugs, (b) protection money, (c) some weird gang warfare thing. They completely ignored Liu's wife, who kept telling them it was political, until it was too late to get the toothpaste back in the tube. Liu had been killed by a gang all right, the Bamboo Gang, a big criminal syndicate on Taiwan. The trouble was, the principal organizer of Liu's assassination had been given a farewell party before he left for the States by the head of the Intelligence Bureau of the Ministry of National

Defense—and was so stupid that, after the killing, he'd called this same Intelligence Bureau from San Francisco International Airport to report that his mission had been successful, a conversation that was recorded by the CIA. Ultimately, this was leaked and the cops picked up a couple of the small fry. They talked. All these articles— which I was reading—got themselves written, and that led to bills going through Congress about trading arms to countries that demonstrated a "consistent pattern of harassment and intimidation" against U.S. citizens. For Taiwan, it was a disaster; they were absolutely dependent on American arms, American trade, American goodwill. The KMT government did its best, but it was out of control—and no spin doctor would be able to get it back under control. However you measure face, a lot of it was lost. Top people got fired. A certain Vice-Admiral Wong, the Intelligence Bureau director, was sentenced to life imprisonment. And CCK's son, Alex, who probably hoped to continue as head of the family business, had to be disqualified—it turned out he was just a little too close to the Bamboo Gang and the security people who'd gone after Liu. In fact, the Henry Liu case had turned out to be the catalyst for a major liberation of Taiwanese politics, which was still going on now. A political opposition had been formed and even run candidates in elections. Local government was reformed. And in 1987 martial law was formally lifted—though it was replaced by a security law almost as restrictive. Taiwan was still a police state in the grip of the KMT . . . but the grip was loosening.

All of which was fascinating, especially for me. As I

rewound the last reel of microfilm, I was remembering 1985. In 1985, thanks to some of Alistair's contacts, I was working for an oil company in Chile. Which meant I had no opinions about Henry Liu—and certainly had never argued about him with Robert Young, or anyone else, at the AIT. I thought about that. And I thought about the way Robert Young had just "turned up." With Laurie, there were some questions I preferred not to think about—that condom, for instance—but this, I decided, was one answer I was going to get straight.

8

TAIWAN ... FORMOSA ... THE REPUBLIC OF CHINA ... the Taiwan Province of the *People's* Republic of China—whatever people call it, they all agree on one thing: it's a great restaurant.

Some people say that Taipei has the greatest collection of Chinese restaurants anywhere, and I wouldn't disagree. Better than Hong Kong, anyway. You can get wonderful noodles at the Ching Chao I, superb *xioa lung tang pao* at the Ding Tai Feng, and there's no doubt that the Chi Chia Chung serves the best *kou rou* on the island—and all the Taiwanese specialties as well ... and don't worry, after a while you actually do catch on to the names. Szechuan, Cantonese, Peking, Jianghze—in Taipei you can get anything your heart desires ... so naturally Young had told me to meet him at the Mama Roma, a gourmet pizza place in behind the Sheraton. Well, he was a lawyer. It was the sort of place Arthur, my lawyer brother in L.A., would have taken a client, although not a terribly important one.

I got there first and watched him come in.

This time he was wearing a blue suit, but Young wouldn't have looked formal in a tuxedo; it was something about the way he walked, it was the sort of easy walk you pick up on the beach in Malibu, so relaxed— one hand was in his pocket toying with some change while a half-smiling, faraway look played around his eyes as though he was hearing the Beach Boys in his own personal celestial space. A gold chain slipped down his wrist as we shook hands. "How's it going?" Maybe he guessed the way I'd been thinking because he said, "If I'm not *talking* Chinese, I'd rather not be *eating* Chinese—does that mean I've been here too long?"

"No, but my Italian's lousy."

He laughed at that. He thought that was real funny. But he knew wine, and he knew that restaurant; he bullied a fine bottle of Barolo out of them, and I think it was for his own pleasure, not to impress me. We sipped it and nibbled breadsticks and a bowl of spiced olives, although somehow Venice, California, seemed about as close as we were going to get to Italy. He seemed in no hurry, almost inviting me to feel him out personally; so I asked him when he'd first come to Taiwan.

He smiled, hunching forward a little, his wineglass cupped lightly in the fingertips of his hands. "A while back, when I think of it. I might as well have been born here—I sometimes feel I've been here that long." He took a quick sip of his wine, then leaned back in his chair. "Ever hear of Admiral Kimmel?"

"I don't think so."

"Few have. I once looked him up in a big encyclopedia—he wasn't there, *K* stood for Jean-Claude Killy, but not the good admiral. No, we don't want to remember poor old Hubby E. Kimmel. You see, Hubby was the fellow who ignored all those ciphered messages and radar intercepts, and refused to put up any air reconnaissance over Hawaii on the morning of December seventh, 1941. And he was the fellow who allowed those warships to anchor in the harbor, some of them only five hundred yards apart. He was, God bless his heart, the officer in command of Pearl Harbor. My father was a very young captain on his staff."

"He was disgraced?"

"No—he was too far down the line. But none of them were, in the end. They couldn't be. It was essential that they be exonerated in order to preserve the myth. You know, the Day of Infamy. The sneaky Jap attack. America, upright and proud, ambushed by the Yellow Devil."

"And the reality was?"

"Pearl Harbor was a great feat of arms, perhaps the most remarkable of the twentieth century. A brilliant stroke—*almost* a master stroke. But of course the whole thing meant that my father didn't have an especially good war. He went from one backwater to another. He got lucky at the end, though. His father, my grandfather, was a banker in San Francisco. In the thirties, he came out here on a business trip, and my father went with him. My father was just in his teens. They spent about a month on the island and my father got to travel all over, hiked and climbed, even hunted. Anyway, toward the end of the war the U.S. almost invaded here—most people don't know that—but my father, partly because he'd made that trip, got on the team that decided not to. He was able to point out, for example, that most of their maps were wrong. And he also made them think about what side the Taiwanese would fight for—"

"That was a question?"

"Sure. Everyone forgets that the Japs took over Taiwan in 1895—they were here a long time—and although nobody loved them, they ran it pretty well, built the railways, roads, public services. The place prospered. And of course a lot of older Taiwanese still speak Japanese. So it was a question all right. It helped convince the army to pass up Taiwan for Okinawa, a wise choice as it turned out . . . which earned my father a little reward, at least he thought it was a reward. After the Japanese surrendered, he was posted here, with a little team. This was before CKS arrived. He was here all through that, made a lot of contacts. Later—he went into banking too—he kept those contacts up and was here quite a bit. I came with him a few times. You know, sort of repeating that first trip he'd made. But I always loved it. And he made me learn Chinese. After I finished law school, I went into the foreign service pretty much looking to come here."

He was very easy with this, very relaxed. It came out smooth as . . . But I told myself to reserve judgment a moment. Yes, he was smooth; but then he must have been called upon to give this account of himself a hundred times. And it was believable. I believed it anyway.

But then, when I tried my hand, I don't think I was quite as smooth myself. "I guess it's changed a lot," I said.

"No kidding. The first time I was here, 1969, CKS was still alive . . . or at least convincingly stuffed. It was like the old days. No matter what you said about Mao and his crew, *this* place was a military dictatorship. Now . . ." He shrugged, and took some more wine. "Of course you don't want to exaggerate the changes. Despite the high tech and the high-rise, these people still burn paper money to pacify ghosts."

"Yes, but you could say that Henry Liu didn't die in vain."

Young smiled. "That's an interesting way to put it. And you're right, I guess. The Liu case, the bank scandals in eighty-five . . . that all put pressure on the KMT. But the big points were CKS dying—that ended so much—and then Carter recognizing Mao. And of course the money—don't underestimate that. All the money they made." He thought a second. Then: "The trouble with the Henry Liu affair was the symmetry. It rang too many bells. It showed how much the KMT *hadn't* changed. Chiang Kai-shek rose to power in Shanghai by using the Green Gang to wipe out the Communists. And with Liu you had Chiang's son, and his son's sons, working with the Bamboo Gang to get rid of someone they found a pain in the ass. The parallels were too close. It was just too much."

I tried to be cool. Probably I wasn't. "I was trying to remember. . . . Weren't we arguing about Henry Liu?"

Young looked blank, genuinely blank. "What do you mean?"

"Yesterday, you were saying that we met at the AIT and argued about Henry Liu. I was wondering—"

"Really? Henry Liu?"

"Really."

"I don't . . ." He waved his hand. He laughed. "No, no, has that been worrying you? I know I arrived on the scene a little strangely, and I remember now, about Henry Liu, but it wasn't for real. You didn't understand. That room is bugged, everybody knows it. I wanted them to overhear. I wasn't talking to you, I was talking to *Kang*, reminding him of the trouble you can get into by breaking the rules."

"So we didn't meet at the AIT?"

"Sure we did, I wouldn't have recognized you otherwise. But we talked about . . . tires, I think. Isn't that your business?"

Well, he was definitely smoother than I was, and everything he said was perfectly plausible. But surely he was too smooth. He answered questions almost before you could ask them, and somehow the answers still struck me as funny. No matter what he said, I didn't like the coincidence, his being in the cop shop like that. And his personal history hadn't reassured me; his family background, the connections to the military, his ties to the AIT—he was too close to the security apparatus, to power, and I didn't see how that put him on my side. But when you're in against someone like Young the best strategy is often to let things ride. He certainly wasn't going to beat himself. So I smiled and didn't push him, just tossed out a few pieces of bait to see if he'd rise to them. But he always played it cool. I told him a little about the deal I'd been working on—since he seemed to know something about it anyway—and he asked, "Why did you go to Cao Dai?"

"Well, he's got the money, God knows, and he's got tire plants. And . . . let's say, I have a little confidential information that I thought might help."

But he didn't even offer to nibble, though I had a story prepared just in case he did. With a grunt, he said, "Cao's an incredible man. He must be eighty if he's a day . . . though I gather he can still manage something with the ladies. All that rhino horn, I guess. . . ." He shrugged. "No one's ever got a real take on him."

"What do you mean?"

"Oh, some people say he was a little too close to the Japs when they took over Shanghai—his first wife was Jap, you know, a couple of his kids are half-and-half . . . no one knows what happened to her. So he came here— this is one story—rather than Hong Kong because he was afraid the Brits might have something to say to him. On the other hand—and with people like Cao there always is another hand—some people claim he may have been working for the CIA all along."

"What do *you* say?"

"I say—to you—be careful." He hesitated, then smiled. "Or maybe *I* should be careful. We're mirror images, you know."

"No. I don't know."

"I mean, you're Chinese but you're almost a Round Eye. Inside your head, what are you? Do you know? I know I don't . . . I mean about myself. I've been here so long, I spend so much time thinking in Chinese, that I'm not sure what I am anymore. When I look in the mirror, I'm almost surprised to see a white face."

"We have the best of both worlds."

Young shook his head. "No. You do. Race counts, after all. It doesn't matter how good my Chinese is, my gorgeous blue eyes mirror too much history. All those damn Brits in their funny hats, all those damn Baptist missionaries, and that jerk in his airplane over Hiroshima." I didn't say anything, since he was probably right. Young shrugged. "We're going down. Fast. It's their turn now. *Your* turn. I'd say, with your connections—the way you can move back and forth—you've got it made."

I hoped he was right, of course; maybe I was even counting on it. But I was diplomatic. "I don't expect America—the West—will quite disappear. And there are other factors. . . ." I was thinking of my father. "I mean the language, the culture. English will still conquer all."

Young smiled. "Maybe you're right. Hell, we'll be saved by the computer. You just can't reduce ideographic languages to ASCII code."

Our pizzas came, covered in shrimp. I was hungry. As we started in, I noticed that Young shared out the wine rather carefully, glass for glass, filling my glass precisely to the level of his own. He noticed me noticing, and smiled; but he couldn't stop doing it. So finally, maybe, he was showing a weakness. A lack of control. But, as I ate and thought about it, it only seemed a confirmation of the story he'd told me of himself. I could imagine the boy traveling with his father, trying to please his father, trying to be perfect for his father, trying to make amends for the unspoken slights the father had suffered, trying to erase the shame the father was a reminder of. But the gesture would always fail—would only be another form of reminder—and provoke the father's irritation . . . which would lead the boy to try harder still, to try to be even more precise; and now he couldn't help himself. Yes, the very last of the bottle was shared out, drop for drop. . . . Which was maybe a lot to read into a single gesture, one quick nervous look on his otherwise imperturbable face. But it gave me a handle on him; and though it confirmed what he'd said, it also put me more on my guard. Young was all California, slick and smooth as Coppertone on a perfectly tanned back, but there was something underneath the slickness, something more complex, which I didn't understand. Part of me wanted to come right out and ask, Who the hell are you? What's going on? But I sensed that would be disastrous, and hung back. . . . Everything has a season, turn turn turn, and now it was my turn to play along. So I said—we still hadn't got down to cases—"How goes the poking?"

"Okay. You heard any more from them?"

"The police? No."

"Good." He made a face. "This whole thing is screwy, Nick. I don't get it. You can forget this witness, for one thing. Supposedly it's a girl, some friend of the victim, but they're not even going to put you in a lineup. I don't even think they believe her themselves."

I said, "She'd have to be lying. No one saw me at seven o'clock. Take my word for it." I held up my hand as he began to interrupt. "Let's just take that as given. No one saw me at seven o'clock."

"Okay, Nick, no one saw you, agreed, except we might have to go into that, what you were doing at seven o'clock. But for the time being, it's almost beside the point. Here's the question that gets me—how did this girl, this witness, know it was you, Nick Lamp?"

"What are you getting at?"

"Well . . . you never saw this Yuki—"

"No."

"Never went out with her, danced with, never were at a party with her—"

"No."

"Not even one of those big bashes, half a dozen tables, like the Chinese sometimes throw or—better yet—the Japs."

"No. Absolutely not."

"Well, how in hell did this girl know who you were? She knew you by name. The police didn't find you through some description, or after combing the city, et cetera, et cetera—or even on the basis of some tip. They had your name. They must have. They just showed up at your hotel, right?"

"Yes . . . I get it. I'm being set up, framed."

He smiled, held up a palm. "Objection, Your Honor. That's a conclusion, unwarranted on the evidence. All we

know is that something's going on ... but over here,
that's par for the course. It's more likely a screwup, or
something political we just don't understand. All they've
done is ask a few questions—if they wanted to get you,
they could do a hell of a lot more than that." He leaned
back in his chair. "Manage a sambuca?"

"No. Thanks."

"Come on. You can chuck half of yours in my coffee
and just chew the beans."

I gave in. Then he said, "What bothers me is the question of the quote bodily fluids unquote. I don't like that
part of it."

"What happens if they ask me. To give a sample."

He smiled. "Say you're a Christian, say self-abuse is
against your religion, and call me—fast. But I don't think
they will."

"If they do, though, would they cheat? I mean, divide
the sample in two and say one half came from Yuki and
it matched mine?"

"Very difficult."

"What if they had a sample of my semen from a different source? Could they have put it—injected it, whatever—into her . . . Yuki?"

"But that's the problem, isn't it? Where do they get
this sample?" He leaned forward and, with a strangely
prissy look on his face, lowered his voice. "Even those of
us with a lousy sex life tend to know it when we come. I
mean, we have a rough idea where and when we deposit
these substances."

"Well, I have a very good sex life and I know *precisely*

where and when, and with who . . . and the list doesn't include Yuki Yamoto." I leaned back. "And the list is not so long that there could be any chance of confusion."

"So, that's clear enough. You're absolutely sure—you didn't . . . not even a little bit?"

"No." And then I added—it seemed appropriate— "Scout's honor."

"All right then. I don't think you have to worry much. . . . To pull something like you're talking about, they'd have to really want to get you. Do you have any reason to believe they might?"

"Think about it. You said yourself that Kang only works on big cases . . . so what's he doing with Yuki Yamoto? Maybe he's worried about something else altogether."

I was again hoping to see if he'd rise, but he only smiled. "That is sharp, and I did think about it, my friend, first thing. And it could mean something, I don't know. So far as I can determine, the good people of Taipei aren't slaughtering each other any more often than usual. At the same time, I'm not sure there are any especially big cases on the go right now, so Kang could simply be taking his share of the load. But. As you say. You expect a little more with Kang. The question is—what?"

"Cao Dai? I told you I'm involved with him—I presume he's what you mean by big. . . ."

"Yes, maybe. . . ." He made a grimace that showed a lot of his teeth. "I don't know. If I'd realized you were into something with Cao, I would have checked it out, but it would take very special influence to get the police into a business deal." He smiled. "Of course, if he gives you a lowball offer on those tire rights in the next twenty-four hours, we'll have our answer. Meanwhile . . ."

Again, this was very smooth. Did Young know Cao was dead, or did he not? I had no idea. But even though I couldn't answer such a big question, I felt I was onto him a little, I was picking up a few vibrations, and I was sure now that we'd reached the point of this meeting, which meant I had just a moment's mental preparation. And although I wouldn't put myself on his level, I've done a few deals in my time, and I don't think my face gave anything away . . . as he reached into his pocket, took out a photograph, and slid it across the table toward me. He said, "That's a copy of course, but do you think you've ever seen it before?"

I looked down at it, squinted, shook my head. "No."

"Cao, since you mention him, is third on the left. Behind the blond girl."

I looked down at the photo again. It was black-and-white, about five by seven inches—bigger than a snapshot, anyway. It showed a mixed group of men and women, Chinese and European, in various states of evening dress, party dress, and undress. It must have been taken at night, or dusk . . . but no, it was dawn, of course it was dawn, the dawn after a long night of partying. It had been a night, you could guess, of stylish dissipation, discreet debauchery. Now, they barely had enough energy to strike poses of gay exhaustion. A Chinese couple, arms around each other, held champagne glasses at a tipsy angle, bow ties had been loosened, one of the white women had her shoes in her hand. I squinted at Cao, since Young had pointed him out. He was just a young, good-looking Chinese man in a tux, and the girl he was with wasn't a blond—she was a lovely Chinese girl in a blond wig that hinted at Marlene Dietrich, with eyes as gaudy as a peacock's wing. It was quite a good photograph, it had a certain style; anyone, looking at it, would have thought of the thirties, the early forties, nightclubs, cocktails, shingles and bobs, ebony cigarette holders, big bands, swing. And of course they were in Shanghai—where else? A city on the brink. And they were right at the edge. They were dancing at the top of a precipice, and they didn't care, they just danced faster, closer and closer, daring the fall. They were laughing. This was the end, they seemed to say, but it wasn't quite the end, there were still a few seconds left. And why worry? They were strangers in a strange land, but they would be going home, and on their faces were the superior, complacent expressions of imperial power. Who cares what happens? We won't have to live with the consequences. In fact, they were grouped around a perfect expression of that imperialism, a great stone lion—one of the white ladies was sitting astride it, her dress pulled up to her thighs—and the background seemed to be an English park, transplanted from Bournemouth or Lyme Regis or Torbay, but faded, like a memory, or an old picture from the *Illustrated London News*: a park with a delicate line of trees, a curving path, a pavilion where a regimental band could play on Sunday afternoon. It was a strange, distant, long-lost world—which, ultimately, I was descended from. I stared down at it. All around the edge of the photo was a faint dark line or stain—the original must have been framed. And in the background, near the trees, I made out a funny white mark.

"What's that?" I said.

"Don't know. They didn't let me see the original. . . . And you're absolutely certain *you've* never seen it?"

"Well, I can look at it some more . . . but no. Should I have seen it? Why is it important?"

"I'm not sure it is, but Kang found it in Yuki Yamoto's purse."

"I see." Then I shrugged. "Or I don't." I looked up. "At least it's not a photo of me."

"Thank God for small blessings." But Young said this almost perfunctorily, as though he'd lost interest; and in a moment he was looking at his watch, taking a quick gulp of his cappuccino. Whatever he'd come to do, he'd done—and I was sure the photo was the heart of it. Was he delivering a message? Setting me a test? I couldn't have said.

As he organized the check, I asked: "What now?"

As smooth as ever, giving nothing away, he slipped his wallet back into his jacket. "I want to look into this Cao Dai connection. Cao, as you say, *is* big. And isn't it interesting that he turns up in that photo—and that Kang pointed him out to me? I want to poke some more, ask a few questions."

"And what should I do?"

"Sit tight. If anything happens, let me know pronto. Okay?"

I watched him go, and decided it was no accident that he'd left the photo behind, even though it only increased my suspicion. Why would Kang have let him have it? It only proved, it seemed to me, that he was altogether too close to the police. But that was the least of my worries. Finishing my coffee, I picked up the photo and studied it some more—for of course I'd seen it a hundred times before, exactly this photo . . . except for that small white mark. Cao was third on the left; my father was third on the right, standing beside a tall Scot named Warden. Although my father never quite made a lot of money— his "big pile"—he came closest in a deal with Jack Warden, "and it wasn't even the son of a bitch's fault that it fell through." Yes, I could hear my father's voice, and see that photo, one of the souvenirs he'd managed to keep from his time in Shanghai, from before the war, before the time he'd met my mother—along with one case of Clover Beer, finally consumed on my twenty-first birthday. In his retirement, this exact photo had hung with a few others in his den, his inner sanctum, the one room in the house where my mother allowed him to smoke his pipe. Even as a grown man, I'd a special feeling when I was with him there and often enough he told stories about that time, quite a few about Warden. I guess I was his last chance to relive those memories— and it was one of the reasons I knew that he'd had some sort of friendship with Cao. I wondered what kind of friendship it had been. Cao had been a crook, pretty much. But not my father. This opinion was not mere filial piety. My father knew crooks, dealt with crooks—thugs,

gangsters, truly ugly people—and he knew how to sail
very close to the wind himself. Once, in fact, he had
killed a man. This was in Macau. It had been a gambling
brawl, the other man had pulled a gun, and my father had
thrown a knife—my father was very good with a knife.
But when he'd told me this story, he'd made absolutely
certain I understood that he'd acted solely in self-
defense, as a last resort, and that the whole affair had
been a catastrophe, not something he took pride in. And
when he'd instructed me in handling a knife myself, he
was only teaching me a necessary gentlemanly skill, like
properly tying a bow tie, not a violent pursuit. Of course,
you could look at all that another way, but it remained
true; despite the world he functioned in, he never went
beyond a certain point. He had something to lose, a view
of himself that was certainly connected to his British
passport, but was more than that—the passport was only
a symbol. My father was Chinese, his life was in
Shanghai, but he knew there was a world beyond
Shanghai. He had direct money connections in London
and New York; for reasons I've never understood, he
knew people in the British military, connections that
were essentially political. Those links were valuable to
him, both concretely and emotionally. Jack Warden was
a case in point. Their friendship went beyond their business dealings, they had deeper claims on each other;
people trusted my father and there were people he could
trust. Of course, this was a romanticized view, but there
was truth in it, an essential truth. You could even see it in
this photograph. My father was half a step removed from

the others, a separate figure. And then, as I stared down
at this ancient image, I could see something else as well.
My father had been a very handsome man, elegant in his
dinner jacket, standing with his hand on his hip, a quietly
arrogant look on his face. A woman, her head turned,
was watching him—and I had no doubt that she was his
mistress, at least for that night. I smiled to myself . . . you
don't often see your father in that light. But just then my
phone rang. I flipped it open. It was Laurie, in the office.
"I'm sorry, Nick. . . . Is it okay?"

"Yes, we're done. I'm just finishing my coffee."

"And?"

"I'm not sure. I'm still not sure about Young. He says
that this witness doesn't really exist. Something funny's
going on."

"Maybe it is. You'll never guess who I was just talking
to. Cao Feng. He wants to see you."

Cao Feng was Cao Dai's number-one son.

I found I was whispering, "There's still nothing . . ."

"No, I've bought all the papers and there's nothing on
the radio. If they've found anything, they're still not
saying. And Cao Feng—"

"Was it him, personally?"

"I think so. He said so. He's sending a car at eight
o'clock. He would like to have a drink and a little talk. I
told him to send the car to my place."

"God, you shouldn't have let him know we're
involved. There's no point—"

"But I am involved."

I didn't say anything.

She said, "Aren't I?"

"Yes."

"Good boy."

"Laurie, it's just . . ."

"I know. I've got the same feeling too. Something's going to happen. *Is* happening now. But maybe that's good, Nick. He wants to talk. You never know. He's a dealer. He'll want to make a deal—from his point of view, that's all there ever is to talk about. And he'll want to wrap this all up as quickly as possible."

"Maybe."

But I was far from sure; sitting there, looking down at the photo, I doubted it could be so easy. In my mind, I went back to the night when I'd gone to see Cao. He was going to see me. He was, as I'd hoped, going to pick up the link between him and my father. That's what the photo meant; he was going to show it to me, it would have been witness to our long-lost connection. It was so strange. Everything had been reversed; I'd hoped to use the past to make him feel an obligation to me, but he'd hoped that I'd feel obliged to him. But what had happened to change everything around—what, after so long, had made *me* useful to *him*? Then I realized something. I made myself imagine the way he'd lain there, sprawled on that carpet. And I realized he might well have died with that photo in his hand. But though I'd instinctively snatched up the magazine from Cao's pooling blood, *there'd been no photograph.* I was sure of it—there'd been no photograph *because Yuki had already taken it.* Which told you something. Yuki was a whore. Whatever

Yuki did, she did for money. She knew what that photo was worth . . . maybe she didn't know why, maybe she didn't know how, but she knew it was cash in her hand.

9

IN CHINA, FAMILY IS EVERYTHING. MAYBE THAT'S TRUE everywhere—but in China it's more true than anywhere else. Family loyalty, family traditions, and family interest almost come before personal interest, and certainly the country. Chinese families are governed by a hierarchy of respect and obedience that extends even to the dead: you respect your father, he respects *his* father, and everyone respects the family's ancestors. Western families may have a family Bible that goes back a few generations; many Chinese families, and their clans, maintain *zong pu*, histories that can stretch back centuries. Because of this, almost all Chinese people can tell you the name of the village where their family began, and in the same way that Muslims will dedicate their lives to seeing Mecca, Chinese are obsessed with the idea of returning to the seat of their family's origins—in fact, the Communist government, for years, issued a special travel permit to overseas Chinese for just that purpose, "Introduction for Return to a Native Village." Of course, Chinese families are a great joy, and children are pampered in a way Westerners would find incredible—adolescents, for example, are still considered children, and the idea of their working or living outside the family home strikes Chinese as incredible. But families are also a burden. Personal responsibility is almost inseparable from family responsibility. I am Chinese; if I am disgraced, so is everyone in my family. This, too, can even affect your ancestors. A scholar named Zhuang Tinglong wrote a history of the Ming dynasty, not entirely unfavorable, and even though it wasn't published until after Zhuang's death, it so angered the ruling Manchus that they dug up his body and burned it—and then burned his father's as well. As for his living relatives, they were simply beheaded. Anthropologists and historians presumably have fancy explanations for all this, but my own is simple. Every Chinese knows how cheap life is, how tenuous its meaning. The soil of China is fertilized with the bones of a billion dead, and yet one in four babies born yesterday was Chinese. What does your life mean? Who cares? In 1906, the San Francisco earthquake, which killed 503 people, made its mark in history—on July 28, 1976, the Tangshan earthquake killed 242,000 Chinese and no one gives it a second thought. You're nothing. You're infinitely replaceable. Every Chinese knows this, but naturally no one wants to accept it. So you invent meaning. You do that in the family, that's where you find your place; they care for you, you care for them, and you elaborate and underline that meaning even to the point of absurdity—you insist that all those dead care too. Or at least that's my theory. Cao's family, of course, had never considered the question for a single instant. They just *did* it, lived it. Now, it seemed, they were doing it to me.

The car they sent was a Mercedes limousine, stretched, black, with tinted windows and an aerial on the trunk that would have made Captain Kirk happy. The chauffeur was a young man in a black suit who looked more or less normal, but there was another man with him who was not normal at all; he was big, big in the shoulders, big in the chest, big in the thighs. He was standing beside the car as I came out, his eyes looking everywhere at once—you had the feeling that any sudden move in his direction would get a response that might be martial, might be artistic, but would certainly be violent. The chauffeur held the door for me, then got in himself; the car was already moving slightly as the second man ducked inside, and before he had the door shut we were already accelerating, hard, up the street. Which was clearly all routine.

Outside it was drizzling. It was one of those nights when the rain and pollution combined to make the darkening sky more livid, the colors of welts; the air had the sheen of a bruise, of injury; light glistened with the colors of wet, rotting wood, of water washing against pilings too long in the sea. But we went through this, climbed above it. We passed the airport and the freeway, for a moment the Keelung River was a dark, wet coil beside us, then we were clear of the city and climbing rapidly north. I'd checked out the Cao family well enough to know where we were going. The dark shadows of trees wrapped around the headlights as we reached the Yangteh Road, and then lights, clean as stars, sparkled above us as we climbed more steeply: Yangmingshan. It's a high, hilly park above Taipei where there are hot springs and fumaroles, orchids and cherry blossoms, monkeys and macaques—sometimes, even the magic of snow. And of course it's here, in an area called Green Grass Mountain, that the rich people live. The Caos must have been among the first to settle here, for their estate was choice and huge. The big car followed a long, dark road through a forest of firs and pines, and then had to slow carefully as we edged around a cliff, with Taipei twinkling in the misty gloom below. Small outbuildings hung back in the trees; a guard with a big light waved us on; we reached a second set of high iron gates, these thrown open: and then the road circled a huge fountain and we stopped at stone steps running up to a door.

Again, I expect, it was routine: the second man, the big man, got out; then the chauffeur; and then the door was held for me.

Another man, also in a black suit, appeared. He greeted me by name. For a moment I felt cold air on my cheek and the sharp smell of wet pine needles filled my nose. Then I was passing through large, varnished cedar doors into the house. A bronze chandelier, burning real candles, lit the entrance hall. Silently, someone took my coat. Then I was led down a long passage with closed doors on my right hand, tall, narrow windows on my left—but windows which had no view because of a high cedar hedge outside. The floor was a plain, earth-colored tile, there were a few rugs, there were more rugs on the walls; but the effect was Mediterranean rather than Oriental. It was like a villa, a summer home. And maybe it had started that way, but at the end of the passage was a room fit for a palace. It was huge, hexagonal or octagonal—but irregular; it must have been built right along the edge of the cliff—and with a very high ceiling, for the walls ran right to the roof beams. A fireplace, with a huge blaze roaring away, filled the left side of the room. Across from this was a wall of glass, or several walls of glass, like the panels of a Chinese screen, which offered a fantastic view; you could see for miles down the dark hill, across the city, all the way to the river. The great fire made the rest of the room seem dark, but in the middle was a smaller pool of light, and here four couches were set around a low table. The two men sitting there rose as I came up. One was much older than the other—and he wore a long gown, the traditional costume of the Chinese gentleman. The younger was in a dark suit—like the chauffeur, but a superior cut. They both bowed. This was China; this was formal. I bowed back.

"Mr. Lamp, I am Cao Feng. This is my younger brother, Mr. Cao Kai-shek. We are so delighted to see you, and are honored that you have found the time to visit us. We only wish that we could have met you earlier."

"The honor is mine, Mr. Cao Feng. It is a great privilege to know your family, and to be here, in this wonderful house."

"Thank you, but this is really my father's house, not my own, and its merits only come from what nature gives us, the fresh air, and the mountain, and our view. You must eat. . . ."

"Thank you, no, I have already eaten."

"Really, but I insist."

"No, truly, I have already . . ." In China, you get good at being polite and this could have gone on for hours, or at least several more rounds; but the younger brother, Kai-shek, cut it off. It was subtle; a quick, impatient movement, a setting of his face—and something he muttered to his older brother so quickly, and low, that I missed it. So we settled, in the end, on Shao-Hsing, which the younger brother fetched from an elaborate rosewood bar, as Cao Feng offered me an apologetic glance—or a glance that flitted back and forth between the cultures, because it was the Chinese's smile of embarrassment and a Western request for indulgence all at once. Then, when the younger man came back, Cao Feng thanked him and called him Ito—and of course that rang a bell with me. So this was the man who'd taken Yuki to Cao Dai's apartment, the man she'd phoned first for instructions: in fact, one of his sons.

As we toasted the pleasure of new acquaintances, I looked around the room. In here, in the dark, there was a traditional feel; a few lamps glowed, but the flickering fire created the effect of lanterns. Silk found a luster in this gloom; rosewood, intricately carved, caught the dance of the light. All the furniture was Chinese, probably antique; it all looked very hard—no doubt it was good for both your posture and character. But what I particularly noticed was a large painting hanging on one of the angled walls, just to the left of the fireplace. I couldn't tell whether it was old or a copy, but I recognized the subject. It was a portrait of Koxinga, the last of the Ming generals, who'd almost driven the Manchus from Nanking, but had finally fallen back to Taiwan. For the Chinese, he was the island's true founder—but in fact his mother was Japanese, and you could see it in the portrait, you could see it in the eyes. Just as, I realized, you could see Cao Feng's Japanese mother in his face, his eyes. Was that, I wondered, why the portrait was placed so prominently, a reminder that his particular mixture of blood had a long pedigree on this island? I looked at Cao Feng. He was upright, but a little heavy; probably in his fifties, but his flatter, Japanese face made him look older. Ito I put at thirty, and despite the name—to me it had a Japanese sound—he was pure Chinese. He looked tough. When he looked at me, I got a sense that he wasn't seeing much at all.

As we settled back with our wine, Cao Feng began: "Unfortunately, Mr. Lamp, we meet at a rather sad moment for us. It distresses me greatly, but I have to tell you that my father has died."

"This is tragic news, I am deeply saddened to hear it."

"It is kind of you to say so. But this sadness, in a sense, is why we wanted to see you."

"At such a moment, I would do anything I could to help."

"Thank you. In fact, there are two things we would like to ask you."

"If I can be of service in any way."

"I believe you met my father at an apartment he maintained, a small place in the old city." He looked at me, obviously wanting me to acknowledge this, but I didn't want to give anything away; and I don't think my face did. So he went on: "I am sure you realized it was not a place where he often met business associates. It had a different purpose in his life, a private purpose. I think it testifies to the great confidence he had in you, by virtue of his long association with your family, that he saw you there at all."

This was like chess moves, or putting pieces of a puzzle into place: "The friendship of our fathers honors us all," I said.

"I am so happy that you say so. I count on that, Mr. Lamp. You see, he died in that apartment. But it would hurt my family, and my father's memory, if the existence of that place should be revealed. Do you understand? We are hoping, all of us—isn't that so, younger brother?—that we can assume your discretion."

In Chinese families, position is everything and there are separate words for "older brother," "younger brother"; Arthur was my *geh-geh*, for example, and Ito was *di-di* to Cao Feng. And now *di-di* made his first contribution to the conversation: he nodded.

I said, "Mr. Cao Feng, I wouldn't think of mentioning it. No one will hear anything ill of your late father from me."

Cao Feng bowed. Sitting in his long gown, with his hands on his knees, he bent forward from the waist and delicately inclined his head. A bow ... yet this whole business, I decided, this theater, was essentially contemptuous; they were reminding me of—who I was? where I was? how I ought to behave? Something like that. The Chinese can be as snobbish about their accents as the English, as arrogant about their families as Spaniards, as ugly about money as the French. And they expected me to be intimidated. Which I was ... but only because Ito, leaning back, revealed a leather strap circling under his arm. He was carrying a gun. And what I realized then—felt then; of course I'd known it before— was that I was nothing, a five-dollar chip in a game of big stakes.

Now, perhaps, a hint about the game was revealed.

Cao Feng had relaxed. Everything was going as he wished. I don't mean that he gave anything away, but I was able to read between a few lines—and he might have been better to hold those lines back. "Always," he resumed, "we must consider our families. We say it is the Chinese way, but surely it is the only way. We must always honor the connection between families and build upon it. Our fathers, very different in many ways, nonetheless both began in Shanghai. I was born there. Am I not right, your older brother, Arthur, was also born there? Yes? And our fathers were friends. They worked together, perhaps. They did business together. They shared the pursuits of young men. Isn't that so? Did your father not love the great clubs of those days, all the pretty faces? Yes?" He leaned forward and took a cigarette from a small marble box on the table; as he lit it, I was thinking of the photo they'd found in Yuki's purse—suspecting that this must have been in Cao Feng's mind too. That was it; at one and the same time we were in Shanghai and the old man's private whorehouse, that was the key. "Of course your father left Shanghai. A British passport! In those days, that was everything ... it is amazing, to think of the British, so important. Of course, all that was before Singapore, before they were swept away, in such a few weeks. Still, your father could leave, whereas mine had to bow before the wind, the Japanese wind. And the Japanese endured even less than the British, they were supreme for so few years—no time, in the time of history. But men live by days and months—that's the trouble. So my father had to bow down. But then the wind changed, so he came here. And now, of course, the wind is changing again. My father accepted that gladly, by the way—if his passing saddens me, it is especially so because he did not see Shanghai again. He longed to move back there. Perhaps it is the same for you, Mr. Lamp. Back to Shanghai! The future lies in the past. Which means, sometimes, that the past is an obstacle in the way of the future."

None of this seemed particularly difficult, and I wasn't quite sure why he was oblique. He was telling me that the problem he faced, the problem that the old man's death had raised, involved accommodating, restating—regularizing—the family's history with the mainland. There was some obstacle. Cao Dai's association with the

Japanese? Everybody, even my mother, seemed to think that had something to do with Cao's case. Or was it something else? I couldn't be sure—but there was something.

I smiled; I was pleased with myself. So I decided to give him some of his own medicine. "Surely it's true. The past and the future hold all our problems."

At this, Ito's face managed to look even more blank. But Cao Feng was enjoying himself; Chinese people, like the characters in American soap opera, love banalities, the more profound the better. And of course he wasn't afraid of me. He smiled, languidly drew on his cigarette, then leaned back into the gloom behind him and a light came on, illuminating a table I'd barely noticed before. It was an architect's model: plaster towers, tiny painted trees, miniature pedestrians and cars. I rose to look at it. There were even tiny street signs on the corner buildings. I said, "The project you are planning in Shanghai? It is truly impressive." It was; a billion dollars, give or take a few hundred million, is always impressive.

Cao Feng nodded. "Thank you. Now it must be a final memorial to my father."

"Of course."

"Nothing must prevent its completion."

"I am sure nothing will."

"But his death, naturally, creates difficulties. And we must attend to every detail."

"Again, I would be honored to help."

"I wouldn't wish you to be distressed, Mr. Lamp, but it seems you were the last person to see my father alive."

"Ah."

"My younger brother and myself were wondering if he had said anything that might have caught your attention. Or perhaps shown you something, or given you something. Anything. Papers of some sort. Or perhaps, inadvertently, you took something away with you—perhaps something you picked up while you were waiting."

So, this was it. . . . Now I could feel Ito's eyes. They were hunter's eyes; they watched for movement. But just because of that, they could paralyze, immobilize. I shrugged, turned my head, looked right at him, then away. I said, "I am a little unclear, Mr. Cao Feng. Your father and I . . . our business together had nothing to do with Shanghai. True, we did talk of my own father. . . ." I stopped there; I'd said enough to be polite and I wanted to see more of their hand. I leaned back.

"There was nothing he showed you?"

Showed you. "Only . . . a photograph. Could that be what you mean? It was taken in Shanghai, I believe. It showed your father and my father together, after a party—as you were saying, they were young together then."

"Do you have it?"

"No, Mr. Cao Feng. Your father only showed it to me—he certainly kept it. It was important to him . . . in that way. But my father had the same picture. I saw it many times in my father's house. My mother must still have it now. Is it important?"

Ito and Cao Feng exchanged a glance, and I wondered if they'd ever seen the photograph before, or knew about it now. Possibly not. If the police really didn't know about the connection between Yuki and Cao Dai, it was conceivable the brothers didn't know that she'd taken it; it was even possible that Ito wouldn't know that she was dead. But eventually—this was my reasoning—they were going to find out and see the photo, so I couldn't lose much by admitting to knowing about it.

"He didn't, perhaps, ask you to do something for him?"

"In particular . . . ?"

"I was under the impression that he might offer you . . . a commission?"

"I don't quite understand. A commission to . . . ?"

He smiled; it was clear neither of us was going to give anything away. "Perhaps he didn't."

"You understand, Mr. Cao Feng, that our discussion was very preliminary."

Cao Dai said, "I only hope—"

But Ito cut him off, speaking quickly, harshly, the words held back in his throat. "You took something. You took something out of there."

There was an instant of silence. I looked right at Ito; and then, slowly, I turned toward Cao Feng. "I only took what I came with. I only took away what was mine."

In a sense, Cao Feng was now trapped. It was partly a question of face, about *geh-geh* and *di-di*, who was senior, who was in charge. But there was more; that room, the careful politeness, his long gown, his cigarette—for tobacco is as Chinese as rice—had created an assumption. We were playing by Chinese rules, we were all Chinese together. Now I was making him live up to it;

and he had to, or bring a great deal more into the open. Did he want to be explicit about what he thought—what he was afraid—I might have taken away? No; with a quick bow he said, "Mr. Lamp, our apologies. That was an unfortunate manner of speaking, and I am sure my younger brother meant nothing. Of course you wouldn't have taken anything that wasn't yours, it is only, you see, that we wish to tie up all loose ends."

"I know of no loose ends."

"We seek only amicable cooperation. Friendship."

"I do not see how I could be of help."

"But no, Mr. Lamp, I insist. You have already been a great help. And a comfort. Your assurance . . ."

"Of course. I do not mean, Mr. Cao Feng, that I don't wish to help. Anything I can do, I naturally will do. But . . ."

Gradually, I let myself be pacified. If I thought of anything more, I would tell them. They were certain that any proposals of a business nature would be looked upon sympathetically. I could always reach Mr. Cao Feng at the private number on this card. . . . In a few moments, he was offering me tea, a clear sign he wanted me to go. Ito hung back, but our good-byes were cordial enough, under the circumstances—Cao Feng even tried out his English:

"It will be a pleasure, in the future, to do good business together."

Bowing, I was relieved. Only now did I feel how tense I'd been. I'd found something out, and I wasn't sure I liked what it meant. Now, I just wanted to get out of there. In that strange dark room, with the leaping fire, the city I could see twinkling through the window seemed very far away, and I wanted to get back to it, fast. Heading down the passage, I was only wishing I had my own car. That was it; I wanted to be in control. . . . Then, as we reached the chandelier with its candles, there was a little disturbance. The servant who was showing me out was met by another flunky—another black suit—who'd emerged from the opposite side of the hall. There was a quick argument; and then I was beckoned. "If you would come this way, Mr. Lamp. . . ."

I didn't like it. "It is getting late. I would like to return."

"Please, sir. It would be better. . . . It will only be for a minute."

He wanted me out of sight; he was disobeying some order—I took a certain comfort from that—but I was unnerved as he led me down a passage, identical to the one that had led to Cao Feng's aerie, but running in the opposite direction, and I stepped uncertainly through the door that was held open for me at the end.

But inside there was a nice surprise: a beautiful Chinese woman, in a blue cheongsam slit well above her knee—a gorgeous woman.

She exhaled cigarette smoke. "You look frightened, Mr. Lamp. At least that shows you have sense. . . . But don't be frightened of me. Ito's the one. All his friends are gangsters. He thinks fucking a whore makes him a man. He's that kind, you see. . . ."

For a second I didn't know what to say. You never

expect a Chinese woman to talk to you in that kind of language, and especially not this one—Cao Dai's wife. She introduced herself but I'd seen pictures and I knew who she was; her given name was Su-liang, but years ago she'd acted in Hong Kong as Suzy and she looked like that, sleek and almost too sexy—her face was lovely, but it was her body you noticed, the long run of her legs, her full, high breasts. She was still marvelous, but I guessed she wasn't as young as she looked; probably she was in her early forties.

Finally I said, "I know about Ito."

"Good. Like a drink?"

"No, thank you, I have already—"

She made a dismissing gesture with her hand. "Christ, do you want something or don't you?"

I smiled; she'd spoken in English and that's how I replied. "A little whiskey, then."

"I have bourbon. . . ."

"Fine."

This room was a complete contrast to the other; it was bright, modern, and as European as *Elle Maison*. There was a glass wall, but we were on the other side of the house and it looked onto a garden, not over a cliff; flickering candles in bronze holders marked a pebble path around carefully tended flower beds, past a pond, and then through a stand of cherry trees. But the candles and the cherry trees—and Suzy's cheongsam—were the only traditional elements in view; everything else was puffed furniture, track lighting, and Sony.

Suzy raised her glass, but with only one hand on it.

"Cheers," she said. She took a sip. "I hope you don't mind, Mr. Lamp, but I was curious to meet you."

"Why was that?"

"They were talking about you. A family conference . . . you can imagine, at a time like this. They even had to include me. Someone said that Laurie Stadler works for you."

"Yes, she does."

"Well, I knew her as a little girl. I knew her mother. The family . . . well, I never really knew the Colonel. Or the Captain. Whatever he was."

"I didn't realize."

"She probably wouldn't remember me. I was just someone she had to be polite to. How is she? How did she turn out?"

"Very well. On both counts."

"Good." She hesitated. "You're not bad-looking. Are the two of you . . . ?"

I smiled. "Your English is very good."

She waved her hand. "You don't have to tell me. I always know. I'm a witch. Coralee loved to say that. Laurie's mother, you know. But she was the witch, really. Witch. Bitch . . ." She stubbed out her cigarette but immediately began lighting another. "You're right, my English is good, and that's partly Coralee's doing. I made her correct me, every mistake, and she did."

"This was . . . ?"

She seemed to want to talk. She tossed her head back, spewing smoke at the ceiling. "This was years ago. Years and years ago, it seems. I met her first in Hong Kong.

Captain Jack was at a military conference and the wives were given tours, one of which included the film set I was on. I was hauled out to make nice because of my English . . . it was pretty good even then . . . I always wanted to try making it in the States but I never had the guts. . . . Anyway, we ended up going shopping together. And other things. Then I met her here all over again."

She stood up. She knocked the ash off her cigarette. She went to the bar and poured a little more whiskey into her glass. She didn't actually pace, but all this was pacing; the words came out like that. She was stretched tight as the silk across her thighs. Cao Dai was dead: that was now, clearly, an established fact. And she was a widow. What would become of her? For her the whole world had changed, but in which ways and how much? She would have a certain amount of money, a certain position, a certain freedom; but what did "certain" mean? Not a hell of a lot, I suspected. I could see why she'd spoken to me, pulled me in here. Right now she was feeling as trapped as a girl in a harem; the sultan was dead, a power struggle was on, meanwhile the eunuchs were in charge. She'd be desperate for any news, for any connections, from the other side of the seraglio's walls.

"Are you still in touch with her?" I asked.

She shook her head. "I haven't seen Coralee in years."

"She's back in the States."

"Too bad. She was quite a lady, she was my kind of lady. There were problems, though. I mean her husband." She took a good slug of her drink. "He was a spy, you know."

"I thought he was in the air force."

"Sure. He was a spy in the air force. He was a spy after he left the air force. That's why he stayed here. And he was even a spy before that, you know, over there." *Over there, the other side*—in Taiwan, there are many ways to refer to the mainland. Suzy had one cigarette burning in an ashtray, but she lit another and came back to the couch where she'd been sitting before. "Of course," she said, "Cao was a spy too. I think they all must have been spies. My God what a place."

I smiled. "And who did your husband spy for?"

"Big Moo? Anybody . . . or that's what I'd guess. Whoever paid. Whoever had him over a barrel. You know, he survived. He was an amazing man, Mr. Lamp. People think I've suffered all these years and maybe I have, but you can't take anything away from him. I didn't see him much, and only for one thing, you know. But . . ." She laughed. "He knew what to do with me. I never *didn't* want him to come." She laughed again and said, "That was the big thing, you know, that we shared, me and Coralee. She liked her men. Especially, she liked her Chinese men. My beautiful Chinks, she used to call them. She used to tell me, they've got perfect cocks for sucking. That was something I could do for her—being a Chinese actress, I had a supply, you see." She waved her cigarette and smiled. "So now tell me, does the little girl take after her mummy?"

I wondered if she was drunk or on something, or if it was only adrenaline. I said, "You don't really expect me to answer that."

"Apologies. None of my business. I was just remembering Coralee. . . . Those were good times. We had good times. Of course she always went too far. In the end she was bound to get into trouble."

"With her husband?"

"Sure. After a certain point he never touched her—which means he didn't have anything to complain about if you ask me—but a few of Coralee's escapades were pretty . . ." She broke off and shrugged. "But who remembers the details? There were problems, though. For him. With his work."

"How much does Laurie know about all this?"

She paused long enough to think, if she was capable of it; then she said, "I couldn't even guess. But Coralee always said Laurie was closer to her father, that she and her father really loved each other." She shrugged again. "But I really couldn't say." She stopped and frowned; something else had come into her mind. She got up then, looked at her watch. "They'll be wondering . . . you should probably get out of here."

"Just a second . . ."

"Yes?"

"What did Coralee—"

But now she held up her hand. "Never mind. I've already said too much. And you've got to go; they'll start looking."

Half of me didn't want to; from her, I suspected, I could learn things I couldn't get anywhere else. But I didn't want to be looked for; I didn't want to be found, in that house, anywhere I wasn't supposed to be. I said nothing and told myself it didn't make any difference; she was in the sort of mood where she'd talk, and might say anything, but a direct question would only spoil it. I watched her cross the room to a phone; she pushed a button and said something I didn't catch. She didn't look at me. She came back to the couch. There was a TV remote lying on it; she switched on the set, which was high up on a chromium stand against the wall, like the monitors in a television studio, and Bernard Shaw appeared, reading the news: but she muted him instantly. Now she curled her legs up on the couch—her cheong-sam was so tight, I guess this was the only way she could get at her feet—and took off her slippers, then slid on a pair of low-heeled shoes. On account of an old girlfriend, I can speak a little Italian—crucial words like Bruno Magli—and I was able to make a shrewd guess at how many lire she was now putting on. Finally she curled herself upright and said, "Come this way."

We passed through a sliding glass door into the garden. The rain had stopped, but a soft, cool mist hung in the air. I took a breath of the air; that's what the rich are buying up here. I followed her along a path of smooth, perfect pebbles that curved gently around the side of the house. Then there was a little slope. With an easy gesture, she took my arm for balance. We reached the drive, a soft, dark openness in the night. She looked along it, toward the house, and said, "They'll be here in a moment."

"You don't have to wait."

"That's all right." But she seemed distracted, falling

silent, returning to her own problems after the diversion I'd provided. With a little shiver, she hugged her arms and then, as lights appeared, she smiled. "Say hello to Laurie for me."

"Yes."

But now the car slowed in front of the house, and someone came out; there seemed to be an argument and I felt a little tightening of anxiety; I wanted to go, I wanted to go. But Suzy said, "Don't worry, they're squabbling about who should get the old lady."

"Who's that?"

"I had several predecessors, Mr. Lamp. The first one— the very first—is still alive. They hid her away in Tayuling but now they have to get her, of course. She's mother to number-one son."

"I didn't know she was still alive."

"Oh yes. Barely. She's Jap, you know. You knew that? That was Big Moo's taste, *his* special weakness." Her smile was almost invisible in the dark. "Coralee always used to say, 'Who can figure men?' and I always used to say to her, 'The same person who can figure women.' "

Now the car came on and Suzy seemed a little calmer. So was I. There was no bodyguard this time, only the chauffeur; and he seemed resigned to a familiar, boring drive. Familiar, boring, resigned . . . words attached to the normal world. I couldn't have asked for anything more.

I got into the car. But when I rolled down the window to say good-bye, Suzy was already gone.

10

LAURIE, SITTING ON THE EDGE OF THE BED, SHOOK ME gently by the shoulder. I was only half-awake, but the headline on the paper she was holding cut through the fog. Cao was dead. . . . So, at last, it was official.

It was still very early in the morning and she'd gone straight out; she was barely dressed. Her raincoat was open and under her blue cashmere sweater her breasts were free as . . . but nothing in the world could be that free. I rolled over, leaning on my elbow. "That's what they were doing last night, clearing the decks, getting their act together. That's why they had to talk to me."

"Nick, it's going to happen. Now."

She was frightened. "I know." From under the sweater her left breast popped out as easily as a cheerleader's. I kissed her. I moved my hands. Her body was so clean, so slim, so white. Flushed, engorged, aroused—these changes were so violent I could imagine that they were almost frightening. I whispered, "I'm going to terrify you."

"Nick . . ."

I kissed her mouth. "Don't worry. Either it's too late, or we've got enough time."

Surely her lips were full of love? Why should I hear betrayal in her sighs? There was no reason to think of Coralee and Suzy and the air force spy. And body heat can't tell lies.

She kissed me, whispering that she wanted to go down, but I didn't want that, I just wanted to kiss, to make her tremble, to feel the roundness of her shoulder inside my palm. Then I slipped it into her, and now I had to be feeling the truth, if there was such a thing at all. And despite everything I didn't want to let her go, give her up, I wanted to believe, I wanted to give her everything, and at last she cried out and then her flesh was rolling under me like a wave, breaking, then rolling forward again.

For a long time afterward we lay there. We were both trembling. I kissed her cheek, and could feel her going off to sleep, and I felt happy. But in the end I couldn't sleep myself; we'd worked out a plan, and I kept running through it in my mind. I wasn't sure—I wasn't sure of anything. I suppose that was the whole problem. I didn't know if the police were really coming after me; and, if they did, I didn't know whether the reason was Cao Dai's murder or Yuki Yamoto's. Was Cao's family against me? That too remained unclear. Young—another question mark. Everything remained unsettled . . . so I was going to lie low, drop out of sight, and maybe things would sort themselves out. There was no point running if I didn't have to. On the other hand . . .

Forty minutes later, I headed up the Tunhua Road, past the Adventist Hospital, and then turned to pick up the freeway.

It was jammed, it's always jammed, but after the airport exits it got a little easier. I made good time against the rush hour traffic. It started to rain. For a while it came down hard, but in Mrs. Stadler's Mercedes—which she'd left for Laurie when she'd gone back to the States—you barely noticed; the wipers flicked the drops away and out there, on the other side of the windshield, it was a different world altogether. I wondered about importing these cars; it had been impossible, at least for a long time, to bring in cars from Japan—they were building their local industry—but maybe not Germany. On the other hand, it probably hadn't made much difference, for Suzy had been telling the truth about Stadler—he certainly had lots of *guan-hsi*—connections, pull—as my destination proved. It was a summerhouse, in the mountains around Chiayi, which had been given to him by the government on his retirement from the air force—and if the pictures Laurie had shown me were anything to go by, it was a hell of a lot better than a Rolex, especially the kind that is made in Taiwan. From Taipei, it was perhaps a hundred and forty miles. That's a fair trip on an island that's only two hundred and fifty miles long, but the new freeway was fast. Around Chungli I tucked myself in behind a container truck and let the miles roll by. The rain eased off; the mountains humped up through the clouds, the central range that is the spine down the center of the island. There were no cops. I only saw a couple of army vehicles, and those were only briefly below us, on a parallel road. Finally we crossed over the Choshui River. I guessed that the truck I'd been following was headed for Kaohsiung, a huge seaport at the southern end of the island, but I turned off and went into a small place called Huwei. That was part of the plan. Laurie never went there. The big car would be noticed, but nobody actually knew who it belonged to. I took a break, bought some things. Then I crossed back under the freeway, zigzagged along minor roads, and came into Kukeng from the south. Here, the Stadlers and the car had been known for years, so I didn't stop, and left the village, heading east, following the only road you could follow, up, up, up, then down, down, down. All around were dark hills, covered in fir, pine, cypress. A river glinted below, probably the Alishan, but now I was following Laurie's hand-drawn map. The road got rougher and I slowed right down. Even so I almost went past the logging trail she'd marked. But I backed up a little and then turned, running up it about two hundred yards. There was a hut here, and an open space where Laurie had told me to leave the car. With luck—and if I didn't light a fire—no one might know I was here at all. I got out two backpacks from the trunk—clothes, a lot of sweaters, the food I'd bought— and went back to the road. It wasn't much better than a track. I began walking. It was still raining, and mist curled among the trees. After a mile or so, the way rose steeply and the trees thinned; looking ahead, I could see a small house with a bright yellow roof, surrounded by a deck, clinging to a high hillside. The Taiwanese like that, those bright roofs. Farther on, and still higher, I could see a second, bright blue. But it was the yellow one I wanted. A trail, with neatly cut steps, ran up to it. Fifteen minutes later, I was at the back door.

My boots were muddy; I left them outside, under a covered shelf, placed there for exactly that purpose.

I did not light a fire.

I made tea, but I used a little propane stove, and after I was finished I washed everything and put it away.

The bedding was all rolled up; the mattresses were bare. I left them that way and lay down, in a sleeping bag, on a couch. My own body warmed me, and I slept.

At ten past three in the afternoon I was awakened by rain pounding on the roof. For about twenty minutes it came down like a monsoon, then slackened off to a good, steady downpour. Even when it lightened up, the cottage was filled with the pounding of the rain and its quick rush off the roof, and then, watching at the window, I could hear the trickling of the thousand streams it made down the hill. With the rain, it was already getting murky; beyond the deck, the hill ran down to a dark cedar forest—it would be close to night among those trees— and then, a fair piece off, was the river in its valley; but now that was almost lost in darkness and mist.

I felt cold and put on a second pair of socks. I realized I was restless. The quiet, the emptiness, of the cottage were vaguely unnerving. But when I found a radio, I didn't turn it on; I sensed that an outside noise, artificially breaking the silence, would only amplify my unease. The place was barren, without personality, or perhaps it just reflected a personality I didn't like. The sofa and matching chairs were heavy, with a lot of polished wood—"western," as in cowboy—and almost aggressively overlarge for this space. The rug was brightly colored, vaguely Navajo or at least southwestern, there was a coffee table in the same "ranch" style, and beside one of the chairs stood a crystal ashtray on a brass stand, the sort of thing you'd have found years ago in a hotel lobby or a train station. Lastly, a glass-fronted cabinet bulked against one wall, also reminiscent of a Jimmy Stewart western, for it contained a rack with three guns, presumably Colonel Stadler's, a shotgun, a bolt-action rifle I couldn't identify, and a Winchester lever-action rifle, the sort of gun I'd often seen in South America but which, I suspected, was out of place here: "the gun that won the West." No doubt it had fitted the Colonel's image of himself, or at least the image he wished to project. I rummaged through the cabinet's drawers, discovering a gun-cleaning kit, cloths, patches, cans of oil (Gun Life Lube, Cor-O-Dex), which clearly hadn't been used in years. But, more interesting, I also pulled out three leather-bound guest books. The latest, only half-filled, dated from Coralee's time—"What a wonderful week we had" . . . "We hated to go" . . . "You live in such a lovely country" . . . "Coralee, so lovely to see you again"—but the others, much earlier, involved the Colonel. His guests, American and Chinese, had almost all held military rank, air force and army generals, a vice-admiral or two. "That was one helluva bear" . . . "Good shooting!" . . . "A real pleasure, Colonel" . . . I

closed my eyes and imagined the parties—the beer, the
plaid shirts, the fancy shades, the jokes. I tried to think
how the Chinese would have taken this—there weren't
many "remarks" beside the Chinese names—but they
would have fitted in; nervously at first, but then, once the
ice was broken, they would have become as giggly as
Cub Scouts around a campfire or frosh on a drunk. He
was a spy, Suzy had said. I could believe it. I wasn't
exactly sure what that meant, but I could see how his life
had been woven into a world where the military, diplomacy, and "security" would have been hard to distin-
guish. And Laurie—I had to think of this—had been part
of that life. She would have been presented to these
guests, all decked out in a fancy dress with ribbons in her
hair, and they would have smiled, and bowed, and
shaken her little hand, and some of them—coming back a
second time, or a third—would have remembered to
bring her a present, candy, a toy, a memento of their
travels: a carved mahogany box from the Philippines, a
gold bracelet from Burma, a silk kite from Siam. She'd
been part of that world, and was it a world you could ever
really leave behind? That question concerned Laurie. But
as I watched the rain, I began to think of all the other
women, Coralee, Suzy, the women who'd signed the
guest books, even my own mother. One way or another,
they'd all had to survive. One way or another, they'd all
had to find their men; men like the ones who'd come
through this place, soldiers, crooks, politicians, spies,
traders, businessmen, adventurers. For a moment, however brief, they had to make history stop, find a little

space between the wars, famines, massacres, atrocities—
the endless calamity. I suppose I was just another link in
that chain. I thought of my parents. My mother had been
the daughter of a merchant who'd traded out of Hong
Kong with half a dozen ships. So there'd been money.
But that would have been a necessary precondition, not a
cause, of their marriage. They'd loved each other, which
must have been a miracle . . . although even as I thought
this, I realized I had little idea what love really meant, at
least in their case. But the trust between them was easier
to grasp, my father's loyalty, my mother's faith—she'd
been prepared to follow him to the ends of the earth, she
more or less had. How had that trust come about? What
doubts had they overcome? Could you still find it today?
Wrapped in the sleeping bag, with the rain beating down,
I found no answers to these questions, but at least managed to doze off for twenty minutes or so.

Finally, at four o'clock exactly, I dialed Mary Williams's apartment—Laurie's girlfriend—in Taipei. That
was the plan. I was to let it ring seven times. If Laurie
picked it up before that, something was badly wrong—
the police, say, were with her. But she didn't pick it up.
So I hung up and dialed again. Laurie answered; I asked
for Mary, in English, but Laurie replied in Chinese that
she couldn't come to the phone. That was the signal—I
hung up immediately. Well, now I knew. . . . One way or
another, it seemed, the police were after me. . . . Was I
surprised? No. I told myself not to panic. I told myself it
was exactly what I'd expected. Still, there could be no
doubt now; I had to get out, get off the island. The police

were after me and, almost certainly, the Cao family was arrayed against me—I couldn't fight that. I waited by the phone. The idea was, by getting off at once, that the police wouldn't be able to trace the call. At the same time, there might be something I'd need to know, and Laurie was supposed to call me inside five minutes. She didn't, though. This meant Plan B now came into force. Tomorrow, I was to drive about fifteen miles north to a local tourist site, a memorial garden which is supposedly where Wu Feng was decapitated. Wu, the story goes, was an early Chinese government official who came to Taiwan and befriended a tribe of aborigines, learning their language, customs, and so forth. They loved him, but refused to give up the one thing he wanted them to . . . head-hunting. One day Wu told his native friends that a man on a white horse, covered in a red robe, would appear in the valley and they could take his head, but it would be the last. Accordingly, after an ambush, the aborigines cut off the head of this man, only to discover that it was Wu—and so, horrified, they gave up head-hunting forevermore. Chinese believe all this is the literal truth— "Righteous even in death" says the memorial dedicated by CKS himself—but it offends the descendants of the aborigines, who pulled down a statue to Wu in Chiayi. But the memorial temple's still there and, half a mile away, the garden which marks the spot where he supposedly died. I'd never been there, but Laurie said it was enclosed by high walls; she'd be at the entrance, leaning against one of them, if it was all clear, but positioned out in the middle if I should get lost. She was supposed to bring money, clothes, tickets—boat tickets to Okinawa, maybe plane tickets to Hong Kong—and whatever else she could think of. I had some money, and my passport, with me.

All this had seemed a good idea at the time—above all, it meant that I'd never gone back to my hotel or the office—and now I still didn't see how we could have worked out anything better. Of course, hindsight is twenty-twenty vision. Yes, I could have run right away. Yes, I could have run as soon as Young got me out of Kang's clutches. But what would that have meant? I would have escaped, that's all. And what I knew now— what I'd sensed all along—was that there was something more than that. Sure, I was just a pawn; but I was a pawn in a very big game. Sure, I was just one piece of a puzzle—but the puzzle made a very important picture. It had something to do with the man who'd been in with Cao before I'd arrived, it had something to do with that screwy magazine, and above all it had something to do with the photograph in Shanghai and the "commission" Cao had wanted to give me. I was going to run because I had to run, but now—I felt this—I could run to win, even if I didn't know the prize. I got up, I was *up* again—I was frightened okay, but I was also excited, at last it was happening—and I began moving around. And I looked out the window. God knows ... I'm Chinese, this was Taiwan, so maybe it was Zen. But that was sure a great time to look out that window.

Down in the valley, along the road I'd come up, I could see men with lights.

Instinctively, I moved back from the window, although it was already too dark for anyone to see me.

I peered forward.

Two flashlights.

Four men, maybe five.

I thought hard. I only had minutes and I knew I had to get this right. Obviously, they mustn't find me here. But—*unless they already knew it*—they mustn't know I'd been here. That was crucial. I could get out, I could get into the trees; but if they started looking, they were sure to find me.

They mustn't know I'd been here. . . . It was as simple as that.

I rolled up the sleeping bag and put it back in the chest where I'd found it.

I smoothed the couch.

The propane stove was cold. . . . I'd used one cup for my tea; it was dry, but using my shirt I made absolutely certain.

The remains of my apples and the wrappings of the chocolate I buried in one of the packs.

I took a last look around; the place was dark and cold and empty.

Stepping outside, locking the door, I picked up my boots. They'd been very muddy, but the rain had been hard enough to wash that off the deck, and now, in stocking feet, I carried them off the porch. I looked back. I could see faint footprints, but it was still drizzling and they disappeared even as I watched. I put my wet feet into the boots, but didn't take time to do the laces.

Behind the cottage, I was screened from the men, and it was dark enough . . . but going up the hill I'd inevitably kick down a trail of rocks and branches: they'd hear me even if they didn't see me. I'd already seen what I wanted, though; a hundred and fifty yards up the hillside was a huge protruding boulder, with five tall cedars growing up around it. I made for that, the two packs humped on my back, the boots half on my feet, working a little sideways to keep behind the cottage. When I reached it, the boulder jutted up like the prow of a ship, with dead leaves and branches drifted up against it; the cedars were actually rooted underneath, their trunks curving out and up, rising thirty feet above my head. I scrambled up, circling around, and got down onto it. I kneeled there, panting. Because I was high up, I felt exposed, but I knew the trees hid me completely. Doing up my boots, I peered out through the dark boughs. In the west, the sky was still light and I could see a glint of the river, a wide stretch, perhaps even a lake; but as soon as my eyes dropped below the horizon, the trees and the hills swelled with a blue-green darkness and I couldn't pick out details. Staring down the slope beyond the cottage I thought I saw a light . . . then I did see it, then I lost it again; and then I saw them definitely, emerging through the trees, two lights. They came on. I could tell when they reached the steps; they fell into single file and their bodies moved with a steady, plodding motion, almost innocent, honest men doing a wet, tiring, tedious job of work. I picked a spot and stared at it; then I watched the men pass through it one by one, counting carefully, one two . . . four. . . . Four. I was certain. They all wore windbreakers with hoods, the lead man had a flashlight and so did the one bringing up the rear. Now, against the dark background of the cottage, they almost disappeared, but I still had a sense of them. Did they have a key? They didn't, they didn't, I hoped to God they didn't because if they did it meant . . . Maybe the wind shifted, because I caught a word or two, and one of them definitely went around the deck to the front, but though the door was glass it was strongly locked, with a bar. So it must have been a window, I thought; one of them forced a window and let the rest in . . . though I knew it was too dark to be sure.

I didn't move.

There wasn't much to figure; if they searched, they'd find me; and if they didn't search, they'd wait. I tried to work out a couple of things but nothing was conclusive. Or maybe it was. If they searched right away, that would prove they knew I was here—but maybe all that meant was that they'd found the car. Yes. But the corollary to that was plain. If they didn't search, that meant both that they didn't know I was here and that they hadn't found the car.

In any case, all I could do was wait.

I waited for forty-seven minutes, until almost half past five.

At no point did they show any signs of making a search.

At ten past the hour, two of the men came out. Two only. One of them had a light and I watched them head back down the steps, the way they'd come—just walking, just moving on, no sense of urgency at all. So the other two would wait. Until they were relieved, probably in the morning. I decided they'd be almost as miserable as me; they wouldn't be able to have a fire, or show a light, for fear of scaring me off . . . maybe they wouldn't even find the propane stove. Small comfort. I was already as miserable as I could be.

Or so I thought. At twenty past, the rains came down, a deluge, like the afternoon's. And the clouds descended, literally. One slid down the hillside, a thick cold mist—but not mist, a cloud. I shivered. Somehow, water kept trickling down the back of my neck. I remembered my mother, You're not made of sugar, you won't dissolve. . . . Yet it was this rain that decided me. I remembered how it had drummed on the roof that afternoon; it was all you could hear, the pounding of the water. So, if I moved now, they wouldn't hear me, and unless they actually stepped out the door—and why do that?—they'd never see me. This was my chance. To the car—but what if they'd found it? I had to go another way, and I had these five seconds to decide; I did. I switched stuff between packs, I only wanted one, buried the other, found a heavy branch for balance, and made my break up the hill, running, slipping, sliding, stumbling down to one knee, and lurching up again, the edge of my boot dug in like a ski, the branch pole-vaulting me across a stump. That first dash almost killed me. Finally I had to stop. I looked back. The rain was so heavy you wouldn't have seen the cottage if you hadn't known it was there.

Catching my breath, I started up again. Twenty yards on there was a thick clump of trees; in a moment I had disappeared.

I'm not sure how I survived the next eight hours—the next day, for that matter. I suppose it helped that I never thought how long it was going to be. I knew where I was; in my mind, I had an idea where I was going and what I was doing. But I never actually made a plan, which meant I was never tempted to make the obvious judgment: I didn't have a snowball's chance in hell, so why not save everyone the pain and just give up? One step at a time; that's what my strategy came down to. And the steps were so painful and exhausting I didn't have the energy to think of anything else. I kept on. I kept on through the trees and the leaves and the fallen branches and over the rocks; I kept on through the rain; and then I kept on through the dark. At first, the going wasn't that hard. Once I'd dropped over a low, treed ridge, the cottage passed out of sight and I followed the slope of the hills, keeping the glint of the river on my left. The pines and cedars were old, a good size, and it was easy moving between them; the worst of it was the wet, for though the rain eased up, the ground was already waterlogged, very muddy in the bare spots, slippery across rocky patches— I fell and skinned my knee—and the thick leaves on the ground were soaked, and soon my boots were sodden, my socks, my pants, everything. Then the light went. Now I was imagining the river as much as seeing it. And I knew, in any case, that eventually I had to angle away from it . . . though I'm not sure, when I finally left it behind, whether I was following a conscious decision or merely the path of least resistance, in this case a shallow valley where the ground was somewhat more open. Along there, too, I had a little luck; I found a stream, and it was easier walking beside it. It also told me that I was heading in the right direction, for the water was coming toward me and really roaring along, so there had to be higher ground ahead. Incredibly—again, it wouldn't have done to think about this—that was what I wanted: to climb. Soon enough I got my wish. After the first long, exhausting slope—I finally grabbed a tree trunk and pulled myself up to a flat spot where I dropped onto my knees—I tried to check my watch, to work out if I had enough time; and maybe once more I was lucky that the thing had stopped, and I didn't actually have to contemplate the hours ahead. Anyway, by then, all I could do was go on. My legs ached, then throbbed, then went numb. My chest was heaving. The only sound I could hear was the roar of my breath. I blessed the rain now: I could look up and let it cool my face, I could lick it off my lips. As I went higher, the darkness made this all worse, but then a different darkness came down upon me, a soft, damp, suffocating humidity. I knew what it was; I'd climbed into a cloud, one wave in "the sea of clouds" which the Chinese imagine cover Taiwan. It was eerie. For a moment I stopped and tried to look around, and when a tree emerged from the strange, gray gloom I had the feeling it was watching me. I was in an alien world. I moved through it with dread, led on by the pitch of the ground, expecting every step forward to drop me into an abyss. Rain rushed at me, then a cold wind; the mist stretched and tore. Ahead of me I could see that the way up was a ledge along a cliff, so narrow I had to inch ahead with my belly to the rock, my back turned to a long dark fall. I made it. Beyond that was a steep, wooded rise; I pulled myself up, tree to tree, wedging my foot against each trunk. And somewhere after that I collapsed; there was a hollow full of leaves and I sagged down into it. I was very frightened. I was panting but the sound was close to sobbing. I was shivering, my guts were shivering. But then of course you see the humor of it. You remember an old hotel with a huge print, Landseer's *The Stag at Bay*. That's you. You remember a comedy record your father used to play, a parody of an Anglican minister, a sermon, *and so we climbed and we climbed and we climbed, higher and higher and higher, until England lay like a green carpet beneath us, at which point my friend suddenly, and violently, vomited. Isn't life a bit like that?* It sure seems to be. And you remind yourself of the alternatives: sitting in jail, talking through a grate to some guy in a suit who's making a hell of a lot of money off you. Which last thought gets you back on your feet, and you keep on, higher, and higher and higher, and then, all at once, the wind comes up, you see a swirl of mist, and overhead a sky full of stars. And a moon, bright enough to make me squint. Etched against this silver light was Alishan's summit.

I reached it, at a guess, forty minutes later.

The top was a lookout, an open area with safety fences—I'd clambered over one. To the left were parking lots for tour buses, a road, and a walkway with steps for the more energetic.

There was not a soul around, only the wind.

The stars and the moon shone down, and below the summit of the mountain—in the valleys of the hills around—the clouds shone like a silvery sea. It was a magical sight, you thought of spells and fairies, of lost souls sailing away to heaven, of how the sky made love to the ocean and brought forth the land. But then you felt the wind and you got down low behind a hut. Remarkably, I still had the pack. I ate all the food. I'd kept one dry sweater and a pair of pants, saving them as my funeral clothes. Now I put them on. I felt a little warmed and tried to sleep, but couldn't, and so I waited—waited for the sun to rise. It was probably an hour later, which meant it had been about two when I reached the summit I'd climbed for seven, eight hours. Anyway, it was still dark when the crowds arrived. Tour buses. People walking. At three-twenty in the morning—I asked someone the time—I was mingling with three thousand chilly people, laughing and chattering in every species of Chinese, Japanese, Korean, even English. They pushed and shoved to get to the edge of the mountain . . . and then the show, perhaps the most popular tourist spectacle in all Taiwan, began: the sun came up. It rose over Mount Morrison and the eastern ridges and shone down on the clouds, the light dancing in shimmering golden waves as all those shutters clicked.

Having seen it all before, and feeling a little tired, was standing at the back.

A hand tapped me on the shoulder.

I turned around. It was Young. Robert Young. Blond, handsome, in a ski jacket—all decked out for Aspen.

His voice was calm, inquiring, kindly, and concerned. "Nick, the cops are everywhere, looking for you. I assume you know that?"

I was too shocked to speak. He looked at me, his glance friendly but a little curious. But his voice grew harder. "Take this. It's a ticket on the train that runs back to Chiayi. You're part of a group, Chinese Americans, Japanese Americans—be careful, they speak English. Get on the train. Someone will contact you. Do exactly what they say. You got that?"

He handed me an envelope.

I was going to say something but he interrupted. "No questions. We can't talk now. . . ." He hesitated. "You need some money?"

"No."

He grinned. "But I bet you could use a drink."

He had a flask and gave it to me.

11

YOUNG. ON TOP OF THAT MOUNTAIN. I WAS STUNNED. . .
But then maybe I wasn't as stunned as I should have
been. Somehow, it was horribly logical that he should be
there. But "somehow" doesn't explain much of anything
Was he reading my mind? And then, before I could make
my mouth work, he disappeared, though it wouldn't have
made any difference—I wasn't going to believe anything
he said. I stood there, rooted to the spot. What the hel
was going on? Who could I believe? Young had no way
of knowing that I was going to be here, even in the area
and he hadn't followed me, I was sure of that. My earlier
notion, that he was a cop, seemed hard to believe—why
hadn't he just taken me in? So who was he working
for . . . I was thinking of the cottage, I suppose, of the
Colonel's old guest books, of all the possibilities tha
raised. And of course I was thinking of Laurie . . . Laurie
had known I was coming; after the phone call she'd
known I'd arrived. It was the only explanation I could
think of—

Laurie. But I told myself that was a conclusion I didn'

want to reach, not now. I was feeling half-dead. I was very cold; even the clothes I'd just put on were wet. Besides, up here, for the moment, I was safe. Right now, right here, I didn't think anything could happen to me. Or that's how I felt. Maybe I was wrong; maybe it was just the result of being on the outside of this strange scene, thousands of Oriental people crowded together on a mountaintop, staring off into space, as the sun shone down on the clouds flowing through the valleys below. It was beautiful, of course; but it was their self-absorption which . . . excluded me. That's what I felt—apart, different; blissfully ignored. These people were all caught up in themselves, in one of their myths, also known as self-deceptions, also known as lies; namely, that they love nature. In fact, they hate it, it frightens them, nature is earthquakes and Godzilla and floods down the Yangtze; they only really like nature when it's reduced to a pattern in a carpet or a few deft strokes of calligraphy. You think you're used to it, but then it hits you again: Asia is a crazy place. It occurred to me, even though I'd come up their mountain the wrong way, that I had a better idea where I was than these people did, the Japanese, the Chinese from Hong Kong, the Koreans. They'd arrived by 747. Now they were absorbing *chi*— life force—from the mountain air. Tonight, back in Taipei, they'd be drinking cobra bile to jack up their potency. And next week they'd be sitting in front of computers designing widgets to go into cameras so that Americans could take perfect pictures of themselves eating hot dogs on the Fourth of July. No, I can use chopsticks and speak their language, but I am just not one of these people. As the sun shone, the clouds glittered, and the shutters clicked, I bought some breakfast from one of the pushcart vendors and then quietly moved down the slope; I don't think a single one of them noticed.

There's no real town at Alishan, but about an hour's walk down from the mountain—there's a good road and a walkway with steps—you find a collection of hotels, and some restaurants and stores near the train station. I made it down there before anybody else and sat in the station until the restaurants began opening. I ate some more—I was still very cold. I drank an awful lot of tea. By the time I was finished, most everything was opening, ready to catch the trade from the tour buses. I bought some new pants, a shirt, a sweater, a hat, and ended up advertising Mount Ali in half a dozen languages.

It was seven-thirty; the train down to Chiayi would leave at eight-forty, and my ticket was reserved. I hadn't seen Young, but then he was probably in one of the hotels. Was I going to go along with him? I was suspicious of him; the trouble was, he'd turned up twice and saved me both times. Why? Because he needed me. Or somebody did. But I had no more idea why Young might need me than why Cao had changed his mind and decided to see me that very first night. Still, I told myself it might be unwise, not to mention ungrateful, to run out on him. And there was another side to that coin, one I had to face up to now; should I go ahead and meet Laurie? For a long time, I'd been pushing a hundred doubts to the back of my mind, but I couldn't any longer. Objectively ... but how could I be objective? Even to ask these questions buried me under an avalanche of guilt. *And yet, and yet* ... I had as much reason to doubt Laurie as I did Young, that was the plain truth, and I was certainly going to be very careful with him. *Everything happened so fast.* Always, there was that, and there was also Laurie's father, his career, everything Suzy had said, the hints I'd picked up in the cottage—could you put that together with Young, the way he kept showing up to shepherd me on?—and then there were all the questions that had troubled me for so long: above all, as Young so delicately put it, the question of body fluids. And now, of course, all these questions had a force they'd lacked before. The fundamental situation had changed. Up to this point, everything was "maybe." I hadn't even been sure I was actually under suspicion—which meant my own suspicions and doubts could be conditional. No longer. I'd just escaped by the skin of my teeth. Once the police caught me, would they ever let me go? The police never like admitting they're wrong; in this place, it was unheard of. No, I was in real trouble, and I just didn't see how I could go forward if I had to keep looking out the corner of my eye, or trying to see out of the back of my head. It didn't make any difference whether my doubts were real or false, I couldn't afford them either way. It made me feel half-sick, it made me feel like a traitor, but I made up my mind and found a phone and dialed, like a coward, knowing she would have already left the apartment. Her machine came on; I listened to her message, listened for anything funny. Everything sounded okay, so I said, "Hi there. Me. Can't make our rendezvous. I ran into Father Knows Best, and there's been a change of plan. . . ." I hesitated then; my mouth went dry. I'd told a lie; at least I hadn't told all the truth. But that was important too. Because I didn't say, I'm frightened on account of what they found in Yuki. I didn't say, I can only think of one way they could know so much about me and my plans. I didn't say, Sometimes I think you're too good to be true. I didn't say any of that. Instead I said, "Don't worry, I love you, I'll be in touch, keep yourself safe." And then I hung up. And all at once I was out of breath. I walked off a little way . . . and then my legs began to tremble and I had to lean against a tree.

Now I was emotionally exhausted on top of everything else. But I felt better at the same time—I was rid of something, now it was only myself I had to doubt. And she'd be all right. I told myself, *Things either work out or they don't. Give yourself credit for what you didn't say too.* I said that over a few times, and caught my breath and recovered. It was still early. I stood there, breathing the air, thinking I could do with some *chi* myself. Then I decided to kill some time and made myself walk all around the place, keeping a lookout for Young. It was a beautiful spot. I thought of Colorado or Banff, and the neat, red-painted wooden buildings gave it the feel of a national park. The sky was clear and now perfectly blue—color brushed purely across damp rice paper—and everywhere you looked the land fell away in rocky ravines and gorges, vaulting views of bluffs, the moun-

ains, stands of pine. But of course this was Asia; everything was a little too perfect, already a postcard. Which is
why Japanese and Chinese people so love the American
West, the real thing. Little do they know—the whole
world is Disneyland, nature is just another program on
PBS. In any case, I didn't find Young around any of the
hotels and so I finally gave up and went down to the station. A crowd was already forming. Almost everyone
was part of a tour, and guides were herding their charges
together like so many sheep in a pen. I decided my group
was the one where you could hear some English, and a
pretty Taiwanese girl asked to see my ticket and nodded
happily when I showed it to her. Finally the train came
up; there was a big argument because one of the
groups—they were Koreans—claimed that they'd been
promised a steam engine for the trip back, but finally
they canned it and we began climbing aboard.

Steam engine or not, it was a great little train; the track
was narrow gauge and the cars had a miniature feel. It
was crowded, but not packed, and I ended up sitting with
two Chinese, an older man and his wife. It was only then,
as we were getting settled, that I saw Young—but only
because he was checking on me. He was clearly going
through the cars. When he saw me, he came over and
said in English, "Do you have the time?"

"No. My watch is broken."

He seemed disconcerted. "Seriously?"

"Yes."

I suppose to make things look natural, he turned to the
Chinese and asked him, but in fact this gentleman didn't

speak any English, so Young smiled and began walking away.

"Just a minute," I called.

"For Christ's sake, shut up," he said, and walked off.

Only later did it occur to me that he might have been marking me, identifying me, for someone else. I let him go. So far as Young was concerned, I was now fairly certain he wasn't working for the police—why not just arrest me?—but for the time being that was a very strong point in his favor; I could put up with his rudeness. Besides, there was nothing to do now but get to Chiayi. The train was rattling on, swaying through curves and dips like a roller coaster. It's about a three-hour ride, and you go through something like fifty tunnels and cross even more bridges. The Japanese built the railway to get at the timber in these hills—pine, cypress, cedar—and they took most of it, but the whole area has been reforested, and the scenery's spectacular: gorges, rocks, great twisted trees, sudden vistas of the valleys and mountains. People chattered happily. Shutters clicked ceaselessly. Camcorders whirred. We flickered in and out of tunnels—a quick black roaring going in, then a whoosh and clicketyclack as we came back into the open—but then we were in one so long that a child screamed; and when we finally came back to the light everyone began smiling and laughing.

I waited.

Someone was going to give me instructions. About what, I didn't know. And why couldn't Young instruct me himself? I'd no idea; Young hadn't betrayed me to

he police; in fact he was acting as my guardian angel—
but where was he guiding me *to*? What was his interest? I
just couldn't work it out. Laurie's father, the spy; the
AIT, where Young had worked and was still well
known—could you really put that together and imagine
Young as an employee of one of those agencies best
known by their initials? I couldn't know, and I couldn't
trust anything he said. But no matter what he said, I was
determined on one point—I wanted off the island.
They're working on it, they're making progress, but
Taiwan, bottom line, is not a democracy, not a place
where you can rely on due process. That's where I'd
started, and by God it was still true. I didn't know what
Young had in his mind, but I knew what I had in mine: I
wanted instructions on how to get to Hong Kong . . . or
Okinawa, maybe on the ferry or . . .

I waited. And it was a long time coming. But finally it
came. . . .

Maybe he was bothered by the Chinese beside me.
Because they moved—some rearrangement of seats was
made down the car, and their son came and took them
away. Five minutes later a Japanese man sat down in
their place.

He was fair-sized, my weight and build, dressed in a
yellow nylon windbreaker with a blue herringbone pattern on one shoulder and sleeve. Not inconspicuous; at
the same time, there were a lot of Japanese and Koreans
in that car, as well as Chinese, and he didn't stand out.
Maybe he was a little low class. Or was that an act? He
sat directly opposite me, hunched forward, his knees

spread; and he put his hands on his knees—I thought of the opening posture of a sumo wrestler, and just because he didn't have that kind of size, it looked a little artificial, assumed. Still, he struck me immediately as tough, and I don't think that was part of any act; he had thick, meaty hands—dark sienna in color, darker than the rest of him—and hard, intelligent black eyes. You did not automatically think, looking at him, This man is probably Buddhist.

"Lamp?"

"Yes."

"Young told you I would be here?"

"Yes."

"I will ask several questions."

"All right. But I'm not interested in questions. I want to get out of here. Off Taiwan."

"Yes. Arrangements can be made ... it is being arranged."

"How?"

"First I must ask questions."

"I have my passport. *Some* money—"

"No, no. Not questions like that. That is taken care of—"

"Young didn't say anything about questions." I wasn't just kidding around; I was deliberately trying to push him. Whatever he wanted, whatever he had to offer, I had to know who he was before I could decide. I said, "I can't speak Japanese. Would you prefer Mandarin? Canton—"

"English."

"Okay. What's your name?"

He looked perplexed, as if it hadn't occurred to him

that I might ask such a question. He leaned back slightly. "My name is Ushida, Mr. Lamp."

I believed him; for some reason, it seemed, he hadn't come prepared with a false name, and his brain, at short notice, had failed to supply one. "All right, Ushida-*san*, ask your questions."

He hesitated. Then, slowly, he said, "You saw Cao that night."

"No. Not really. I saw his body. I didn't kill him."

"Yes. We know you didn't kill him."

"Good."

"But someone was there before you—"

"Obviously."

"Yes, and did you see who that person was?"

"No. I didn't see anyone."

"Maybe you saw such a person coming out of the door, or walking on the street?"

"No. If I saw someone, I didn't notice. I don't remember anyone."

Outside the window, the land was leveling and the colors were changing from the hard gray and green of the hills to the soft, sun-washed brown of winter fields and orchards. The views were less interesting and people had settled back into their seats, into themselves; a few were asleep; they'd been up since two or three in the morning. And they didn't have as much adrenaline in their systems as I did. I watched Ushida. He'd given me a clue. He knew I hadn't killed Cao, it wasn't even a question— because he knew who had? Even if he didn't know, I thought, he realized that the logic of what was happening excluded me. I came into it by accident . . . but of course that wasn't entirely true. Something had happened to make Cao want to see me. According to Cao Feng he might even have had a favor to ask, a commission. Did Ushida know anything about that? I wondered as well if he'd ask about Yuki, but he said, "Okay, you didn't see anyone, but you took things."

Everybody seemed to know I'd taken something.

He prompted, "Yes?"

"Yes, no, maybe. What did I take? How do you know?"

"Mr. Lamp, this is very important. You understand?"

I couldn't quite place him. He wasn't a bureaucrat, or a policeman, or a crook—although what does a Japanese criminal look like, sound like? He could think, his mind had force, but he wasn't a thinker. I decided on an engineer, one who's moved over into management; an engineer who now runs people. He could run a Toyota plant, nothing grand, something on the outer fringe of the empire, in the Philippines or Georgia. He could run the plant that would make my tires. An engineer . . . The train, on its narrow-gauge tracks—laid at the direction of Japanese engineers just before the First World War—swayed through a gentle curve; in the distance, I could see two figures, probably women, their *doulis*—the traditional Chinese conical hat—silhouetted against the sky. And all at once, with a crackle, my ears cleared—we'd come down so far—and the rush and swoosh of the train was suddenly louder. We were almost there. I leaned forward against the noise and said, "Young knows about the photograph."

"Yes."

"Why is it important?"

"That is for you to tell me."

"I don't know why it's important. All I can tell you is that my father's in it. He's one of the people in it. You understand?"

His face gave absolutely nothing away, but then he said, quite easily, "I didn't know that, Mr. Lamp. That's very interesting." Then he looked at me, seemed to come to a conclusion, and added, "*You* interest me, Mr. Lamp."

"Well if you're so interested in me why don't—"

"But you did take something, Mr. Lamp. There was something else besides the photograph. You took that. I have to have that, what you took."

I'd known he would get to this, just as Cao Feng had done. With Cao, I'd more or less denied it, got up on my high horse with Ito. Which hadn't gained me anything. I didn't see how, but it was possible that my denials had even triggered what had followed, their decision to release the news of Cao's death and come after me. So I took a different tack.

"Maybe you can't have it," I said. "Not unless I get what I want."

"All right. That is no problem. No problem. But what was it exactly, Mr. Lamp? I must be sure. . . ." He smiled. "I must be sure we have the same things in our mind."

"Let's say it was a magazine. A magazine, and something in a magazine."

He sat very still; the jostling of the train rocked him slightly. I realized—he'd heard what he wanted to hear. "Yes," he said, "good. That's what I had in mind. Do you have this magazine?"

"Maybe I have it, maybe not. Maybe I know where it is."

He said, "We will go between the cars. Bring that—"

"I don't want to go anywhere."

He moved . . . or the train jostled him again . . . I didn't really see what happened but now there was a gun in his hand. He held it down between his legs, against his right thigh, casually but definitely pointed at my chest. He said, "Some things you know are valuable, other things you know are dangerous. You have to see that, Mr. Lamp. Please. And please take your bag too."

I saw it all right. I hesitated just a second, then I grabbed the pack and stood up. One or two people might have glanced our way for a second, but no one noticed us. I opened the door between the cars and stepped onto a small platform; there was a panel or gate on either side, waist-high, but otherwise it was open—everything was shaking, the wind rushed against my face, the noise was deafening. Ushida was right behind me. You would have had to shout to make yourself heard and so he simply gestured with the gun. He wanted me to open the pack. I undid a couple of straps and buckles, then he held out his hand. His eyes never left mine. He began feeling through the pack, but kept the gun on me, easy and level. No one, from inside, would have seen anything; the doors were small, their windows opaque with reflections. Behind Ushida the countryside rushed past, now a few farm buildings in the distance. I wondered what he was going to do. What would he do when he didn't find what he wanted? *You wouldn't think he'd shoot you, not here, and not so long as he thinks you still have something to tell him. . . .* Yes, I began talking about myself like that, which is what you do when it's happening to you and you're trying to pretend it isn't. You make up little dialogues that ignore the fact there's a gun pointing at your chest and you work out an ironclad chain of logic that proves it can't possibly go off. Then something happens. In this case it was the sound of the train, a shift of its pitch . . . and I knew we were heading into one last tunnel or maybe just under a bridge. But I had that in mind, I was ready for it; and when we flickered into the blackness, I swung at him, a right cross aimed at his chin. If it hadn't been for that first instant of blindness, maybe he could have done something fancy, judo, karate, tai kwon do—he might have kung fu-ed me. But he never had the chance: he was my size and weight, but it was no fair fight. I didn't get his chin, only the side of his head, but I hit him so hard it almost ripped off his shoulders. Weakly, he flailed at me with the gun but only scratched my neck, and already my left fist was driving into his belly. He sagged back; he had no air; and I grabbed him by the hair on his head and banged him backward into the car, once, twice, again, bang bang, picking up the rhythm of the jolting cars. Then I let him go. He slumped down into the corner between the car and the side gate, and from some black hole of violent lore I knew enough to kick him, stomp him, in the angle between his neck and his shoulder. The bone snapped—I felt it go under my heel. And if your collarbone's broken, all you can think of is supporting your arm. Desperately, in agony, he was trying to do that, but then I kicked his head, and I kept kicking him until he stopped moving. I thought he was dead. His whole body jerked. A dark trickle of blood came out of his nose. . . . Now all the strength drained out of me; I was limp, gasping, trembling. I looked down at him. I felt sick. I said, out loud, "What did you expect? What the hell did you expect?" I leaned against the gate, sticking my head out, and let the train rush air into my mouth. The train was roaring. The train was roaring though my head. I couldn't get my breath. I hung there, looking down: the rush of the gravel of the roadbed, shadows flickering against my eyes, the flash of water in a ditch. . . . I was leaning there at least a couple of minutes, anyone could have come through, but finally I got myself together. I kneeled down, and he wasn't dead. He was still breathing, gasping now. I got the gun. I opened his jacket. There was a zipped pocket inside, passport, billfold, a few papers. . . . I took everything. Then I grabbed him. I'd hit him that hard, but he was already coming around. I lifted him under the arms, pushed him up against the gate . . . I was going to find the latch, it would have been easier, but he was already coming around, so with a great heave I got him up on the edge, he hung a second, then I pushed him hard, over. And out.

He was gone. But I pushed him hard enough that he didn't go under the train—I saw him bounce and roll once, then he disappeared and I could hear the train whistle up ahead. . . .

I had to get my breath again. Now it was my own body that weighed a ton; it was hard for me to think clearly, but I was pretty sure that Young, coming through the rain, had walked up the other way, and he'd never walked by the two of us as we were talking. So I went into the next car, then one more—a few people looked up, that was all. Everyone was tired now, they only wanted their trip to be over. I went into a toilet. I looked at Ushida's gun; it was an automatic, strange, not made of steel—it had a slightly slick feel, like nylon, carbon fiber, or something. I pushed it into the pack. Then I checked his passport, some of which was in English, and I'd guessed right, his name was Ushida. I put it away; it might come in handy. And he had money, also useful, a lot of it, a lot of N.T. dollars, yen, and some H.K. dollars too. I kept it all—kept the whole billfold. The rest was receipts, a couple of notes in Japanese which I couldn't read anyway; so I sent them down the toilet. And then I sat on the toilet until the train slowed, and the conductor was going through the cars, calling out the station. And finally the train gently glided to a stop.

We'd arrived in Chiayi.

It's a fair-sized town, with about a quarter of a million people. Since it's on the main rail line the station is large and crowded; during the day, there's probably one or two trains every hour, either running north to Taipei or south to Kaohsiung. In any case, as the crowd spilled off our train and mingled with people waiting on the platform, it was easy enough to lose myself, to keep out of Young's way. But in fact I wanted to see him. I worked myself into a knot of people around some pushcart vendors and bought some noodles, easing back into the shadows and wolfing them down. I relaxed a bit. I figured I was away now, I'd done it; in an hour or two I'd be in Kaohsiung, and a few hours later, courtesy of Ushida-*san*, I'd be in Hong Kong. So I could afford to satisfy my curiosity and I waited until I saw Young's blond head moving above the crowd. He was looking for me—or Ushida. And I was wondering, you see, which of us was uppermost in his mind. I'd assumed that Robert Young was the man in charge, but Ushida's manner and bearing had made me think otherwise. Now, as Young turned, the anxious expression on his boyish, innocent American face confirmed my suspicion . . . which is something else you have to remember about the new Asia: more and more often, the white man is working for the yellow.

12

I LOVE HONG KONG. I ALWAYS HAVE. IT'S A GREAT CITY,
period. If you travel a lot in Asia, it can kind of become a
second home. You can relax, almost forget what part of
the world you're in. I feel at ease there in a way I don't
feel anywhere else, not till I get back to Honolulu. I
don't mean it's a Western city, but sometimes, in the
summer, coming into the Miramar or the Oriental you get
the same hit from the air-conditioning that you do in L.A.
or New York. You see Western women in the street, you
hear a lot of English—and that can be a relief. There's
English TV; you can catch up on the news. The phones,
the subway, pretty much everything, work. Sometimes,
it's only after a couple of days in H.K. that I realize how
tense I've been. And on this particular trip, of course, this
was true in spades. I looked like Ushida, Ushida looked
like me, so I'd done the obvious thing ... especially
since I had his passport. But there'd been a few tense
moments. I got through them, though, by speaking
Fukienese, and mine is bad, bad enough to be convincing
as the Chinese a Japanese might have spoken. It had

worked, anyway, though the trip had left me exhausted. Once I'd cleared immigration, once I'd registered at the Imperial and showered, and once I'd taken an easy stroll through Kowloon Park and listened to the birds—I could have slept like a baby. Could have, and did. I'd left Kaohsiung in the early afternoon; sometime around six I lay down to have a little rest before dinner; and when I woke up it was after nine, the next morning.

Over breakfast, I worked out my next step. In a way, that also tied in to the reason Hong Kong is such an easy city for me. I mean the fact that my father spent so much time here . . . enough time, certainly, to meet my mother. Of course Shanghai was his city, and in those days it was a lot bigger than Hong Kong. But Hong Kong was special because it was British, and my father always had interests there, and ever since I can remember I've had an account at the Hong Kong & Shanghai Bank—that's where my birthday and Christmas money was duly deposited. Hong Kong was a refuge. Everyone in Shanghai knew that someday the music would stop, and Hong Kong was a nice, comfortable easy chair to sit down on. My father went there just before the Japanese invaded Shanghai and had enough sense to see what was going to happen next and get himself and my mother to India. But after the war, he went back, and in the years before the Communists moved in, he probably spent as much time in Hong Kong as Shanghai, and did fairly well.

He had a number of special Hong Kong friends, and to understand that photograph—which seemed the clearest lead I had—I needed to speak with one of them; and now

I considered the possibilities. Alistair Cameron had been
the closest—my brother was named after him—but he
had died a few years before my father. There was a Chinese named Chen Yun, whom I'd met, and he was still
alive, but I was pretty sure he was living with one of his
children in Kuala Lumpur; so he was out. And I wasn't
sure why, but toward the end of my father's life something had gone wrong between him and Bob Ring Lee,
one of his oldest and dearest friends from his Shanghai
life. He still lived in Hong Kong, he'd know what I
wanted—but would I be welcome? I wasn't sure. All of
which left Mac Maclean—another old Scot—the Far
East is full of them. I suppose he might have been my
first choice anyway. He was younger than my father, so I
wondered if his memory went back far enough, but he'd
always liked me. I had a terrible time in school—my
school days were the worst period of my life, I just knew
school wasn't for me—and it had been a tremendous
relief meeting him. "Quit," he'd said. "You know enough
to make money once you can read and write and figure.
Unless you want to be a teacher yourself. Or push paper
in the government. Or be a churchman." And he'd
laughed his big booming laugh—he laughed with a
brogue, you might almost say. I hadn't quit, not then; but
having his permission made it easier to go on. I knew that
he and my mother still kept in touch, and I'd looked him
up two years ago. He lived on Lamma Island. I decided
to surprise him and didn't phone ahead; around ten I took
the ferry Hongkongside, then a tram to Kennedy Town.
From there, you get a *kaido* out to Lamma.

The trip took forty cold, gray, choppy minutes; by the time we reached Yung Shue Wan, the village, a misty rain was falling. I had only three fellow passengers and there was no one on the dock as we came in. A stray dog crossed the road. . . . The place is like that, small houses hunkered down around the harbor, a few bigger buildings in behind; expats, mostly. There's only one street, and Mac, I remembered, was up the opposite way from the power station and the temple. I had a little trouble—he was closer to the water than I thought—but eventually I found it, a small house with a red tile roof and a big hedged garden, gray vines clinging to trellises; he'd built it years ago.

"Mac?"

I gave him a second to recognize me. Then he smiled. "Nicky boy, Nicky boy. Well, well." He laughed. "Now tell me, how many shillings in a florin?"

He looked older; but he still had all his hair, and it was still jet black. But he was stooped—a tall stooped man with an ash stick in a big hand spotted with freckles and scars. He wore a dark, indeterminately colored suit jacket, with gray flannel trousers that didn't match; and a cardigan of too bright a blue. "Two," I said. "Two shillings in a florin. Two and six in a half crown."

"There's a lad. *Entre dans, alors, dépêche-toi, dépêche-toi.*"

He'd hated Britain's going decimal and when I was a boy, twelve or fourteen, had brought me a proof set of all the old coins and made sure I knew the system. "Us two,"

he'd said, "we'll remember, we'll be the last to know."
And maybe we were.

I went into his sitting room; I doubt if a single item
had changed since I'd last been there. Although he'd
spent his life east of Suez, there was really nothing Oriental about it at all. Home, once upon a time—at least for
his clan—was Edinburgh, not Glasgow, something you
wanted to be quite clear about, and the furniture was like
that, British, middle class, and proper, ancient, over-
stuffed, covered in brocade; it would have gone out of
style in the U.K. years ago ... but I suppose that was
partly the point; it was keeping memories alive. Though
why he bothered I don't know. There was an electric fire
whose ruddy bar popped a welcome as I came in, and a
strong scent of lemon oil. For so masculine a man, the
room felt feminine—the chairs even sported doilies; but
it was the sort of femininity that might be traced to an
aunt or a grandmother, some immemorial source. I don't
believe he had ever married. But I could hear someone
moving about in the back of the house, the clatter of
dishes. As I came in, it occurred to me that I couldn't
actually swear to where he'd been born, the U.K., Hong
Kong, possibly India or the F.M.S., but all his life, I
expect, there'd been a yellow servant in the background,
doing for him, amahs, houseboys, his batman. . . .

He sat me down and I said, "So you're still hanging on."

"To life? Barely. One whiskey a day, wine only at the
weekend. No brandy at all ... if you cut a Scot off from
France, what's left to him?"

"I meant, you're hanging on in H.K."

"I like it here. I like this house." His fist clamped over the end of his stick, though he smiled. "I was here first, after all." He leaned back. "Of course, nowadays, there're a lot more expats and the power station and the quarry and . . . all the rest."

"I keep wondering, at the last minute—July, ninety-seven—maybe you'll all turn tail and run."

He chuckled. "But where to go? Tell me that, old son?" He shook his head. "It's sad. Over home, it's finished. They worry about *pay equity*. Here, it's *making money*. That's the difference between winners and losers, and they don't understand it. Soon enough, they'll have no pay to be equitable about. And it's such a long flight, at my age. Coming back's all right, but going . . . I don't know. The summer's too hot, the winter's too cold, but then you think of the alternatives. Singapore? I'm too old and too much of a Brit; the very word fills me with such shame. K.L. is not too big, it has that going for it. A nice backwater. Tell no one, but at my exalted age I have finally decided to own to a prejudice against the Mussulmans. My God, the Koran is boring. Those yodeling prayers . . ." He shook his head again. "Of course there's Australia, but there I have my class prejudices to think of—it's true, you know, the poor Aussies are just working-class Brits who've discovered protein. No, I don't think I could take it. I might as well put paid to things here."

Perhaps he'd pushed a button; perhaps it was automatic. But an old Chinese woman appeared with a tray of tea—two pots—and biscuits; Peak Frean bourbon creams . . . when I was a boy they'd always been a special treat, and I wondered—I couldn't remember—if Mac had introduced me to them. Probably. Sitting there, I realized how much I owed him, and how much I'd looked up to him.

"What'll you have?" he asked. *"Bo lay—"*

"Not if that's English breakfast—"

"Irish. And if I'm not offended, you mustn't be."

"I'll have it then."

"Ah, you are your father's son. . . ." He poured; milk, then the tea. It was the color of mahogany—talk about working-class Brits. After I'd sipped, we chatted about my mother, the rest of my family, the reasons my father had ended up in British Columbia, some of what I was doing. But of course Mac was shrewd. After a decent spell of this, he leaned back and said, "You've got a problem, Nick. What's up?"

"Well, something you can help with."

"Your mother told me about your tires—that might work, I thought."

"They come into it, in a roundabout way. But I wanted to tap your memory."

"Surely. An old man's delight."

"What do you think of this?"

I passed him the photograph, now a little the worse for wear. Holding it above his head to catch the light, he tilted back. After a moment, he murmured, "Have I seen this before?"

"My father had the same photograph—that's a copy,

though not of his. I remember it always hanging somewhere near his desk."

He brought it closer to his face and grunted. "Goes back that far, I'd say. . . . Dear me, you have folded this right through the middle of a pretty girl's face, and I think I even remember her name . . . Sun Weishi. A tart. No. That's unfair—to a lady, probably dead. An actress. Actually, so are these other Chinese girls. . . . That's your father, of course. And a man named Warden. A real scoundrel, your father always called him—"

"His greatest compliment."

"Of course."

"But about the girls . . ."

He lowered the photograph and squinted at me. "Now Nick, you mustn't ask me anything that might embarrass your father's memory. He was a good-looking man, you can see that. Ladies liked him, he liked the ladies."

"That's not the problem, I promise you."

"You're sure now? After he met your mother, he never looked at anyone else—and I think I was in a position to know. He was crazy about her, right from the start. I remember him saying, 'I'll marry her, Mac, I'd be mad not to—she even laughs at my jokes.' "

"But that photograph was taken before he met my mother."

He squinted at it again. "Yes, I'd say so. They met here, didn't they? Hongkongside?"

"Right."

"And this is Shanghai. Early thirties . . . something like. Going by the girls' hair. Always up-to-date, they

were. Paris had nothing on them. . . . Of course, I was
younger than your father. Your mother and me, we're
only a few months apart, you know. In fact, I was likely
still at Harland's when this was taken, that job my father
got me."

Amazed, I think, at how long ago that had been, he put
the photograph down again and his eyes lost focus as he
remembered. "From there, I went to the bank, Shorty's,
then I was on the *Mercury*, and then my granny died." He
looked up at me. "That gave me capital, you see, something of my own." He was silent a moment; but though
his mind wandered, it never went very far, and his gaze
snapped back and he shook the photo. "These people
were all in pictures, Nick."

"You mean motion pictures?"

He grinned. "I mean *talkies*. Or I guess they were
talkies by then. Here . . . just a minute."

He got up; not with difficulty, but it was a calculated
movement, as though rising had now become a trick. At
the back of the room, he shouldered through a curtained
doorway. Listening to him rummaging in the room
beyond—banging a drawer open, scrabbling through
papers; expressing the frustration, rather than patience, of
old age—I thought of Granny and her capital; perhaps
the furnishings of this room still honored her. He came
back with a magnifying glass in his hand; enormous,
worthy of Sherlock Holmes. As he got himself settled, I
poured more tea. He peered through the glass a moment,
but then leaned back and eyed me. "You do know there
was a picture industry in Shanghai?"

I nodded. "Pretty big, wasn't it?"

"Yes, I suppose so. Well ... I don't know. As I remember, most of the pictures were American, same then as now. ... But there were Chinese films and stars. Magazines. I put a little money in a few—even got it back. And your father, come to think of it, made quite a bit—"

"So it's not surprising that he'd be with a group like that?"

"Oh no. Not at all. ... It was a business. Chinese have always been mad about the pictures. They had studios. I'd say the biggest was called Mingxing. This girl here, you see—she's dressed herself up as a blonde—she worked there I remember. Can't think of her name, though. But this is the really extraordinary one ... look here. At the back. Maybe there's the reason your father liked to keep this photo near him."

He shoved the photo and the glass over to me, and I examined, across the decades, a lovely, elegant Chinese woman, a cocktail glass in hand. She was leaning toward the camera, more self-consciously than the others, with her free hand and forearm draped across the shoulder of a man in front of her; he was kneeling. "Mac, are you saying that my father and this lady ... ?"

"You never know." He chuckled. "But I doubt it. Your father was game, but if he was having it off with her, he was taking quite a chance. Her name ... I think her real name was something like Hu Die, but everyone called her Butterfly Wu. Ring a bell?"

"No. Actually, I think you're making it up." Except it

did ring a bell. Yuki had mentioned it, as something she'd overheard Cao talking about with his visitor, the man who'd been in the apartment before me. And Yuki had mentioned that they'd talked about Mingxing, too.

Mac, with a smile, was shaking his head. "Oh no I'm not. She even has her little place in history. Whatever she was doing with your father, she was in fact the mistress of a man called Dai Li, who was head of the Blue Shirts in Shanghai. . . . Hitler had the Brown Shirts, Mussolini had the Black Shirts, and we had the Blue. I suppose they were a little different. Just thugs, to beat up the Communists . . . or I suppose that isn't much different really. Anyway, Dai was a real tough chappie. He became head of Chiang Kai-shek's secret police." Leaning forward with a smile, as though revealing the punch line of a joke, he added, "They called it the Military Statistics Bureau, if you can credit it. I suppose it meant they kept track of dead bodies. . . . But anywho, skip ahead. Nineteen forty-six. The Americans were in it then, trying to help Chiang beat the Reds—if only the sweet silly bastards had helped him more—and they gave Dai a C-47, in which he flew one night to meet his lovely Butterfly in Shanghai. Except a storm came up, they diverted to Nanking, and the pilot put the plane into a mountain. End of story. But she was real enough. . . . What's curious, though, when I think about it, is the rest of the company. Not where you'd expect to find her, actually. . . . Mingxing, that was one of the big studios. Commercial. But there was another one that was artier, left wing. Dian Tong it was called. The fellow she's leaning on there . . .

it's hard to see his face, but I remember him, met him a few times, he was an actor but also a director or producer or something. His name was Yuan Muzhi. Remember him quite well."

"How did you meet him?"

"He wanted money of course. That sort of chappie always wants money. And the other Chinese girl, the other pretty one . . . I think she was there too."

"What about this girl with her dress pulled up, on the lion?"

"Couldn't say. With Warden? Could be. The sort of European girl you saw around a certain sort of bar."

"And Warden and my father . . . they would have known these people because they might have put money into films?"

"Your father, yes. Not Warden . . . he'd be along on this sort of junket as your father's pal."

"And the gentleman at the very end?"

"Him? I don't know how much he put into films, but he regularly put his all into actresses. Cao Dai, he was called. A businessman, and maybe he was putting up some money—actually, your father knew him pretty well, but not like Jack Warden."

Mac was shrewd, all right; I'd thought I'd worked around to Cao fairly discreetly, but he grunted and said, "That's what this is all about, isn't it?"

"Yes."

"Tell me."

I hesitated. "Mac . . ."

"Playing it close to your vest?"

"I think I better."

"Sure? Talk a little. Do you good. Besides, think of the pleasure you'll give me. That's what old age offers, you know, *vicarious thrills*." He gave me a grin, a little toothless now, almost lewd. Then he got up to his feet. "Actually, I shall now give myself a very favorite thrill, and fetch *you* a drink." I was going to protest, but he waved that down and crossed to a high mahogany cupboard, dark as Clydeside soot, returning with a decanter and a glass. He poured me a drink. Brandy. Because that's what my father drank.

I sipped. I felt his eyes watching me drink, drinking right along with me, and as I took a longer slug, I knew I'd have to tell him something. So I began, giving him an edited version of events; but the more I talked, the less editing there was. He was right—it felt good to get it out. He listened carefully. At his age, I suppose his personality was, to a degree, an act, or at least had been elaborated in response to so many different situations that it was no longer freshly created; there was no need; he had an inventory of thoughts, gestures, feelings, which would meet virtually any occasion. He'd seen and felt everything before, and it was probably an effort to try to feel again. But I think he made that effort. At a certain point, telling him about Ushida on the train, he brought out a handkerchief and swished it across his nose, as if wishing to dispel a bad odor; and after that his concentration deepened. He stopped blinking; his eyes grew a little watery, even rheumy. But you could see the intelligence in them and . . . the knowledge. He had so many facts—

names, faces, times and places, voyages, acts, refusals, triumphs, failures—at his disposal. Then, for some reason I couldn't see, he looked sad, and a little blank. In any event, when I was finished, he sat silent for a time. Then he leaned back on the couch and laid his stick, rather formally, across his knees. "Quite an adventure, Nick. Of course, you are now up to your neck in the proverbial."

"And sinking slowly."

"I don't know. I'd say you've done well. Of course, you're worried about the girl."

"Yes."

"Well, one always is . . ." He made a face. "No. That's cheap. I take it back." Shifting forward, he cupped his hands over the end of the stick. "I can give you the obvious advice. Run. Scram. Get clear of the whole mess." Saying this, he levered himself to his feet. "Probably wouldn't be hard. If you must be wanted for murder, perhaps Taiwan is the best place for it; no one recognizes them except the South Africans and the Koreans. Are there any extradition treaties? Rather doubt it."

"The trouble is—"

"Oh, I know what the trouble is. You want to do business there."

"And here. In fact, Southeast Asia generally."

"Difficult, if you're wanted for murder . . . and if you have the Caos ranged against you."

"Exactly."

"A fair reach that family must have." During this dialogue, he had gradually migrated to the cupboard and back, bringing another glass.

"The smell can't hurt me," he murmured and poured himself the tiniest tot; but he smacked his lips over it. Then he leaned back, resting the glass on his stomach—a pose that must have brought back the taste of a thousand brandies in the past, the taste of the past itself—and said, "Cao was a fairly tough chappie, as I remember. I was never close to him—he got used to seeing me around that bank, you know, kowtowing to everyone, and I never had enough face. Besides, he didn't like Europeans, he didn't really like anything European, European thinking—your father did a little business with him, but I wouldn't say he liked him. That's why, you see, Cao liked the Yapanese. He bought their line, you know, Asia for the Asians. As I recall, he even had a Yapanese wife, and after the war, before Mao, he had to tread rather carefully."

"Everyone says so. And maybe it explains why I had such a hard time getting to see him. But in the end, of course, he did agree to see me. That's where the photo comes in. I think that's the key—"

"Hang on . . ." Mac waved his hand gently, as if dispelling a fog. "You're probably right, but look . . . a moment ago, when I said it was Cao you were interested in, you thought I was pretty smart, didn't you? Well I'm not quite that smart. One of the ladies in your picture brought something back to me and I was able to get the jump on you. Ever meet a friend of your father's, Chinese, a man named Chen Yun—tall, thin as a rail? Well, I guess you wouldn't—"

"Yes. He lives in Kuala Lumpur."

"That's the one. His daughter's there. Anyway, he was my friend too, we were all friends. And he stayed on here, long after your father and mother had gone. But here's the point. About twenty-five years ago—a long time ago anyway; I could still run for the ferry—he came to see me. Said Cao had come to see *him*. He wanted to know what had happened to a lady back in Shanghai, the lady in your picture right there . . . an actress." He leaned forward and prodded the photo with his finger. "She worked in Dian Tong, the arty studio I mentioned. I expect, looking at this, that she probably came with him, this one, Yuan Muzhi . . . the fellow who tried to get money off me. But that would have been later."

I looked at the photo, looked at the girl through the glass. "She was beautiful."

"She was."

"Do you remember her name?"

"Her name was Jin Shi. She was never famous but she was . . . a real actress."

"And Cao came to Chen Yun looking for her, and Yun came to you—"

"That's right, he wanted to consult. Neither of us had ever much liked Cao, you understand, didn't trust him. We knew where Shi was—in Shanghai—but we weren't necessarily certain we wanted to pass the information on."

"You both knew where she was . . . you and Chen? And my father?"

"I think we tried to call him, but never made connections. Look . . . it's hard to explain. You know? You would have had to be there. Then. In Shanghai, I mean. We shared most things, your father and me and Chen. Sometimes we shared everything. Everything. But you mustn't get the wrong idea. Yes, we were young men, yes we were wicked, but we also accepted our responsibilities. We took that seriously. In a way, they were really responsibilities to each other . . ."

"Mac—"

"Nick, there's no point going into it, we were naughty boys but don't throw stones—you know? So let's keep our eye on the ball. I said this was twenty years ago, when Chen Yun came calling around, but I can be more precise than that. It was the summer of seventy-one. Do you remember what was happening then in China?" I was staring at him. I couldn't believe what I was thinking, and he kept things moving, made me keep up— he went right on, "Of course you do. The Cultural Revolution. It was in full cry, the madness of it. In the countryside, people were denounced and killed and eaten—eaten. Did you know that? They destroyed their Chinese culture all right, and turned into barbarians. Cannibals. But that autumn, in September, Lin Biao did his thing . . . do you know who he was?"

"Yes I know who he was. The general."

"That's the one. He was the defense minister. And that September—September, seventy-one—he tried to depose Mao, in a coup. He and his son, and his wife, tried to kill Mao—B-52 was their code name for him, rather good you must admit—and when they missed they took a plane and tried to get out to Russia. But it crashed in Mongolia ... these Chinese will keep flying planes into the sides of hills."

I took a breath; why was I upset? "So you're saying the coup, and Cao's trip, had some connection."

"I'm not saying anything, necessarily. But it's the timing, you see. It was so confused, that year and a half. Early in the year, in fact the end of 1970, Mao began cozying up to the Americans, informally invited Nixon to come and visit—'Ping-Pong politics,' you remember. Then there was the coup attempt in September seventy-one, and the next year Nixon came. . . . You see? And there's something else, about your photograph. . . . Think about it. All those people were in the pictures, Butterfly Wu, Jin Shi, Kang Jian, all of them. Sun Weishi. Actresses. But can you think of one actress who *isn't* there?"

"Mac, I don't see what you're driving at."

"Think now. She had several names, you know, the way Chinese do. Li Yunhe was one. Lan Ping was another—that's what she called herself in Shanghai, when she was in the pictures. And finally Jiang Qing. . . . Ring a bell?"

"Yes . . . Jiang Qing was Madame Mao."

"That's it. Mao's wife was an actress, just like Reagan's—about the same level, when you come to think of it, not much of an actress, but you'd see her in the magazines, she had a pretty face. I met her. She knew Shi, fairly well in fact because they were both in the left-wing studio, Dian Tong. I bet they didn't make fifty yuan a month."

I was working it out now. "So did Cao—?"

"That's what you wonder, isn't it? I will swear he didn't have anything to do with Shi, but he sure had a lot of other women, a lot of girls like the ones in your picture—so why not Jiang Qing? Your father could have. *I* could have. It's all so curious. In seventy-one, she was still the leader of the Cultural Revolution, the real power in China, right with Mao. And here, in Hong Kong, Cao shows up, looking for Jin Shi in Shanghai. . . ."

"As a way of perhaps getting to Jiang Qing, you're saying. But why?"

"I don't know. That's the simple answer. But later, when I learned about the coup, and when Nixon stepped off the plane the next year, I asked myself a lot of questions. Say the Americans learned what was going to happen. In general, Mao must have seen it coming, but say the Americans had the specifics, who, where, when, how. They could have got that. Lin Biao, you see, was trying to negotiate something with the Russians—the Americans might have picked it up from that. Their electronics. The satellites. So what do they do? If the coup goes ahead, you have chaos in China, with a military dictator running the show, and the chance of China getting back in bed with Russia. It would have made a lot of sense to warn him. Mao, I mean. Lesser of two evils . . . lesser of a whole lot of other evils."

"Okay. But why use Cao Dai?"

"Oh, I think you'd warn him half a dozen ways. The

trouble would be, how to get a warning to Mao himself and then how to make sure he believed it. No, no, you'd get as many lines in the water as you could, and Cao could have been one of them. Cao to Jin Shi, Jin Shi to Jiang Qing, and Jiang Qing to Mao. I mean, those connections were real."

"If you accept that, you're as good as saying that Cao was an American agent."

"Nick, old son, I expect Cao Dai was an agent for everyone at one time or another." He leaned forward. "I was less promiscuous—please forgive me all my sins— but even yours truly has been known to do the odd patriotic act."

Sometimes we shared everything. You would have had to be there. Then. In Shanghai . . .

Well, that was true enough; you would have had to be there—and I've never been happy making moral judgments, especially about other people's sex lives. Including my father's . . . I suppose. And this was complicated enough already. I thought of Young and Ushida, and Yuki Yamoto; maybe things were starting to make sense, but I still didn't see it all—I didn't see the half.

Mac leaned forward. "That's it, Nick. That's all I know. But I think *you* should know. If you're going to go on with this, you should have all that under your bonnet."

I shook my head. "Mac, you know something else. Come on. And I'm going to find out anyway. All I have to do is speak with your lady friend, Jin Shi. She must have some answers."

He smiled. "No doubt she did, but she's been dead five years. Five years next July."

"Christ."

He frowned; did he have some scruple against taking the Lord's name in vain . . . presumably his granny did. But the moral situation in his mind was more complex. "I'm not sure I want to tell you this."

"Mac, it's important . . . and you wanted me to tell you. You didn't have to hear a word of this."

He sat up straight. "No. You're right, I didn't. I suppose I asked for it . . . and perhaps it's for the best. Just don't ask any questions, Nick . . . we have our pacts, us old fellows, even with the dead, *especially* with the dead. So just listen. Jin Shi had three children, two sons and a girl, and of course they had fathers, but no, no, I told you I won't answer any questions and I don't know anyway, not for sure. But the younger boy is still in Shanghai, at her old address." Plucking a scrap of paper from his breast pocket, he deftly scrawled some characters. He passed it over. "We could've got her out, I could've, but she wouldn't come. She told me she was a Red—and I don't know, she might have been." His eyes broke away and he picked up the decanter. With a grunt, he poured some brandy out. "That's better. Now that's what I call a pony." He drank it straight down his throat, and gave a delicate little cough. "By God, that should either kill me or make me well."

I didn't want to say anything; I could see that's how he wanted me to play it. At the same time I felt I had to say something, but as I opened my mouth, he shook his head.

"Forget it. . . . Anyway, lad, you should be on your way. You've your visa to arrange—you know that you can pay and get them quick?"

"Yes."

"Good. You don't have to take a *kaido*, there's a ferry in twenty minutes. Give yourself a little stroll."

I got to my feet; as we went to the door, he said, "Now if only I had a woman here to smell this lovely liquor on my breath." He leaned against the jamb, gave a toss of his head. "When you're in Shanghai, you should go there . . . where they took your picture. You know it? I forget what they call it now, but just ask for Jessfield Park, people will still remember. That's where they had those lions—the one the tart was sitting on. No Chinese or dogs allowed . . . but of course money talks and, that hour, they'd look the other way."

"If there were Europeans in the party."

He smiled. "Don't worry, Nicky, they'll be having their revenge."

He stood, stooped, in the doorway as I went out. The sky had lightened, but remained a cold steely gray, and the wind was up; it was cool. On such a day, Lamma was not so different from those islands around Scotland.

"Mac, you have to tell me—"

"Nicky, there's nothing much I can tell."

"You must know—"

"Not for sure, I swear. But Nick—remember now— this was all before your mother."

I shook his hand. He was an old man; I wondered if I'd see him alive again. He must have been thinking that himself, for he said, "Come see me when you get back, and if I'm not here, you'll know where to find me . . . 'Bury me where the soldiers of retreat are buried, underneath the faded star.' "

He'd always had a joke; he'd always left me smiling.

"Mac, I'm not sure, but I think those lines may be American."

"Damn their eyes!" He suddenly looked all fierce and Scots. "But then they're finished too!"

No matter. I gave him a wave and headed for Shanghai.

13

UNDER STEELY GRAY SKIES, AND WITH A LIGHT RAIN
starting to fall, the ginkgo in the garden seemed to shiver
with cold and the house itself looked smaller, shrunken;
frigid. The pillars on either side of the drive, originally
brick, had now been coated with cement, but the two iron
rings—the remains of hinges—had been given a fresh
coat of black paint as if expecting the gate, with its elaborate cinquefoil design, to be finally replaced. There was a
car in the drive; that was new. And someone had built a
large cold frame against the front wall, where it would
catch the sun. I would tell my mother: she would
approve. "They're taking care of it well," I'd say, and she
would reply, "Good, so I might as well hang on to the
deed." Because this house, of course, was where my parents had lived . . . though I always found it hard to picture them here because the architecture—the cream tile
roof, the arches across the porch—had a rather Portuguese air. It was just inside the old French Concession.
My father had bought it with his first real money, had
then left it to the mercy of the Japanese—they'd taken

he gate—and had returned after the war, with my
mother, to find it miraculously intact: my brother had
been born in one of the upstairs rooms. Somehow, it had
also survived the Communist assault of the city, but after
1948 my father had never returned. I had no idea who
was living here now; I suppose I could have found out,
but I didn't want to. Party people. A top person in one of
the big state enterprises. Something like that. It was no
mansion, but it was a fairly big house.

I sat there for a long time, looking at it. I just let my
mind move the way it wanted. Say this all worked out.
Say, despite everything, I had some kind of future. I'd
come here, wouldn't I? Not this house, maybe, but this
city. It was unavoidable. Like London in 1880, New
York in 1950. How would I live? And of course I began
thinking of Laurie then, she could live here with me, of
course she could, that would be no problem. *If* . . . But
that was a problem, wasn't it? I'd called her from Hong
Kong. Like a fool I'd called from the airport; I couldn't
stop myself. But when she'd answered, I didn't have the
nerve to speak, I didn't know what to say. What *could* I
say? I love you. It's just that I'm suspicious as hell. I love
you, *but* . . . Except there can never be *but*s in love, that's
one of the rules. . . . Yet she'd known it was me, because
she kept saying "Nick? Nick?" and then, after a long
silence, when I still didn't answer, she said, "I guess
you're, you know, *traveling*. Okay. But be careful." And
then she said, "I have to," and *she'd* hung up. I wasn't
sure what it meant. *Traveling* . . . that I understood; it
was about *Breakfast at Tiffany's*, her favorite book, the

way the heroine had put her name on the mailbox in her apartment—*Miss Holiday Golightly, Traveling*. I'd never read it, only seen the movie, which horrified her: "It was a terrible movie—they spoiled the ending. You have to promise to read it, first' thing." I'd promised. We were lying in bed and she'd kissed me. "Of course, as a girl I admit wanting to have Audrey Hepburn's neck . . . but not her tits." She'd laughed. "What do you think? Aren't mine better?" So maybe she was reminding me of that, of us, saying it was all right—but then she'd hung up. Because she had to. Because someone was with her? Because she knew the line was tapped and she didn't want the call traced? I couldn't be sure, of course—in fact nothing had changed, I couldn't be sure of anything. Except that I felt . . . but I didn't want to feel that, I told myself I couldn't afford to, and I leaned forward and said to my driver here and now in Shanghai, "Okay, let's get going. Drive up to Hongkou."

We turned out of these residential streets, back into the city.

Shanghai . . .

Some people ask, What happens if more than a billion Chinese all start marching in the same direction? And my answer is, I don't know, and I don't care, because it will never happen. There are only six, eight, ten, twelve million people in Shanghai—it depends where you draw the boundary line, depends who you ask, no one really knows anyway—and they're always going off in every imaginable direction, in every sort of conveyance, and even if you could get them to agree on a destination they'd all take a different route. And Shanghai's a proxy for the country. No one knows where it's going, least of all the government (or the Westerners who "invest" here, forgetting that the Chinese are the greatest gamblers in the world). Nobody knows. . . . They're printing money so fast that you could have an inflationary blow-off that would make the Weimar Republic or Peron's Argentina look like a model of austerity; as we skirted Nanjing Fenglu—they close it to cars during the day—where every corner was jammed with people making for the big department stores, hyperinflation wasn't hard to believe: a million shoppers go through here every day, day after day. Then again, you could have civil war, a civil war of warlords—factions of the army—as Shanghai, Canton, and soon Hong Kong, the southwest, grow ever richer and find political control from the north ever more irksome. Certainly, crossing the creek, looking down at the tugs and the barges, the miles of warehouses, I had no trouble believing that people would fight to protect the money they were making from anything as arcane as politics. Or, just as likely, you could have some ultimate breakdown of order, a social and ecological collapse in which chaos and revolution would be indistinguishable. All around me the streets were jammed, packed with people; peasants are migrating to the cities by the millions. In Shanghai, they've tried to throw them out but they sneak back in . . . into the sort of place I was going, one of the older industrial suburbs in the northeast—the old Japanese Concession—street after street of workers' housing, cells supersaturated with humanity. And these people are breathing the filthiest air in the world. Eventually, you'd swear, something will have to give, the whole impossible enterprise will break down, and the place will relapse, exhausted, into authoritarian barbarism. But who knows? Only academics, politicians, and other professional idiots would even try to guess.

Jin Shi's son lived on a long street of identical, three-story houses, probably built of brick, but cemented over and painted a bright yellow—they were attractive, actually, like a larger version of an English workingman's cottage, and maybe that was their inspiration because the upper story—I suppose it was really a half story—was timbered, so it had a kind of Tudor look. The street was very narrow; the taxi filled it. There were trees and small walled gardens; as so often in China, a mildly claustrophobic, miniaturized feel. But it was no more anonymous than a lot of suburbs.

I paid the driver in yuan, then added ten American dollars and told him to come back in forty minutes, promising more.

I went up to the house, through a door, into an entrance hall. But it was rather confusing—it took me a moment to work out that Jin Ying Mao was in the top apartment, up a narrow staircase, then along a short hall and up another staircase at the end. As I climbed, I could hear soft voices behind a door, and maybe there was a mild smell of cooking; but there was nothing sordid about this place—I had the feeling it was a decent building, full of ordinary, decent people.

I knocked a little anxiously—I hadn't called ahead.

But I was in luck. The door swung open . . . and no, he wasn't my half brother, he was Mac's Oriental son. There was no doubt about it; he had Mac's height, his build; and though he was a half-caste—that is certainly the term Mac would have used—even his skin revealed his origins, not so much by the color as the texture, a kind of dryness. Maybe I was relieved . . . but for a second I wasn't sure how to play it. I'd been trying to work that out, of course, but everything had depended on who he was. Finally I introduced myself and said, as neutrally as possible: "Robert Maclean gave me your name."

He blinked. Very slowly. He must have been forty-five or fifty, but he wouldn't have looked that old except for his very thick glasses: I watched his eyes move behind them. His glasses were not only thick, but made of clear plastic, and gave him that self-absorbed look nearsighted people often have: obligatorily, their world doesn't extend much beyond the end of their nose.

"Come in," he said. And then, with a smile, he added, "You're wondering if I know who Maclean is."

"Yes. But I guess you do."

"My mother told me. Long ago."

"Mac was a great friend of my father's, of my family."

I was trying to be careful; did he know about my father's relationship with his mother? But he simply nodded, showing no sign that he recognized I was being discreet. "If you don't mind—if I could—I'd like to ask you about that time . . . when they knew each other." And then I added, "I've come a long way."

He didn't directly reply to this, but then gestured me farther into the room.

It was a sitting room, small but pleasant, built under the sloping roof with a bright triangular window just below the peak. It was cheerful; a patch of sun lay across a blue cotton carpet and a pot of red chrysanthemums was blooming brightly on a low table. The furnishings were modern, vaguely Scandinavian: bent metal frames and plump cushions of natural cotton, the sort of furniture you might expect to find in Ikea. But the part of the decor you really noticed was his picture collection, which covered every inch of the walls and one whole side of the ceiling—hundreds of pictures. I didn't have to look at them closely to see they were movie photos, stills, portraits, posters—glossy photos, reproductions, pages from magazines, images of every kind.

I said, "You're a movie fan."

"Yes. But more than that, a historian."

"Ah, I see. The parents make history; the children record it."

He smiled at my effort to find the right tone. "Perhaps, yes. . . . It is part of suffering the consequences. Could I offer you tea?"

Passing through a small archway, he went into the kitchen; I could see his tall, slightly stooped figure moving about, and with his back turned it would have been easy enough to mistake him for Maclean. He seemed very casual and relaxed in his brown corduroy pants, a checked flannel shirt, and big, fleecy, sheepskin slippers; still—and this was also true of Mac—he didn't shamble about, like many big men; he was neat and precise in his movements. I wondered about him. He was so uninquisitive. I was sure Maclean wouldn't have phoned him, and yet it almost seemed that he'd been expecting me. Bringing in the tea, he poured it out, quite easy in his manner, but not saying a word or offering any opening.

I finally said, "Perhaps I shouldn't ask, but have you ever met Maclean?"

He shook his head. "Oh, no. I have never been out of China. I will never leave China. I'm not sure, in any case, that I would wish to see him. Would we have much to say to each other? I don't hate him, you know. I have nothing to forgive. My mother made it very clear that he would have done much more than she permitted him to do. Her fate was her own. Which was what she wanted." I think he was surprised that he'd said so much, but then he gave a little shrug to himself, as if to say, What difference does it make? "As a child, I sometimes had fantasies of his return, his sudden appearance . . . it would solve every problem. I would be the son of a prince. We would be rich, happy . . . you know. But then—" He broke off; he seemed to think for a second. Finally he looked up. "I was going to say that I forgot about him, that I gave up on those dreams, but more likely they merged with the general dream—you understand—the dream that everyone has, that something will happen, something good, something good will come back."

"Has it?"

He smiled. "Well, you have come back. Your father could come back if he wanted to. Is that good?"

I felt embarrassed; he knew all about me . . . but then everyone says I look like my father and he must have been making all kinds of connections. But feeling this— facing him—I was now able to face for myself the fact which I'd been unconsciously keeping vague, indistinct: my father had also had some sort of relationship with the mother of this man, and she had borne his child as well. That child was Jin's half brother or half sister, and my half brother or sister, come to that. So far as I've ever understood these things, I don't think that created any formal relationship between Jin and myself; all the same, there was something. And that's what he'd been assuming, something joining us even if we didn't quite know what it was.

A little uncomfortable, I managed to say, "Well, my father couldn't come back—he has been dead for some years now."

"I am so sorry . . . I am sorry to hear that. But of course that is the other side of it, what has been lost, what will never come back. In your father's life. Mine, too, I suppose."

"Even China's."

"Yes."

"A lot has changed. I wonder how much my father would recognize, even if he could be here."

Jin shrugged. "I don't know . . . I often wonder. What has been accomplished? What have I seen during my life . . . I agree, many positive achievements, but in the long run I'm not sure they are important. More important has been the destruction, the destruction of China's old life. Our villages have been destroyed, much of the land has been ruined forever, many families have been destroyed, and learning, tradition ... in so many ways we now resemble the barbarians we used to despise. But—history is always right—it has been necessary. We have had to destroy ourselves to become modern, to join the modern world."

"You underestimate China."

"No." He shook his head emphatically. "As China joins the modern world, the modern world will change and shift, even dramatically. But that is a question of momentum, not direction. We were too late to determine the direction of the modern world, but we might have influenced it, contributed to that—and perhaps given something important, who can say? We lost that chance right here, in Shanghai. Imperialism was our great chance—"

"Which the Japanese took, didn't they, but China refused?"

"Now that is interesting. . . . Was China weaker or more arrogant than Japan—"

"Both."

"Yes, you're probably right. But we had them right here, the foreign devils with their bright blue eyes. The trouble was—the arrogance?—the International Settlement was a kind of apartheid too. It was to keep them in, keep them away. Keep them from corrupting us with their foreign ideas. They could own land here but nowhere else. Let them have their own laws—they applied only to themselves. And let them trade ... the

Chinese who helped them, and got rich, and who learned to think like them—who learned to think like modern men—well, they could be despised." He smiled. "Of course, as you know, I'm only justifying myself, my lineage, my blood."

"But that's history, isn't it?"

Jin smiled. "That's *writing history*. But of course you must never admit it."

"Are you really a historian?"

"Yes. When they let me, I teach history."

"The history of . . . ?"

"Literature, culture." He made an expansive gesture, taking in the room. "But cinema, Chinese cinema, that's my great love."

"So I see. In a way, that's what I want to ask you about."

He smiled again. "We have more and more in common."

"I asked Maclean about this. He told me to come to you." Behind his glasses, Jin's eyes watched me steadily. And then he reached into the pocket of his cardigan, took out cigarettes, and lit one. I handed him the photograph Yuki had taken from Cao. "Have you ever seen this before?"

He eyed it, squinting against the smoke of his cigarette; then, without saying anything, he walked to the back of the room and took a photograph off the wall. "This is an original print," he said. "That is a copy."

I picked it up; it was in a rosewood frame, there was

no dust on the glass—he clearly valued it. I said, "I know it's a copy. My father had one—my mother still does."

"Really? But of course . . . that's your father, there."

"And that's your mother." Jin smiled at this. We were like a couple of kids playing a game. I said, "Maclean told me something about her. But I wanted to know about this photograph. Why it was taken. What it was all about."

He shrugged. "There's not much of a story. . . . In English, what do you say, 'a night on the town'? I remember my mother said they started out together, the people from Dian Tong—"

"That was the film studio where your mother worked?"

"Exactly. I don't know if your father was with them . . . maybe not. Because they met some of the others in a nightclub, and they were on a treasure hunt—that's why they ended up in the park. Caofeng Park . . . you know? Jessfield Park? Now they call it Zhongshan Park. Those lions, you see . . . this woman is riding on it . . . they used to be there, but probably the Japanese destroyed them, or the Red Guards. But there was a clue that took them all there—it had something to do with one of those first Chinese movies, like *The Burning of the Red Lotus* or *Three Champions Struggle for the Beauty*— you know, they were like a combination of a western movie and knights in armor, ridiculous—but something like King Arthur, I think, because the clue involved a rock, with a split in it, a crack. It was wide enough to drop something down and then, if you knew how to look underneath—you had to dig some dirt away—you could retrieve it. But I think they just found another clue. I don't know why they took the picture."

So that explained the white mark, which was on Cao's photo, but not my father's or Jin's. It marked the rock.

I said, "Your mother was at Dian Tong, but some of the others were at Mingxing—"

"Yes, exactly, you see there . . . Hue Die. She was a great star. Like all stars—it was the mark of being a star—she took an English name, Miss Butterfly Wu. They all had English names, Tiger Cat, Lily Lee . . . Butterfly Wu was in the very first Chinese talkie, *Sing-song Girl Red Peony* . . . which was 1931. But this photo would have been long after that, and probably even after *Sister Flowers*, which was her great hit—1933. She played both roles, you know, two sisters who are separated at birth, one becomes westernized in Shanghai, the other is a traditional village girl. . . . Of course they are brought back together at the end."

I smiled. "Of course . . . But wasn't that unusual—that these people were together, I mean. Mingxing was a commercial studio, Dian Tong was political, Communist. . . ."

He shook his head. "It didn't work like that. Mingxing was big and commercial, but the Communists—the political people—were influential there. That was a deliberate policy of the Communists, they had a film group, and they tried to infiltrate all the studios, Yihua, Dian Tong, Xinhua. They were very successful. Yuan Muzhi—you see him, there—was political, and worked at Dian Tong, but his most successful film was *Street Angel*, and he made that at Mingxing. . . . Still, you're right, in a way. Dian Tong was a little different because the Communists actually bought it in 1934, and it became even more political. The score of one of their films—*March of Youth*—has 'The March of the Volunteers,' which became the march for the Eighth Route Army and then the national anthem."

"So the fact that Butterfly Wu was the mistress—I forget his name, but the man who was head of the Blue Shirts—that didn't make much difference to anyone? To your mother?"

"Not really. She was beautiful, independent, in Shanghai. So she had to be somebody's mistress. His name was Dai Li. Of course the right wing had their studio . . . Lianhua Studio was run by someone close to them. And Xinhua . . . it stayed open during the Japanese occupation."

I'd been working around to Cao Dai, and now I had my opening. I put my finger on his face. "What about him? How did he fit in?"

As we'd talked, Jin had moved over and was now sitting beside me on the couch. I could feel his body stiffen; and when he spoke, I don't think his voice sounded as casual as he wished.

"Cao Dai. A businessman, an investor. He liked beautiful women and he put money into films. . . . A rich man."

"Did your mother know him?"

"I'm not sure."

"She must have—because he came to visit her in the summer of 1971."

Now Jin definitely moved away from me; but then he smiled, suddenly shy behind his glasses. "You knew that. You shouldn't trick me."

And now I smiled back—oddly, it was at this point we admitted that we liked each other. "I'm sorry. I didn't mean to . . . well, I guess I did."

"Tell me . . . what do your friends call you?"

"Nicholas. Please call me Nick."

"All right. And I am Little Ying . . . because I'm so tall. Nick, this is really why you came? What you want to know?"

"That's right. Cao, you see, came to Maclean to find out where your mother lived and Maclean knew . . . because of you, I guess. I'm trying to understand why he came to see her."

"Yes. And that's interesting. Because there is something to understand, I've always known that—but I don't know what it is. My mother never said. She never talked about it."

"Because she was afraid?"

"Not really. You must understand, I didn't see what happened. I was in university, or at least I was trying to study—the Cultural Revolution was still on. I came home one afternoon, and Cao was with my mother. But he'd already been there several hours, and he didn't stay much longer. Whatever happened was already over when I arrived. They were talking, laughing—"

"Not arguing?"

"No, it was different. They were finished with their business, now they were reminiscing. For me it was very curious because I had a sense of what my mother must have been like before—back then. . . ." And, saying this, he gestured at all the photographs on the walls, the sloped ceiling, the photograph in front of us: his mother's life, I realized, which he'd spent his own life trying to understand.

"So she'd told him something? Given him something? Or he'd given something to her?"

He shook his head. "I don't know, she never said. She didn't want to talk about it, and said I mustn't ask. In those days, you realize, it was sensible to be afraid."

"All right, Little Ying—you didn't know, but what did you guess?"

"I thought it was all about Jiang Qing—the wife of Mao."

I nodded. "That's what Maclean thought too. But why did you think it?"

He shrugged. "Cao went back to that time, my mother went back to that time, *she* went back to that time. After he left, you see, my mother did tell me who Cao was, where he came from—that it was all a secret—she told me that much just to frighten me, to make sure I wouldn't talk or tell. And that's what I thought. . . . At that time, with the Red Guards in the streets, what else did Cao and my mother have in common? My mother had known her, Jiang Qing, I already knew that. And I knew . . ."

"What?"

"For me . . . it's so hard to talk about."

I leaned forward and took his arm. "We can't judge what they did, Ying, we don't have the right. They were young girls, they were poor, they were trying to survive. Your mother, Jiang Qing. So they slept with powerful men. Rich men. Like my father. White men, like Maclean. Foreign men—"

"Yes," he said. "Yes, they called them whores, they called my mother a whore—and after she was the leader of the Gang of Four, that's what they called Jiang Qing. At the trial, that's what they called her."

"Was that it, then? Did Cao's visit have something to do with one of Jiang Qing's lovers?"

He shook his head. "I don't know . . . I've never been sure. Because my mother never hated her. She would say what you just said, 'You don't know what it was like in those days, you can't know.' She wouldn't want to hurt Jiang Qing. So maybe it was different. Maybe it was something that could *protect* her."

"And what could that be?"

"Well, some people said she was a Kuomintang spy. Before she came to Shanghai, she lived with a man in Qingdao, a Communist, and he was arrested; some people say Jiang Qing betrayed him to save herself. And then, here, she was herself arrested by the police and put in jail. That was 1936, just before the Japanese came. But she got out, and some people say that the KMT let her out only because she agreed to spy for them. It was after she was let out, you see, that she went to Yanan and met Mao. Many people didn't want her to marry Mao because of that. They suspected her."

"How long was she in jail?"

"Who knows? Weeks, a few months . . . for a time,

undoubtedly, she disappeared and immediately she left Shanghai. It was a peculiar gap in her life. Later she claimed that she was there for a long time, and tortured— but she was always making up stories about herself. That whole time was a mystery. During the Cultural Revolution—there is no doubt of this—she sent people to Shanghai, who were looking for something, something that her old friends might have—"

"Her movie friends?"

"Yes. For example, they ransacked the house of Cui Wanqui, looking for something. He was a writer, a critic, the most famous in Shanghai in the thirties."

I leaned backed and thought about this. It might all fit. The Americans, somehow, induce Cao to warn Mao about the Lin Biao coup. His problem would be credibility. But if he could offer, as a token of his good intentions, documents that might compromise her—prove that Jiang Qing, Mao's wife, had spied for the Nationalists, say—then he would have been welcomed indeed.

But then, as I was thinking all this, Jin got up, picking up the photograph. I followed him as he went toward the back of the room, to replace it. As he did so, I found myself looking at the photographs around it. They were all framed the same way; and they were all very good, with the same flashy, modern style—a hint of irony. Which was part of my photograph, too: the girl on the lion, the Chinese lady in her blond wig. . . . And that's when it occurred to me that sometimes the most important person in a photograph is the one you can't see.

I said, "Do you know who took these?"

"Yes, of course. He worked for all the studios, he took hundreds of stills. He was very good."

"You know his name?"

"Ke Dan. He was well known as a photographer, not only—"

"Is he still alive?"

"No. He was persecuted in the Cultural Revolution and killed himself. But his son is alive, and I sometimes see him. His name is Ke Ling. He is also a photographer, he has a shop. I can give you the address. He has negatives for most of his father's photographs, hundreds of them."

The photograph had the answer; that had been my hunch all along, but now I was certain of it. Actors and actresses, studios, stars; it's not how you think of China, but in the land of Cultural Revolution, why not?

He wrote out the address for me, and then—as though wanting to keep up with me—he smiled and said, "*Dianying* . . . in English, it means 'electric shadows,' does it not?"

"It's a good word for the movies." I smiled. "And I think that's what this is all about."

We chatted a moment longer, then I began to take my leave. But as I reached the door, he stopped me . . . and turned away, then returned, with two more photographs. The first showed an older woman, perhaps ten years older than Jin, but the other, of the same woman much earlier, seemed oddly familiar. As I stared at the photo, I had no doubt—she had my father's high cheekbones and thin mouth combined with that extraordinary Chinese beauty that is both elegant and sensual at once.

"You must take them," Jin said, and his eyes smiled behind his thick glasses.

"What is her name?"

"Yunnan."

South of the Clouds . . . a lovely name for your sister to have.

14

I DIDN'T HAVE TO GO FAR, TO MY CABBIE'S REGRET. The address Little Ying had given me was still north of Suzhou Creek and a little to the east, where the Huangpu River begins to straighten out and head for the Yangtze estuary, and the sea.

It was a scruffy, semi-industrial area, wet, gray, not very inviting. The street was narrow; an idling truck clouded the air with diesel exhaust. There was a place that repaired pumps, a small warehouse, then a garage—they'd fix cars, bicycles, scooters, and all the other things in Shanghai that move—and then Ke Ling's shop. It was square, built of cement blocks; cement steps, with a rail of pipe, led up to the door, and there was a single small window—not very encouraging, I would have thought, to retail trade. But in fact he wasn't even open for business. A handwritten sign stuck on the door said he'd be "Back Soon."

That was all right with me; I was hungry, and I walked over a couple of streets and found a restaurant. As I ate, I thought about Jin and the life he had led, trying to make sense of him. It must have been a secret life, I thought, a life of alienation, and all the more alien because his real concern was continuity, the maintaining of links—to people, ideas, history. Which were forbidden. Or at least that might explain something of the attitudes he displayed. He'd liked me, he'd wanted to talk and tell me things, yet he'd also been incurious. On the one hand, he'd wanted to show me how much he knew; on the other, he must have sensed that I, without even trying, knew more. Returning from the past, as it were—a link myself—I also had a surer grip on the future. Maybe, obscurely, he resented this, wanted at some level to deny it; probably there was some guy at the University of London, say, who knew far more about Chinese films than he could ever hope to. It was a curious part of the general Chinese problem; from Taiwan, Hong Kong, San Francisco, Singapore, Vancouver, Manila—all those places where bits of the Chinese past had been washed up—they were now importing both Chinese history and the country's future. Looking at the photograph of my sister, I wondered what sort of life *she* had led. She was older than Little Ying, quite a bit older; born before the war, while he had come after—reassuring, at least from my mother's point of view. I smiled at that; actually, I think my mother has always been secretly proud of my father's sexual reputation. Did she not tame him? You could certainly see a good deal of him in his daughter's face, as you could in Denise. There'd been many photographs of Jin's mother in the room, and I wished I'd asked for one—it would have been reasonable—

although, thinking of what she looked like, I realized that Yunnan didn't much resemble her. Which made another odd point: looking at her, I could sense more of a resemblance than Jin could have done.

With those thoughts in my mind, I headed back to Ke Ling's shop, taking my time, giving myself a little tour of the neighborhood ... which, all of a sudden, seemed familiar. There was something here that nagged at me, a connection I couldn't quite make. It was only as I stepped into the shop—he'd reopened—that it came to me, and it changed everything. In a second, walking across to the counter where Ke Ling was standing—at least I assumed it was him—a penny dropped, maybe even a nickel. For one thing, it was clear that the store didn't simply deal in photographic supplies; there were cameras, all right, and film, but also electronic gear of various kinds, and signs saying he'd print menus for you, business cards, letterhead—he was running a desktop-publishing enterprise of some primitive sort. There was a smell of toner in the air; through a door behind him I could see the gray glow of a computer screen. And as I came right up to the counter I noticed, piled behind it, a bunch of empty cartons, and at once I recognized the company logo on them: one of Cao Dai's companies in Hong Kong. That's when I figured it out. Ke Ling's store was part of Cao's huge development project; I'd seen exactly these streets, these blocks, modeled in Cao's living room, with that portrait of Koxinga staring down from the wall and Taipei glimmering brightly at the bottom of Green Grass Mountain. In one way or another,

Cao's family owned this place, *and it was just the sort of place that could have turned out that strange copy of* Asiaweek. Which changed my whole approach ... I started to say one thing, I was going to introduce myself as coming from Jin, but I completely switched tactics. Ke Ling was a tall, thin man, with a hollow chest and a stoop, a little older than myself. His face puckered in anticipation of my request—five rolls of color negative film, Fuji please if you've got it—and then crumpled as I casually remarked, gesturing at the boxes, did he know that old Cao was finally dead, in Taiwan?

He just couldn't keep the shock out of his face. His skin went gray. Wrinkles suddenly swelled around his mouth and his eyes—I thought he might cry. And that's when I knew, with a certainty just this side of proof, who had murdered Cao Dai.

I offered him no comfort, just paid for my film and left.

Outside, in a lane across the street, I waited.

Two minutes later, the "Back Soon" sign appeared in the door; and five minutes after that, Ke Ling emerged from an alley that ran alongside the building.

He turned away from me, walking fast. At the intersection where I'd left the cab, he swung west, still moving fast, heading toward the creek. He wasn't hard to follow. It was cold, damp, nasty; he walked with his head down and his hands in the pockets of his overcoat. I had no idea where we were going, but after a time I damn well wanted to arrive—I was that cold. Ke Ling plodded on. Finally, up ahead, he turned into a crowd around a

doorway . . . the post office. The international post office.
I went in after him and, after looking around a moment,
found him waiting behind someone to use a phone. He
had to wait about five minutes, then he got to make his
call. Was he calling Taiwan—could you?—or Hong
Kong then, trying to confirm what I'd told him? I knew
you could make international calls from here and send
faxes, though I'd never done so; I always used the hotel.
But it all seemed too simple . . . in any case, after a
moment—he was just on the line a minute—he hung up
and headed off.

I wasn't exactly certain where we were, but now we
crossed the creek by one of the bridges, and headed
toward more familiar territory.

Working south, he walked as fast as he could through
the crowds—on Beijing Fenglu, on Henan Fenglu—and
then he turned onto Nanjing Fenglu, where a billion Chinese rode off in all directions . . . or that's what it felt
like. People who think Fifth Avenue or Regent Street is
crowded should come here and see what real crowds are
like. The press, the pressure of bodies, was incredible—
after twenty yards, you're tired; in fifty, angry and frustrated; after a hundred I felt a kind of horror at humanity,
the smell of it, the spitting, the pushing the shoving the
shouting, all you want to do is get out, you start praying
for it to stop. There are no cars, only buses; and they kind
of reminded me of sedan chairs, moving through the
crowds, slightly above them. He kept on—we kept on
quite a way. And then, just by the Overseas Chinese
Hotel, he finally turned into a restaurant. I told myself to

wait five minutes to let him get settled, but—it was bloody cold—thirty seconds after he went through the door, I followed.

He'd already found a table, by himself.

I went past him and found one too. I could see him, I could see the door, and I didn't really care if he saw me; at this point, I doubted that he'd recognize my face.

A waiter came up. It was a place for pastries and coffee; you ordered, then they made the coffee at your table. I chose Hainan beans, filtered. I watched Ke Ling brush his waiter off. . . . He was waiting for someone. . . . That was it; he'd called from the post office, rather than use his own phone—supposing he had his own phone— and set up a meeting here. And about five or ten minutes later, she came in. I must have had a good look at her— she'd walked right toward me—but of course I hadn't known, until she sat down, that she was the one meeting him. And as she sat down, turning her back, I only had the impression of a short woman, bundled up against the cold, probably around fifty.

Now they ordered.

My pastries were excellent, the coffee strong but acid. I watched Ke Ling—I could see him perfectly. He was talking, fast, far too fast for lipreading. His face, though, told a lot; he was fearful, disturbed—and her body also betrayed anxiety, as she leaned forward, then recoiled away.

This was only confirmation, however, for I was already pretty clear in my mind about the general picture.

These people had secrets, these people were afraid, these people . . . were spies.

Ke Ling's reaction to Cao's death, his careful phone call, this meeting, gave them away. It was all very appropriate; here they were, blowing their cover in a sort of Oriental *brûlerie*, only a few blocks from the old French Concession.

Spies . . . maybe that wasn't exactly what I wanted, but it was the reality; I was sure of it. Ke Ling and the woman certainly didn't work for any government; they weren't "intelligence officers" in the sense, say, that Laurie's father might have been. So they weren't exactly "agents"; they were the sort of people agents "ran." Which raised a question, of course; who were they working for? Conceivably they didn't know. Ke Ling obviously knew Cao Dai, but perhaps the woman didn't—and who was Cao working for? Ultimately, himself; his whole career proved that. And conceivably you could run a network of spies as an enterprise, collecting information, then selling it; but that's not what this was. No, maybe it was a carryover from my talk with Jin, but I thought I was now looking at another link, another historical survival. I sipped coffee, I watched the two of them leaning together, I listened to the clink of coffee spoons and happy student laughter, and beyond the steamy windows the new Shanghai flowed by. . . . My father's life in this city had left traces behind, so had Cao's, and this was one of them. Cao had been political, in some way I didn't understand; it was tied to his wealth, it was tied to his long survival, it was tied to the twists and turns of the history of this place. This line of thought led straight to Japan. Cao's Japanese wife, his half-Japanese son, even Yuki, even Ushida—it all tied in. By all accounts, Cao had prospered during the Japanese occupation of Shanghai, and possibly his collaboration with the Japanese had been a little too close for comfort, or at least a happy resettlement in Hong Kong. On the other hand—because, even as I thought it out, I didn't like it—Ushida hadn't acted like someone in charge; he'd been desperate. Had Cao betrayed him? But there was a greater problem; if Ke Ling and the woman were a link to Cao's past—and his faiblesse for the Japanese—this link would have had to survive the complete collapse of Japanese power during the late forties, the fifties, even into the sixties. "Made in Japan" and any other connection to the Rising Sun had been a joke, an embarrassment, certainly a true test of loyalty; and however much Cao had loved Japanese women, I didn't think he was a patriot. A link to Japan would have brought him nothing, except danger; and after the war he'd wanted protection . . . which only the good old U.S.A. could provide. I was never going to prove it, I really had no interest in doing so, but so far as I was concerned that was the answer. It tied in with Maclean's theory of why Cao had come to China in 1971, his attempt to warn Mao and Jiang Qing about Lin Biao's coup—a theory I liked even if Jin hadn't been able to fill in all the details. Yes, whether this middle-aged woman and anxious-looking man knew it, they were American agents. Except now, of course, the old order was changing, the winds had changed direction again . . . what would happen to them? what would they do?

Well, they didn't panic. No doubt they had survived many crises before. They drank their coffee and had a pastry each, and I think they calmed themselves. They made a plan, settled something—or at least I sensed, by the end, a purposeful air. They were quiet together for a time. They were sitting by a window, and Ke Ling reached over with his hand and rubbed off the mist and looked out in silence at the passing crowd; she said something to him, and he smiled. Then they talked together some more, and Ke Ling paid, got ready to go . . . which meant a little decision for me, but I'd already made it. I knew where I could find Ke Ling. But I knew nothing about the woman. So I let him go and eked out a last cup of coffee until she got up. And then I followed her out.

She'd been frightened.

She was cautious.

Crossing the road, she cut into Renmin Park—People's Park—and threw a glance over her shoulder; then, a little farther on, she stopped to watch some children playing, which also gave her the chance to check behind her. But that park is very flat—it's the old Shanghai Racecourse—and although there are trees and pools, you can see quite a way; so I'd already swung off to one side and was in fact parallel to her. I wasn't really following her at all, and on the other side, where the park merges with the vast paved brutality of Renmin Square—specially designed for the masses to voice approval of their leaders—everyone was reduced to a dot, insignificant, anonymous. As we headed up Yanan Jonglu, the old Avenue Joffre of the French Concession, she hadn't seen me, and although the crowds weren't quite as bad here, they were bad enough; a platoon of policemen could have been following here and she wouldn't have known. So I was right behind her as we passed into Shanghai's entertainment district; there's the music conservatory, the art academy, a couple of theaters. She turned into one of these, the Shanghai Art Theater. On my very first visit to Shanghai, I'd seen a performance here of a play by Bernard Shaw, and it had been one of my father's favorite haunts when it had been known as the Lyceum; even now it had something of the look and feel of a West End theater. Ke Ling's friend must have worked there; she went in a side door, and I thought I saw her showing a pass. Unless I wanted to give myself away, I was stuck. I went around the front, but the box office was closed—there were matinees, but not today.

I felt frustrated, but not entirely so. I'd seen her face, I could recognize her now; she had a round, plump face, with a small, protruding mouth as though she was about to plant a kiss on your cheek. My earlier guess at her age was about right, not quite fifty. She could have lost a few pounds, but she had a certain sense of style; she had been wearing an elegant pair of boots, and a cape, not a coat. So . . . I could wait, follow her home after work . . . or I could flag a passing, miraculously empty cab and go back to my hotel.

I was staying at the Peace. It's one of the great old art

deco hotels, once owned by Sassoon. I went up to my room, which overlooked the Bund and the Huangpu, lay down, and dozed off, circa 1931.

When I woke up, it was ten past two. I hadn't quite missed lunch, but if I had lunch, I knew, the day would be shot; in the late afternoon Shanghai's traffic somehow gets even worse. So I washed my face, went downstairs, and had tea, English tea—I needed the caffeine. Then I arranged for a cab—in Shanghai, most of the cabs operate out of the hotels. Now I had two small pieces of luck. Though I asked for him, I didn't get the driver I'd used all morning, so there was no pattern for him to notice; and then I didn't actually go to Ke Ling's address—I got out about ten blocks away, just wanting to check out that I'd been right, that this was the area Cao intended developing.

It was; but all this meant that I arrived, more or less anonymously, at Ke Ling's shop.

The street wasn't much different; there was activity, but nothing special. A truck went by, as I walked down. A man leaned out a doorway and called to someone I couldn't see . . . the vertical door of the garage went up and there was a hiss of compressed air from inside. . . .

Even before I reached the store, I'd seen his "Closed" sign, but I went up to the door anyway and peered in. I couldn't make much out, but there were lights on, there was a light in the back. And since there was a lane at the side of the building, I decided to go up it, hoping to find a window and see if he was actually there. The lane was very narrow, hard-packed dirt; you couldn't have got a car up it—it was wide enough for trash cans, but if you wanted to make a delivery you would have to use a cart. Perhaps they did. Because there was a side door, concrete steps against the side of the building, a small landing, and a gray metal door. Which now began to open. A man stepped out. He stepped right out, and I really do not know how he missed seeing me, I was right in front of him; but then I stepped to the side. This was, absolutely, pure chance. Just at that point, in the opposite building, there was a kind of alcove; one step up, then another. But it didn't lead to a door; there were just a couple of capped pipes—I've no idea what they could have been used for. Maybe fuel oil. But standing there, pressed back against the brick, holding my breath, I was about three feet above the level of the alley, and maybe that helped, being up a little high. I heard steps coming. Then a man passed, a Chinese, a blue and gray windbreaker; another Chinese, a dark topcoat—I remembered, on the mountain, how I'd stared at a particular spot, watching the police pass through it, counting them—there was a third Chinese, hands pressed into the side pockets of his jacket, his shoulder twisted down a little, and then I saw Ito. It was him all right. A short, dark, powerful man; unmistakable.

And then they were gone.

I listened. After a second, I couldn't hear their steps. I strained my ears—hoping to hear a door slam, an engine start. But there was nothing at all.

I was frozen there—a kind of shock. It had all happened so fast. But I made myself look at my watch and wait two full minutes, then I went down a step—I almost broke my leg; my knees had been locked—and peered around the corner, down the narrow little lane.

Up to the street, it was empty. From what I could see of it, the street looked empty too.

Still, I wasn't exactly overjoyed at the prospect of coming out of there, of exposing myself; I wanted to give them lots of time to move on, and that was part of what I did next. Because I emerged from my niche and went up the steps to the door Ito had come out of. And it was open. It was a big metal door, and there was a piece of loose weather stripping on the bottom; swinging back, the door had stuck a bit, and the lock hadn't caught. It just hadn't closed all the way. I grabbed the handle, to keep it from shutting. I opened it slowly, stepped into a dark, narrow room; on either side, metal shelves rose right to the ceiling, piled haphazardly with bits and pieces of electronic junk. Farther on, I could see a light. I took three or four steps and listened. I could hear a fan, a certain hum . . . it was from a computer. I went on and the room got bigger; and then, through an open doorway, I could see into the room with the light—it was the room I'd seen earlier from the inside of the shop.

Ke Ling, tied up in a chair, was obviously dead.

Besides this, the room was a mess, and at first I put it down to Ito and his men, but then I realized that it was just a mess. There was a bench, with a lot of electric out-lets wired together, and four or five computers in various stages of disassembly and repair. Shelves, like the ones I'd passed, were piled high with paper. A table held half a dozen blank TV screens. I thought I recognized an old duplicating machine, a Roneo or Gestetner, and on a big table stood two photocopiers and a laser printer—an Epson, I had one like it in the office. Despite the light, the room was dark; the air had that electronic smell, heat, insulation, silicon, metal.

I went over to Ke Ling. There was absolutely no doubt that he was dead—I didn't go too close to him on account of the pool of blood around the chair. They'd beaten him; the left side of his face was smashed, his cheek torn so badly I could see his gums and jaw. They'd beaten him to make him talk, and then they'd killed him. With a knife—his shirt was sagging with the weight of his own blood.

I don't know; maybe you get used to it. It was bad, but it wasn't as bad as Cao Dai. And this time I had to stick it out. I made myself think. They'd killed him . . . and it was almost as if they hadn't cared much, they'd just done it, got rid of him. They hadn't really troubled over it; somehow, that was a clue. And they'd made him talk. What could he tell them? I only knew one thing—the name of that woman. The person Ito was going to kill next. . . .

That was plain to me. That was what I had to assume.

So I had to find out who the woman was. But I was trying to be deliberate, trying to take it slow; I told myself no one was going to come here now, not Ito, certainly, he was done and gone, and Ke Ling was just one more dead Chinese. . . . Take your time. That's what I told myself, and that's why I decided to check the computer. It was sitting there, humming away, a perfectly good IBM clone, no doubt made in Hong Kong. I checked the root directory; a lot of the programs were in English—desktop-publishing stuff, Coreldraw, clip art, Bitstream typefaces, several word processors, yes, everything you needed to put out a dummy magazine—and I started running through those and found a database program which apparently held the customer records of the store. Under "Address," I tried the Shanghai Art Theater, and an algorithm, doubtless spawned in nether California, chugged out the name Du Wing . . . which is a perfectly reasonable name for a Chinese woman. In another program I found her name two more times, and also a Du Shan, but she was in Xian, a city about eight hundred miles away: a special rush order for frames, about a year and a half ago. In all cases, there were addresses, phone numbers, various particulars; I wrote them all down, and then went looking for a phone.

It was in the store, on a table.

I sat on the floor, behind the counter, so I couldn't be seen in case someone looked in, dialed the number of the Shanghai Art Theater and asked for Du Wing. A man answered. He was not inclined to be helpful; Du Wing, he claimed, worked in the makeup department, a statement he seemed to think explained everything, answered all possible questions, was the very last word, and so I should now go away. I persisted—it was an emergency. He was dubious, but finally put the phone down and went off somewhere. Eventually, a woman answered, but not Du Wing.

"She's already left. She went to Xian."

"Are you sure? She's not in the theater . . . she's not at home?"

"Is this about her sister?"

"Yes."

"She went straight to the airport from here. The plane has already left. I went with her myself."

"Very good . . . I'm a friend, you see. I just heard. I wanted to be sure she knew."

"So it's very serious then?"

"It seems so, yes. It's good that she's gone."

I hung up.

So the sister was part of it too. . . .

And it was a crisis. I tell Ke Ling that Cao is dead; he sets up an immediate rendezvous with Du Wing and tells her; and at once she concocts some story about her sister and heads off for Xian. . . . Why the urgency? It made sense, given what *I* knew—that Ito was after them—but they didn't know that. So what was going on?

That was one question I couldn't answer, but as I looked around the shambles of that place, with Ke Ling's body slumped in the chair, I knew I had a lot of it figured out now—other people knew things I didn't know, but I knew more than anyone else. So I had a chance, but I had to get moving. I left the way I'd come and walked all the way back to my hotel. There, they told me the last plane to Xian was booked solid; but I knew better.

The dead were burying the dead, the old order was changing. I packed a small bag, found my cabbie from the morning, and had him take me out to the airport. I found the flight to Xian, began talking to people. The young man who sold me his ticket would have traded his soul for five hundred American dollars.

15

XIAN LIES IN THE VALLEY OF THE WEI, TRIBUTARY TO the great Huang Ho, which it joins about a hundred miles to the east, and which then flows another five hundred miles to the Yellow Sea. Xian is the capital of Shaanxi Province, where Mao's Long March finally ended. And Xian is the ancient home of Chin, the first great emperor, who unified the country, who gave his name to China, and who lies buried nearby with a guard of terra-cotta warriors to watch his sleep. Now, around the ancient walls, there's a modern industrial town, ugly, filthy, and undergoing a boom which manages to be both Dickensian and computerized at the same time. Du Wing's sister lived in a village beyond, and the morning traffic was insane—the driving. And improbable—the vehicles.

I fitted right in.

For these roads, my driver was the perfect combination—reckless, lucky, skillful; we were going very fast. And his machine was inconceivable anyplace else but China, although here it probably seemed the product of a natural evolution, sedan chair, rickshaw, bicycle.

Technically it may have been a tricycle—I assume there was a third wheel somewhere. But he drove it like a motorcycle—his arms hidden in enormous gauntlets permanently attached to the handlebars—and I was riding in something like a sidecar, but bigger, and enclosed under a canopy; there was actually a fringe on top, and I peered out through a hopelessly scratched plastic window. The noise of the engine, which had probably never had a muffler, was deafening; the cold was bitter—it wasn't too far above freezing. Hanging on, I retired into the cocoon of my own body's warmth and peered out. Soon, the traffic fell off, the landscape began changing; there were fewer houses and roads. And then we passed into the countryside, fields, fields, fields, fields of yellowish brown earth, marked off, marked off, marked off, in every variation on the sole, single, only theme, the rectangle. The Chinese countryside ... maybe it's beautiful, maybe you can write poems about it, but it gave me that funny feeling, a low-grade virus of unease, the way it always does.

Here and there, you could see a tree; but never woods. Bushes grew in rows along the dikes or between the fields; but there was never any brush. This was winter, so the fields were mostly brown—plants clinging to life under the warmth of plastic sheeting—but in the spring they'd turn green with growth; everywhere you looked you'd see plants growing; but nothing would grow wild. Every inch of ground was cultivated, dressed, tilled, *worked*; there was no margin. ... Around Xian they grow wheat, cotton, oilseeds, but I find the rice areas almost worse. Even when the seedling beds are green, or the terraces rich and brown with paddy, I don't see comfort, or abundance, only fear—staved off for the moment, held in check, but always waiting. Harvests here are only the opposite of famine, and you never forget it. I know that nothing is more human than cultivation, it's the true sign of man, but when that's all there is, it's a kind of barbarism. There can't be freedom. Behind the intensity of it—footpaths one step wide; gardens in the ditches—all I hear are hungry cries. Riding now through this landscape, I remembered my father's utter detestation of the good Chairman; I'd never understood it until I actually came here and saw for myself. Mao glorified the peasant, and my father always said, "Let him eat mud, that's what peasants do." He could get into incredible rages about it. "Peasants aren't men, they're backs; they're not women, they're wombs and teats." Maybe he carried it a little far, as a general rule he tended to, but I could see what he meant—I could see it now—and, after all, every peasant on earth, if given the chance, will take a job in the city. Passing through miles of fields tended for millennia, where the ground was no longer earth or soil but some organic compounding of the human, bones and shit and flesh, this ordinary road reminded me again of the first truth about China. Forget two million people in Renmin Square waving their little red books, forget those pictures of uniformed schoolchildren singing in perfect unison. That's all a lie, or at least a desperate attempt to conceal and control the truth, which is that China is a land of fierce, bitter, ultimate competition. It is now and it always has been. In the fifties—easily within living memory—there were famines here in which people ate each other; believe me, nobody forgets it can go that far.

So I had a fair idea of the world we were heading into, but it didn't make much difference. We turned off the main road, climbed a little, picked up another road; but one village was the same as the next: brick cottages, plastered with cement or mud; a street, if the village had some importance; maybe a store. Of course this is just me and my Western arrogance; the endless repetition of this landscape is in fact a topography of infinite variety to those who inhabit it. Every square inch has a separate history, a particular story to tell—and they can tell it. They know this land like the back of their hands, like their own names; but then you also have to remember that the great Emperor Chin decreed that his subjects must take one of only a hundred names so the stories also tend to be repetitions, barely at a higher level of complexity, characters scarcely distinguishable from each other, the same plots, over and over: birth, marriage, death; harvest and famine; floods and drought; repression, rebellion, and yet more death. I'd found a bottle of brandy in the hotel, and though I spilled a lot down my front, it was what I needed to get through this, a kind of dream about losing yourself in a maze. Eventually it came to an end. The land rose slightly; we entered a village—small, gray brick cottages grouped together (people walk to their fields), a manufactory of some sort behind a brick wall, a store. The store was the front room of someone's house. My driver stopped in front of it: relaxing, I discovered that my whole body was vibrating.

With the engine throttled back I could hear him shouting that he was going to ask our way, and a moment later he came back, shouting again, saying the Du woman's house was just over the rise. I'd hired him for a round-trip, and I think he wanted me to let him wait there, where he could go in and get warm, maybe find a drink. But I made him go on. We jolted down the village's single narrow street, to the far end.

My driver throttled back again, but kept the engine running; I suppose, in that cold, so far from the city, he didn't want to risk starting it up.

I unzipped my canopy and got down, feeling a little unsteady on my feet; I almost slipped in a slick patch of mud where a car had spun a wheel. Which was funny; there wouldn't be many cars in a place like this. I looked back toward the village; we'd come over a rise and all you could see were roofs, gray patches against the gray sky. The house was like all the others, a low gray cottage with a small door and two small windows. Two smaller buildings, even smaller and squatter—possibly mud— were off to one side. I had the feeling that there was no one home, but maybe that was just part of the feel of winter.

I shouted at the driver that I'd only be a minute and gave him my brandy as compensation for making him wait in the open. Then I started up the narrow dirt walk, which had been carefully brushed with a broom, except for one long streak where a heel had scraped; Du Shan was a housekeeper. The stone stoop was swept too. I knocked at the door and listened. No one came. I knocked again, and tilted my head to the door, but I couldn't hear anything inside. I stepped back. The two windows, either side of the door, were curtained, and I couldn't see in.

I looked back to the driver, giving him a wave, and then stepped around the side of the house.

Here, too, the ground was neatly swept. There was no grain that I could see, but a few chickens huddled against the wall, around the base of the chimney, and clucked forlornly as I went by.

I walked on and found a side door, painted white, with a window of four small panes. I knocked hard—hard enough to rattle the door on its hinges; but still no one came. I pressed my nose up to the glass, smelling all cold and coppery, but saw nothing except the gray reflection of my face.

I stepped back again. I glanced around the back of the house. Another door. But I didn't bother; it was sheltered by a porch, skinny poles holding up a flimsy roof of branches. A motor scooter was parked underneath this, carefully propped on its stand. There was a bicycle, too, its shape bulging under a neatly arranged tarp. Farther on, there was a tidy pile of rubbish, and then brown garden furrows awaiting spring.

I stood still a moment. My mind was working, and what it was coming up with began to make me uneasy. I stepped clear of the house, looking up at the sky; it looked cold and gray and immense. From here, because of the rise, you really couldn't see the village, only the roofs of two houses and the meager branches of a single

tree; and looking down the hill, I saw only the patterns of
the brown fields and a road, with a single man on a
bicycle, riding along, steadily, slowly, as if he was going
to ride on forever. I stepped farther back, I was just
looking around, that's it, I was just being very natural—
just having a look around—and it just so happened that I
stepped far enough away from the house so I could see
the driver, the dark exhaust leaking out of his motorcycle. I gave him a wave. A nice, friendly, natural wave.
Yes. I wanted to make that contact, *Keep your eye on me*,
because of that tire mark where a car had got away real
fast, because of the deep scrape of the shoe in the walk,
because no one had answered even though the chimney
was warm and both the bicycle and the scooter were still
neatly stowed under the porch. Because maybe someone
had been here before me. Someone had seen Cao before
me, that was for sure. And Ke Ling . . . Now I sniffed the
air. My nose was cold, but it wrinkled with the smell of
dung, of the chickens, of vegetation, earth, but not the
smell of wood smoke or burning coal, and when I
glanced back at the chimney I couldn't see smoke. Did
that make sense? Say they'd gone out for a walk, the two
sisters—it wasn't the sort of day to go for a walk, but just
say they had—they'd leave a fire in the stove, sure, that's
how they heated the house, so wouldn't you see smoke
from the chimney? I wasn't sure. How do stoves work?
How do chimneys work? But if there was someone in the
house, and they didn't want you to know they were there,
they might put out the stove, close a damper—wasn't
that what you did, *damp the fire down*? I wasn't sure, but

I didn't like the way all these details came together in my mind, not after Ke Ling, and I stepped farther away from the house and just then the wind came up, and a door banged, open and shut, open and shut, and I turned toward it. It was the door on the smaller of the two out-buildings, in fact an outhouse. Slowly, I started walking toward it. One of the chickens followed me across to it. I closed the door—to keep it shut, all you had to do was turn a simple wooden latch, but somebody—in a hurry?—must have forgotten.

I glanced behind me. Once more, I waved to the driver. I didn't quite have it worked out, but I was working it out, and I bent down and clapped my hands and shooed the chicken forward, making it run on ahead of me. I wanted to get away from the house. I wanted to make sure the driver kept me in sight. With the chicken clucking a few steps ahead, I went across to the second building. This was larger; a shed, a pen, a stable—of course, at some point in its history, a human dwelling. It had a window, though it had no glass, and a low door. I stood near the window, gesturing toward the other chickens, as if wanting them to come toward me. God knows if this made any sense; they didn't seem to think so. Without turning my head, I looked at the house, at the windows, and I almost thought I saw a curtain move. But I was sure someone was watching, anyway. The scrape on the walk, the slick patch from the tire . . . someone had been taken away, dragged away. But someone was inside, waiting now. And someone was hiding, out here—had they been in the outhouse? tending the chickens? I didn't know, but the motorcycle engine, still running, was pretty loud, and I decided it was safe to shout, maybe it would seem I was shouting to the chickens, so I called, "Mrs. Du Wing, Mrs. Du Shan, you have to come out, you have to come right now. I can't wait here any longer." They have to be inside, I thought, they're inside the shed or they're dead, as dead as Ke Ling. That had to be it. But there was no answer. A moment passed. Still no answer. I wondered if maybe I was wrong, but I didn't think so, and I called again, "Hurry, I have a motorcycle . . . to take us . . . it will be safe as long as I'm here. But I'm going now. I'm going."

And I felt I had to go. It just wouldn't be natural to wait any longer. I glanced at the house. If there was someone inside, I had to move fast, before he could think or get organized. *He'd been left behind.* Yes. That was it. That's when I understood it all, they'd taken Du Shan away, but they hadn't realized Du Wing was there— she'd been outside, in the outhouse—but they thought she still hadn't arrived from Shanghai, so they'd left one behind to wait for her. . . . "Du Wing! Hurry! You must hurry!" I called it out but already I was walking, fast, just this side of natural, because someone had to be watching, from inside the house. And finally I heard the door open behind me, and she ran up, Du Wing, the woman I'd seen with Ke Ling in the restaurant.

My throat was so dry I could barely speak, but I said, "Keep walking, keep walking. . . ."

"My sister—"

"I know. Keep walking, keep walking."

"I was outside. They didn't know I was there, but they sent one back—"

"Now run! Run to the motorcycle!" and then I was running too—the man inside could come right out the front with a gun, but he'd have to shoot us all, that was his problem. And he didn't solve it. He didn't think fast enough. Or we did it too fast, and anyway what the hell could he do? Because in a flash we were up to the motorcycle and I was pushing her into the sidecar and shouting at the driver "Go! Go! Go!" and he could see my fear, which frightened the hell out of him thank God, and as I pushed in beside the woman he was revving his hot engine, and we were gone, over the rise, roaring through the village.

I hung on to something.

A jolt socked me in the ribs. I pulled myself up a little . . . I had my face in her armpit; her thigh was across my crotch. In that bizarre contraption, it was ridiculous and might have been funny, except for her tears, her trembling, and finally her limp exhaustion as I held her in my arms.

16

DU WING WAS VERY FRIGHTENED, AND THE RIDE AND the cold compounded her fear into shock. Back in Xian, it was hard getting her into the hotel; she was close to hysterical, and I was afraid she was going to make a scene, maybe even run away. It was her sister. She had to find her sister. . . . But she spoke a little English, and though at first I brushed that off, I then changed around and made her speak it. That seemed to help her get a grip on herself. Taking her arm, talking to her all the time, I got her past the front desk—I was staying at the Hyatt—and up to my room. Right away, I ran a hot bath. She was frozen. I just sat her on the edge of the tub, in the steam, and left her alone.

When I heard her get into the water, I went downstairs and bought some clothes for her. Everything she had on was filthy; she'd hidden herself in the darkest, dirtiest corner of that shed. So I found her a blouse, trousers, a sweater. She didn't know what to do—she didn't know how to accept them. But finally she did, and I persuaded her to go into the bathroom again and change.

The clothes helped; she became a lot calmer. Switching back to Mandarin, she told me the whole story, which was pretty much as I had guessed. She'd been "outside"—that is, in the outhouse—when a car had pulled up. She hadn't really seen what had happened next, but apparently three men—she was fairly sure of the number—had knocked at the door, grabbed her sister, and pulled her to the car. One shout; that's all she'd heard. It had been so quick—telling me now, the speed of it all seemed to especially frighten her. But there was nothing she could have done; she'd barely managed to get into the shed before one of the men returned to the house. They'd obviously known she was coming to Xian, but they hadn't searched for her because she'd been in such a rush leaving Shanghai that she hadn't taken a suitcase, only the big shoulder bag she had with her. Luckily, she'd taken it with her to the privy, and so they'd never guessed that she'd already arrived. She ran through it all a dozen times. I let her talk. I ordered up tea. By the time it came, she'd begun to run down.

Then it was my turn—of course she wanted to know who I was. I told her a little, most of it lies, if only in the interests of simplicity. But I had to tell her that Ke Ling was dead. She began to weep, one quick convulsion, then a smooth sheet of tears down her cheeks.

"You can't go near his place," I said. "I'm not even sure, at least for a time, that you can be safe in Shanghai at all."

"Why are they doing this? Who are they? They're not the police. . . ."

"No, they're not the police. This is going to be hard to explain. Cao Dai . . . do you know who he is?"

"I shouldn't know, but Ke Ling said that he was the one—the one he saw in Taipei. And before, I think he met him in Hong Kong, and I think long before that too."

"You know he's very rich?"

"Yes, he knows the Americans."

"But he was rich long before he met any Americans. He was rich before the war, in Shanghai, and now he's very rich in Taipei. He owns several companies, very large enterprises. But now he wants to make investments in the new China, especially in Shanghai—he has a huge project there. So, you see, he doesn't want any trouble with the government. He wants to make peace . . . or he wanted to. Because that's what happened, you see—Cao died. Now his sons are taking over the company. They have no interest at all in anything that would hurt their relations with China. The Americans, I think, had some hold over Cao. He had to do what they wanted, I think they gave him protection—and he probably wanted to work against the Communists anyway. But he's dead and everything's changed. In English there's an expression, 'Let the dead bury the dead.' That's what's happening now."

"Ke Ling said that too, that everything had changed." She looked away. "So they're killing everyone . . . Ke Ling, me, my sister. . . ."

"Anyone who knows who they are. They want to cut every connection, every link. Erase every sign."

She was silent for a moment. Then she went over to

the window, parted the sheer curtains, and looked out. Her body twisted as she did so, tensed; she was a short, stocky, powerful woman; I could see the line of muscle running across her heavy thighs to her hips, the tension in the creases of the cloth. She had strong, round hips. For the first time, in a way, she now made an impression on me. I don't mean I felt anything sexual, merely that her physical reality hit me; she was someone, different, over there, another life: Du Wing. I remembered her in the restaurant, with her cape and a pair of fine, high-heeled boots that laced up the front. She saw herself . . . how? I didn't know; but she had some definition of herself that included great risk. And she was suddenly aware of that. She turned back to me and said flatly, "I am in danger."

"Yes."

She nodded. "I'm sorry that I was so frightened."

"That's all right . . . I only wish . . ."

She turned back to the window. Her voice was bitter. "They will kill me. . . . Well, why not? The Communists killed my grandfather, they killed my father, so now me. They killed my grandfather because he had land—the peasants killed him and took it. They killed my father because he had books, and an old, old writing desk. I was there. . . . The Red Guards were searching for the Four Olds and they found a Bible, and they painted the desk bright red and put it on my father's neck, like a yoke, and he was struggled—that was the word they used—for three days. He lived through that, but then he killed himself—he was sure they would come back."

The Four Olds . . . it had been part of the Cultural

Revolution, one of the Red Guards' campaigns against revisionism—old ideas, old customs, old habits—there'd been one other "old," but I couldn't remember what it was. "Your family were Christian?"

"No. But my grandfather knew a missionary, a priest. He was French. They exchanged visits, for dinner, and when the missionary left the village he gave my grandfather a big Bible. It was in French—my grandfather only wanted to study the language."

"Where was this?"

"Guangxi, Guangxi Province . . ."

"It's not the Communists who are after you now. I know, really, it's all because of them, but they're finished here now, everywhere. In a way—"

"But they will still kill a lot of people."

"You're probably right."

"But at least, this time, I will deserve it. I have been a true enemy of the state, a Kuomintang spy, a capitalist roader, a counter—"

"Okay, hang on." I could hear, in her voice, that she was on the edge of something. I had to pull her back. "Listen," I said, "I want you to tell me about that, about what you were doing, you and Ke Ling. It's hard to trust me, I know, but you have to."

"What difference does it make now, to anyone?"

"Du Wing, I saved your life."

"Yes—"

"And something happened, didn't it? You came here for a reason—urgently."

"Ke Ling—I told you—he said everything had

changed, we had to be quicker. It was a question o
time."

I hadn't mentioned my visit to Ke Ling—that I was th
one who'd told him about Cao—and I didn't now
Instead I said, "What didn't you have time for?"

"The way we usually did it. . . . Usually we waited, w
were careful." She looked at me, then shrugged. "Wh
not? I might as well tell you. It concerns a film, a roll c
film."

"What film? Where does it come from?"

"A man. Every time, it's arranged in a different way
he passes it to us in a different way, but it's always th
same man, I am sure."

"Who?"

"I don't know."

"You must have some idea."

"I think . . . I shouldn't even say it, but I think he's
scientist. I'm not sure. Ke Ling didn't even know."

"What kind of scientist?"

"A specialist in rockets. In rocket engines. Propulsio
You see, here—or not far, in Lantian County—there'
a great laboratory to develop rockets. Rockets wit
solid-fuel engines—modern rockets, like the America
Minuteman. It's called the Fourth Academy, the Soli
Rocket Motor Academy."

"And this scientist works there?"

"No, not directly. I think he works at Shuangchengz
in Gansu Province. It's far in the north, very isolate
That's where they test the rockets. But he frequentl
comes here."

"And passes you film?"

"Yes, always film, but it's never done the same way. So we never see him, we never really know who it is—"

"But this time, it's supposed to be a roll of film?"

"Yes . . . at the museum for the terra-cotta soldiers . . . Chin's army, the great display. . . . There's one place where you are allowed to take photographs, but nowhere else—it's strictly forbidden. The only way to take any different pictures is to ask the museum, and of course then you pay a great deal. Well, he will try to take a photograph and they will confiscate his film. He'll protest, he'll even tell them who he is, make a fuss—but they will take his film. But of course it will already be wound up, in the camera. It goes to a woman—my sister knows her. My sister will get the film from her. They've made an arrangement . . . she pays the woman, the woman thinks my sister then sells the pictures. You see? It's all very simple. People always try to take photographs from places where they shouldn't."

I thought for a moment. "You're sure you—and your sister—don't know who he is? Can she identify him? Does she know what he's wearing? What kind of camera—"

"Only that the film will be Ilford film, because that's very hard to get here. My sister will buy it, and then—normally—I would come up and visit, or she would visit. You know the work I do, at the theater? Well, here in Xian there's a large film studio. I often do makeup here. So I'll come for that. I would take it back to Shanghai with me. Then, again, the normal procedure, I would give it to Ke Ling and he would get it out of the country. don't know how."

I was pretty sure I did, having seen that computer. Ke Ling had intended to use another daring bluff: he'd print up a mock version of *Asiaweek*, insert his material in place of a regular story, and either mail it out or get someone to carry it for him. I sat quietly for a second working this out. . . . This was something very big— clearly. God knows what was on the film. . . . Rocket engine plans? Test results? Strategic parameters and conclusions? There was no way of knowing, but it was something special. Maybe Cao had intended it as his last coup. On that night in Taipei, Ke Ling had probably been the visitor just ahead of me, getting Cao's approval for his method of smuggling the material out. I'd taken Ke Ling's mock-up out of Cao's dead hand and later burned it. . . . That all seemed reasonably clear. But so did something else. Du Wing hadn't worked it out, but I was prepared to bet her sister was alive. She'd have to be, to get the film. She couldn't identify the scientist—so Ito's men weren't going to know who he was till he actually tried to pull off this stunt. By then, though, it would be too late— the film would already have been confiscated. So the only way to get hold of it was exactly as the sisters had planned, through this woman in the museum they had contact with. And if they killed Du Wing's sister, they had no way of making that contact. Unless Ito had really screwed up, Du Shan was alive.

I said, "When is this scientist likely to be at the terracotta soldiers?"

"After two. He's been told that. It's a question of shifts, when my sister's friend will be working. But it could be anytime afterward."

I didn't like this. I thought about Ito's men. I was sure he had two teams—this group wasn't the same bunch who'd killed Ke Ling. I wondered where they came from. He could have brought them with him from Taiwan, or picked them up in Hong Kong. Or Canton. Even Shanghai. There's a lot more criminality in China than people let on, outright gangsterism; Canton's the worst, but it's everywhere now. In the seventies, kids sent to the countryside during the Cultural Revolution drifted back to the cities and began a whole new Chinese tradition of gangs and violence—China is a country with a huge pool of thugs. And that's what these guys were; they wouldn't come any tougher. And I didn't have to do anything. On the other hand . . . that film could be valuable in so many ways. Almost from the first, I'd been sure that something big was going on, something that touched me with danger but also opportunity. Now, finally, the opportunity had knocked at my door. That film was a prize, a golden prize, and I was going to claim it. I turned to Du Wing and said: "Here's how I want to play this. . . ."

17

THE NEXT MORNING MY INSTRUCTIONS TO DU WING
were simple enough—though I wasn't so sure about the
ones I was giving myself.

I gave her money. I told her to have lunch, around two,
at the Xian Restaurant—it's just down the street from the
hotel, a huge place, immense, six floors, a dozen dining
rooms; full of people. When she was finished, she was to
go anyplace where there was a big crowd. Then, at five
o'clock, and every hour on the hour, she was to call my
room at the hotel. If I didn't answer by nine, she was to
leave the city, preferably not back to Shanghai—she
began telling me where she might go, but I told her I
didn't want to know.

Having settled Du Wing, I started on my own agenda.

First I went downstairs to the front desk and bought a
ticket to the museum. There were vans to take you out
there, one of which left the hotel at exactly two; I booked
a place—if Du Wing's scientist was early, that was just
tough luck.

Then I went shopping. In the center of Xian, one of the

ights is a great bell tower, about a hundred feet high, and
n the northwest side of this is the Muslim quarter, with a
mosque and a market. In China, you can find knives
verywhere, but especially in street markets; I bought
wo, a long, slender dagger and a smaller knife, which I
ould strap to my ankle. I ate lunch in there, as well—
grilled lamb on skewers, okay if it was going to be my
ast meal—and then I headed back to the hotel. I'd left
my money belt in the safe; I got it back, then returned to
my room—Du Wing had already gone. In the money
belt, I had ten Krugerrands and I put two of them in my
pocket. Then I lay down for a while, doubling a blanket
over my legs because my feet were now getting very,
very cold.

At quarter to two, against my better judgment, I went
downstairs.

Besides myself, there were two couples making the
trip, a pair of elderly Brits and two Canadians; they
already knew each other and they offered to be friendly,
but I preferred to be alone. We headed off in our Toyota
minivan. It was a fair drive, about forty-five minutes:
plenty of time to think what an idiot I was. Of course I
wasn't actually committed. In my mind, I had three separate plans, but, likely as not, none of them would work
out. Was I being sentimental? I liked Du Wing, I liked
in Ying Mao and his movies; they were surprises, both
of them. Did they know each other? How many other
people were like that, hidden away in this extraordinary
place? And what would become of them? Nice sentiments . . . interesting questions. . . . But did I want to die

because of nice sentiments and a questioning mind? No
On the other hand I kept telling myself what that film
could be worth.

The museum complex lay on a flat plain south of the
Wei River. We slowed as a guard waved us through the
gates, then passed into a large parking lot; no doubt this
held hundreds of tour buses during the summer, but now
it was virtually empty: two other vans, a taxi, one private
car . . . which made my first job easy, especially since the
car's engine was running.

Waiting for the British lady to get out, I stood in the
light drizzle and tried to think along with them.

Assume three men.

One stays with Du Shan, the sister. So two come here.
Since they want a fast getaway, one of the two stays in
the car. And the third goes inside, because they have to
identify the scientist, whom they'd either frog-march out
or ambush when he left. Yes, I thought, it had to be just
that simple. . . . I walked a little distance away from my
companions toward a kiosk, and a fenced area, where one
of the terra-cotta warriors had been set up as a backdrop
for photographs. A cold, bored-looking man with a
camera on a tripod stood ready to oblige. I smiled him
off, wandered back . . . and was able to get close to the
car, close enough to see that the button was up on the
passenger door, and to catch a quick look at the driver's
face. He was young, with slicked-back hair—an extra in
a martial-art film. I glanced back at the statue. Chin's
warrior was powerful, austere, stern; this kid was a surly
psychotic punk. Well, I thought, what did you expect?

Quietly, I rejoined my companions. The museum was in an immense Quonset hut, vast, utilitarian, like an aircraft hangar, but it was afforded the dignity of a broad stone staircase. Ascending this, you reached an anteroom, with several souvenir shops, but we went straight in, through the main doors. Inside, we all stood for a moment—I'd in fact been here before, on my very first visit to China, but it was still impressive, though maybe not in quite the way people expect. Partly it was the size of the place. So huge. And partly the light; the only windows were long, narrow, and high up: on a day like this the light was as gray as fog. And then there was the atmosphere, a cold, earthy exhalation of the pit in front of us. We stood on a wooden, planked walkway with a low railing; below us, maybe six feet down, was the surface of the vault, which had been dug out to reveal Chin's clay army, rows and ranks of archers, spear carriers, and infantry, each life-size, each an individual with a carefully modeled expression, topknot, and mustaches. Everyone went over to the rail and looked out across this amazing phalanx. I went with them, but also checked out the scene more generally. The place was almost empty. The walkway ran all around the perimeter, and about halfway down the hall another walkway ran across the vault; perhaps twenty or thirty tourists—there was one large group—were scattered at various points along this run. To our left, a small, railed area—almost like a stage—protruded into the pit; this was the position from which you were permitted to take photographs, and indeed there was a man standing there now, aiming his camera. Security was not obvious. I picked out three or four men whose army greatcoats almost swept the ground, and I assumed they were guards; also two pairs of bored, husky fellows who could have been plain-clothes policemen—their deliberate gait suggested strolling a beat. Du Wing's scientist, if he was there, was not immediately apparent, at least to me ... although just as I was thinking this, I spotted Ito's man. He was alone, crossing the pit by the walkway at the halfway point. And he was, I realized, doing the intelligent thing: checking to see who had cameras and who didn't.

He was not a big man, and he was older than the kid in the car. His dark topcoat was buttoned right up, which gave him a slightly stiff formality, and I would have guessed he was wearing a suit underneath. All of which was fine; he looked like an overseas Chinese tourist paying his respects to the first emperor. Every few steps he'd stop at the railing and look down, then move on again, in no rush at all. But he was always watching, and every once in a while his hand went into his pocket, reassuring himself, I was prepared to bet, that his gun was still there.

Over the next twenty minutes, I watched him, watching; but I don't suppose—since I didn't have a camera—that he was ever aware of me. At least not until the very last second and by then it was too late.

That was a strange time; it passed with an odd rhythm. The rhythm of my steps on the planks ... like a child, I began avoiding stepping on the cracks between them. The occasional echo of a sound, a hushed voice. His steps. And then the movements of the guards, which I instinctively tried to fit into a pattern, and of the four men I had picked out as likely candidates: each shifting his position around the pit with its endless, frozen time.

But then the pattern shifted, the rhythm broke.

I had the advantage on Ito's man, who must have been eyeing the same people, because it turned out to be someone entirely different. And I saw him first; he was between us, with Ito's man walking away from both of us. . . . An older Chinese man in a raincoat, white-haired, stooped. . . . He didn't have a big camera, the kind you carry on a strap or in a camera bag; he just took one of those small pocket cameras from under his raincoat, went to the rail, and began taking pictures, or pretending to. I stopped and watched; Ito's man kept walking and only realized something had happened when the guards moved in. But their movement, in fact, was quite gentle. When Du Wing had originally described this whole scenario I'd thought it was risky, overelaborate, dumb. Now I wasn't so sure. The guards were perfectly polite; there was no question of grabbing the old man or taking him away. They approached him, two of them; and one gently took the old man's arm. But then they merely appeared to explain the rule, pointing to the little area where you could take photographs, smiling all the while. The old man protested briefly, but finally nodded, opened the camera, took out the film—which, even from where I was standing, was clearly wound back into its cassette. He gave it to one of the guards, who put it in his pocket and then actually offered a little nod that was tilting toward a bow. It couldn't have been more civilized; maybe it all worked just because he was old, impossible to imagine as dangerous. . . . Anyway, it worked. And now everything—from my point of view—depended on what happened next.

The old man, putting the camera away, continued along, walking by the railing, passing Ito's man—who let him go. That was the first point. Would they try to move him out right away, or wait until he left on his own? The latter, apparently, which struck me as smart. There was less risk of creating a scene. Point two concerned the old man's plan: Would he stay for a while, playing out the charade, or leave right away? Clearly, at least for a few minutes, he was staying, for he kept on walking, heading up the left side of the hall. Unless he doubled back, retracing his steps, he'd have to go all the way around before getting back to the entrance.

Now I moved.

I went the opposite way, down the right-hand side. About ten yards before I reached the walkway that ran across the pit, I went over to the rail, looked out, then kneeled down as if tying my shoe—but actually taking a Krugerrand out of my pocket.

I stepped back.

Standing in the gloom, I stared across the pit. I watched the old man—and noted that the guards were watching him too. Which was fine. In fact, it all worked out perfectly. Rather than going right to the end of the hall, the old man turned onto the middle walkway. And in the middle of that, he stopped, standing in front of the rail, looking down at the warriors. Then he came on, and turned toward me, Ito's man following and closing the gap between them ever so slightly: because now the old man could be heading straight for the exit. But that was a long way down the hall; there was no rush. Ito's man was still relaxed. He didn't see me, standing very still, just standing, not moving, but even in that gloomy light he was going to see the glint of the Krugerrand. He had eyes that could spot that sheen in the middle of the darkest night. When he spotted it, in fact, he actually licked his lips—God knows what he thought, probably he didn't think, it was pure instinct. He headed for the rail, barely keeping one eye on the old man, and certainly with nothing to spare for me as I moved toward him. I don't think he saw me, not even at the very last moment, as he bent down—and all it took was a quick lifting push and he sprawled straight over the rail, and down.

At once, I began shouting, pointing. He'd jumped, I tried to stop him. . . .

Whistles blew. I kept shouting. Feet pounded on the planks of the walkways, other people began shouting and calling, some sort of horn went off, and everything echoed in the gloomy vastness of the place.

I stepped back. Ito's man had gone right over, hitting a broad ledge of earth about six feet down, but as he tried to get up he stumbled, staggering backward, and fell straight back, down another six feet at least, into the pit itself. The museum was now pandemonium, with everyone screaming at the top of their lungs, and I stepped farther back, then turned as one of the guards pushed by me.

I began walking away. In ten steps I was up to the old man and grabbed him by the arm. I felt his arm, I sensed the fineness of his white hair, I smelled eucalyptus on his breath—that was all the impression I would ever have of him. "I know who you are, you're in great danger—get away. Get away." I hissed this in his face, and then, *"Don't do anything more until someone offers you a roll of Ilford film."* Which drove it home—he believed me then. But I was already turning, getting well away from him, and heading for the door—I was afraid they might close up the place, especially once they found Ito's man had a gun. It was all too confused, though—no one really knew what they were doing. I went through the main doors; in the anteroom people were looking around anxiously, but they didn't know what had happened. I called out, "Someone jumped into the pit, it's crazy in there," but kept going until I was outside. I paused an instant at the top of the steps, catching my breath, blinking in the light; I could hear dogs barking and then, across the parking lot, I could see handlers with two of them, leashed, but now unmuzzled, running toward the front of the building. I headed down the steps. More dogs were barking now—there must have been a security compound somewhere, and a couple of the drivers in the vans began looking around. But the kid in the car was just waking up to the fact that something had happened when I jerked the door open and slid in beside him, the knife very much beside him, and screamed, "Drive! Drive!" He hesitated; I jabbed him with the dagger and screamed again "Drive!" and then he yelled—there was blood now on his shirt—and his eyes went terrified and he kept yelling "Okay okay okay" in English and then he started ahead. And we were through the gates.

"Keep going . . . where you're keeping the woman. . . ." I was a little calmer now, and then, hitting the main road, he shifted up into third and I said, "Just leave it there and get your hand behind your back, all the way . . . all the way."

He did that, slowly, because he could feel the knife pressing through the cloth of his shirt into his side; and when he had himself in a sort of half nelson, I felt his pockets and then around his belly, and found a gun stuck in his waistband. That made it easier. I wiggled away from him, wedging myself against the door; but I didn't take my eyes off him for a second.

"You understand? Where you've got the woman. You understand?"

"I understand. Okay, okay."

The gun was a revolver; I cocked it. "And don't hit any bumps."

We drove.

And we kept driving. I made him keep his arm where it was; third gear was fine with me. I never took my eyes off him, so I wasn't exactly sure where we were going. But I guessed south; away from the river. There was little traffic, mostly trucks and a few tractors hauling wagons. After twenty minutes or so he turned right, and immediately we began climbing, then steeply climbing. I let him switch into second then, and about ten minutes after that he said, "I need the map . . . up ahead."

I glanced out the front window. The road forked, and grew narrower, about twenty yards on. He pointed to the glove compartment but I told him, "Stop the car and get out."

He did that. There was no one around. I opened the glove compartment and there was a map, and by God even an *X*. I made him step away from the car, then take his coat off and empty his pockets. "Turn them inside out, throw everything onto your coat." With the gun, I motioned him farther off, to the edge of the road; behind, the ground fell steeply into a ravine. Kneeling, I checked through his papers, his wallet. I had everything. His documents. All his money. We'd been speaking Mandarin, but he was from Canton, or, more precisely, one of the smaller towns to the west of the Pearl River Delta, one of the Four Districts where they speak low-class Cantonese, Sze Yap, I can't really do it well, but I tried. I started yelling at him and shaking the gun, telling him to get the hell out of there, to run. And he ran, all right, sliding and stumbling down the hill. I thought of letting a shot off, but didn't; and in a moment he was gone . . . though where he could go, without papers or money, I had no idea. And didn't care.

With the map on the dash, I started down the road. I'd complained about the lack of marginal land—well, here it was, in spades. These hills were barren, eroded, with slaps of scrawny reforestation along ridges, a desperate attempt to hang on to the last of the soil. There were no fields, but after half a mile the land leveled and was covered with a light growth of bushes and dead grass; some goats were grazing here. Then the road swung through a curve and I reached a small village—it was marked on the map—where a woman carrying a water pail eyed my passing. I kept going. But slowly. The road continued on the flat, and I could see down into the plain below, a flash of water, power lines, and the endless patterns of the fields, reduced to the formal outlines of a Chinese painting. And the sky was gray, the sun a weak, watery disk: all this, in a different fashion, was disturbing too.

Then, quite abruptly, the road began to descend—without realizing it, I'd been making my way along the summit—and coming out of a bend, I saw what I'd been looking for.

An abandoned village.

It was on a very steep slope—I could see where the road had once washed out. Just this side of it was a ravine, probably once a stream, but now dry. The dwellings, I counted five, were not actually houses, but structures hollowed into the side of the hill. Not caves exactly . . . I'd seen this sort of thing before . . . the peasants would dig a large chamber into the hillside—the loess soil was easy to dig—and then erect a mud-brick wall across the opening. There was a door, windows. But the front walls of two of these dwellings had obviously fallen in.

I coasted down to a wider spot, where I could pull off the road.

I got out, and worked my way down the hill.

Then I stopped. I wasn't sure what to do. I couldn't see a guard, but he would be inside. I didn't want to kill him.

I didn't want to get into a gunfight—knives I know about, but I hadn't used a gun in years. And there was Du Shan to think of . . . and another possibility: What if there was more than one man?

For half a minute, I stood stupidly by the side of the road. All the guard had to do was step out to piss and he'd see the car. But then, thinking that, I wondered if there wasn't a way to finesse this. And I worked out a way in my mind, decided it was very neat, then saw how I might make it neater—and then told myself not to get smart, some risks you don't want to take.

I went back to the car. I wasn't going to finesse anything—or not much.

I put on the kid's overcoat and hunched over the wheel. Then I started the car down the hill, revving the engine, blowing the horn like hell, blowing the horn and swerving all over the road, slumping right over the wheel so the horn blared continuously, driving down there like hell on wheels, and then fishtailing to a stop in front of the caves.

And no one appeared, not a soul.

I had the gun out; I'd been keeping it hidden under the kid's coat all the time. I got down, training the gun all around . . . and still no one appeared.

Then I realized something. Christ, I couldn't count. Three of them. A team of three: the one in the museum; the kid in the car; and the one they'd left this morning in Du Shan's village. . . .

I called, rather softly, "Du Shan? Du Shan?"

Then louder. And then, from the second of the two caves, I heard a moaned reply, "Who are you?"

I stepped through the doorway—there wasn't a door. I entered a large, dark chamber; the walls were black with soot. A couple of filthy blankets were pushed against a wall. They'd made a fire; open tins were strewn around, and two greasy bowls. Du Shan was at the back. She was tied tight with ropes, knots across her shoulders, her arms, her thighs, her ankles; and a tight noose ran from her neck to a stake in the ground. They'd gagged her with a cloth, but she'd worked it loose.

I cut her free. She began to moan.

"Can you get up?"

She shook her head. She tried to kneel, but fell. "I feel nothing. . . ."

They'd tied her that tight; she could barely move. I eased her up on her knees, then picked her up and carried her to the car. I slid her into the seat, and she had just enough strength in her arms to hold them out against the dash as I started the engine.

She began to cry. She was terrified, she didn't really know what was happening; as she cried I kept telling her, over and over, that she was safe, and Du Wing was safe, there was nothing to fear. Finally she brought her hands to her face, and held her head, and slowly the crying went out of her. Then she leaned back and asked me my name. I told her. She was still disoriented, not quite together. "What kind of name is that?" she said. "Nick. Lamp."

I smiled. "It's the name my mother gave me."

"But you are Chinese?"

"Sure. Don't you think so?" She looked at me. For the first time, expression flickered across her face; whoever I was, she didn't believe me.

18

LOOSE ENDS . . .

Finishing touches . . .

Small confirmations . . .

But mostly the next period was a time of waiting. Either Ito was going to call me, or I would call him. . . . There was no way around it. Certainly, when the call came, the only surprise was the form it took.

Still, there were things to do. Du Shan was not in good shape. She'd been terrified, and I think they'd raped her, although she didn't quite come out and say so. On the way back to Xian, I stopped a couple of times, once just to get her to move around, then to feed her and buy some new clothes; her own were ripped and dirty. But even cleaned up, she was pretty much out of it, and when we reached the hotel, she didn't want to go in; she didn't want to go into closed spaces. I don't know. . . . There was something sullen and stubborn about her. Finally I just left her in the car, went up to my room, and took Du Wing's call at seven. She was at the train station; I told her everything was okay and she arrived twenty minutes later. I let her organize her sister, while I found them both a room.

All this left the problem of the film. I wanted it. I'd earned it. It was the grand prize and I was going to claim it. But though I tried not to take it personally, it was obvious that Du Shan resisted the idea of handing it over to me. She didn't even want to see me. She was fearful, upset, angry—understandably—but also harbored a resentment, which she took out on me, and which I didn't understand. She was suspicious of me. A reflex, after years of caution? Yet it went deeper than that, and finally, after we'd gone back and forth about it, Du Wing came to my room.

I said, "I need the film, you have to understand that. I may need it to bargain with."

"Yes, I understand."

"It's important. It could save you. And what about your sister's friend—she could be in danger. I told you about Cao, about what they're doing . . . if they know about this woman—"

She shook her head. "But they don't. I never told Ke Ling . . . that she existed, of course, but never her name, or anything about her. Today, they made my sister tell them, but she lied. She gave them a different name . . . and do you think those men will still be here?"

I didn't actually, but I said, "Do you want to take that risk?"

"It's difficult to explain. She's upset because it's all over, because it's finished. So am I, but I also feel relief. You understand?"

"No."

"This was her whole life. Everything she'd gone through, everything she'd suffered and our family had suffered, everything she hated—it all went into this. So what will she do now? What will her life mean? You have to give her time."

I felt badly. I'd assumed they'd both be feeling relief, maybe even a little gratitude; and, to be fair, I'm sure they did. But their own lives had disintegrated around them. It was a terrible irony; these two women had fought Maoism all their lives, but now that communism was collapsing, their lives became meaningless. There was nothing left to fight. They'd won, but their victory was hollow; they couldn't enjoy it. I wondered what they'd believed, what had carried them along such a dangerous course. Freedom? Liberty? Democracy? Probably not. Probably it had little to do with ideas as such. It was more a question of who they were, an expression of the central core of their lives. I thought of their father, wanting to learn French from a missionary. What life had he imagined for himself, his children, his country? I couldn't guess, probably the Du sisters couldn't even precisely recall; but the possibilities he'd seen for himself had been crushed. That's what you forget. History is always written by the winners, and so everyone understands the history of modern China in terms of Mao, communism, the Long March; they forget the lives of millions of people who imagined, and who wanted to live, something different. Living in Vancouver, my father made friends with a retired banker, a man from

Montreal, and I remember one day he came over to the house and found my father reading a Chinese paper. "So what's happening in China?" he asked. My father put the paper down, smiled, and replied, "That's not important— not as important, anyway, as what's *not* happening." It took me a long time to understand that, but finally I did. So much *didn't* happen under Mao, so many possibilities went unfulfilled. Including, I suspected, the lives of these two women. What had they lost? *All that they could have been.* And there's no way you can get that back. It's true of the whole country. Often, in Shanghai, I get the feeling of being in an earlier time, around the turn of the century, the twenties, as if they've gone back and started all over again. Mao and communism have become a bad dream, something you want to forget, but what if your whole life had been spent in that dream? It had been a nightmare of banners and slogans and persecution, of having the wrong class background, the wrong parents, of "bad status," of campaigns against the Four Olds and "the One Hit Three Antis," against "hidden class enemies," a nightmare from which you awoke every morning only to perform a loyalty dance to Mao: literally, you were supposed to get up and dance under a portrait of the Great Leader. In the end, all that was left to you was hate. Now, even that was being taken away. The China which Du Shan had hated for years was transforming itself, but—to make it all worse—not into something she could recognize or love. The game had a new name, and the people at the top had monkeyed with the rules, but they'd still be the winners. In Xian, I'd met

China's new breed of thug, but they only existed because of bigger crooks at the top. Crooks in suits, crooks who traveled around in chauffeured Mercedeses. Like the people on the council of the Bank of China who were also running businesses; no wonder interest rates were low, inflation high. They could use their connections to borrow at rates less than inflation, then ship the money to Hong Kong, watch the yuan fall, and pay off their "loans" with virtually worthless currency. Or they ran companies, but companies without real owners or shareholders, so that no one cared about costs; costs like special executive housing and bonuses and your relations on the payroll and all those big cars. China was now a nation of scams. Du Shan had wanted revenge; she'd lost everything, so she had nothing to lose. Du Shan had hated. Du Shan wanted to get rid of *them*, whoever they were. But you never do; all they do is change their names and faces, and come back to take more. Which is the way of the world. Still, the loss of all that you've hated is a loss too.

"I'm sorry," I said, "I wasn't thinking of that."

She smiled. "Why should you? But you see how difficult it is for her, to give up?"

"Yes. She's giving up everything."

"Exactly." Then she smiled. "There is another problem, too. She suspects that you've some connection to the Japanese."

I smiled . . . but then felt the smile fade from my face. I was thinking of Ushida. I didn't have a connection with the Japanese, but maybe they had a connection with me. "Don't worry," I said, "no one loves the Japanese.

They have too much money. Why does she think that about me?"

"Who knows . . . she's very upset. But that was one of the reasons she was always sympathetic to America, because they defeated Japan. She always thought the Communists were hypocrites, for taking credit."

If she didn't give them credit for that, she hated them indeed.

But I said, "I'm not sure Mao disagreed with her, at least strategically . . . though I suspect the Eighth Route Army did have a little to do with it." In a twisted way, there was something logical in her suspicions. I was displacing her; and if the Americans were out of the picture, who would take over but the Japanese?—ergo, I was sympathetic to them. "How did you and your sister become involved in the first place?" I asked. "You never met Cao?"

"No. It was Ke Ling—"

"His father knew Cao, in Shanghai. In the thirties."

"Well—that is interesting. He was a photographer, I know, and so was Ke Ling. I met him that way. He was taking photographs at a theater—I met him several times—he'd ask me to make little changes in the makeup. We became friends. Our families had been destroyed in the Cultural Revolution, and we sometimes talked about it. Then the group I was with went to India and he asked me to take something for him—that was film too, a long piece of it. I took it in my makeup kit, in my nose putty, but later he told me there was nothing on it, it was just a test."

"Which you passed."

She smiled. "Yes." And then she added: "I am not ashamed of what I have done."

"No, of course not. . . . What about this scientist from Shuangchengzi?"

"I've never been sure. . . . Perhaps, in the very beginning, Ke Ling already knew about him and was searching for a way to get his information to Shanghai, and so he arranged to meet me. Perhaps he already knew about my sister here . . . that it could be done so easily. It was about eight months later, I think, that Ke Ling told me about him."

"Do you think Ke Ling knew him?"

"No, not really. Not what he did. Not exactly. I always assumed it was the Americans who found him—recruited him? That had nothing to do with Ke Ling. All he was concerned about was moving the information."

That would be the big problem for the Americans, the need for Chinese people on the ground. That's what Cao had supplied.

Du Wing said, "Can you tell me what you will do with the film?"

"I will try to get it out of China, but I told you, I may need it to bargain. I can't promise anything."

She considered this a moment, then nodded. "All right. I'm sure that is the most honest answer you could give."

The question of the film was resolved the next morning, although not through any reconciliation between Du Shan and myself. She remained withdrawn, hostile; but Du Wing had worked on her. Besides, she wanted to go to her house, and I had a car and a gun; whether she liked it or not, she needed me. On the way, without actually admitting where we were going—I simply followed Du Wing's directions—we ended up at the home of Du Shan's friend from the museum. Both sisters went in, and twenty minutes later Du Wing put a roll of Ilford film in my hand, without saying a word. I drove on, in silence. Indeed, none of us spoke until we reached Du Shan's cottage. Then Du Shan said, "I'm sure no one is there."

From her voice, I suspected she was expressing a deeper hope: that nothing had changed. But it had. And again I was the messenger. "I told you," I said, "I think you're right. But you two wait here."

The place was empty. And a mess. It was a simple cottage, a front room, a kitchen, an alcove for sleeping—in China, though, that was a lot for a single person—and every room had been turned upside down, pulled apart. The chaos was so complete I wasn't sure whether it was an expression of anger, or the result of a genuine search.

I said, testing, "Ke Ling told them you had something hidden here."

Du Shan looked at me contemptuously. "There was nothing here."

Du Wing shook her head. "I don't think so."

Watching their faces, I believed them. Which was interesting; Ito was looking for something besides the film.

I helped them clean up. And then, of course, Du Shan wanted to stay. The danger had passed, she said, they wouldn't come back. Du Wing argued with her for a time, then I stepped in.

"Probably they won't come back. But if they do, they'll kill you."

"Du Wing can stay with me."

"Fine. They'll kill her too."

She stalked out. So, again, we drove in silence. But then, as hydro pylons marched ceaselessly across the landscape, and the city, enclosed in its gray pall of smoke, came into view, Du Shan suddenly spoke, in fact recited ... " 'Nearer at hand I recognize the power station chimney, / Ceaselessly emitting its ink-swirls of smoke, / Painting, in the darkness, lights like stars on the earth, / Painting, in the day light, a black peony on the sky.' " And then she laughed. "Do you know what that poem was called? If you were a good Chinese you would know, if you loved Chairman Mao and the Great Leap Forward you would know ... it is called 'Flowering Homeland.' " And she laughed again.

She was bitter. Well, I suppose she had cause. That afternoon, in the hotel, I was wondering if Ito wasn't feeling bitter too. He had failed; I had caused his failure—by now the reports would be in, his worst fears realized. Even more galling, I had a prize he coveted. You didn't even have to bring face into it. As a simple, practical matter, he had to kill me ... or do a deal. And he had to do it quickly. His fear was the move *I'd* make. I could go over his head, which is to say, I could go to his brother. So he had to get to me before I left China. My own idea was to keep the initiative; keep options open;

avoid trapping myself. I made some progress there. Du
Shan had a friend in Beijing, and I'd already bought her a
ticket, by train, her choice, which was all the better: the
trip took more than a day, so I was relieved of that
burden. Du Wing had insisted on going back to Shanghai, and I had reservations and tickets for both of us—so
Ito would have to move fast or be too late. Or wait for my
move . . . which I was already working out in my mind
when the phone rang.

I picked it up.

"Nick?"

I hesitated. Before I could say anything, I heard
"Nick? Someone here wants to speak to you."

"Mr. Lamp?"

"Yes."

"You know who this is?"

It was Ito. Speaking English.

"Yes."

"Okay. We have to talk. We have to have a meeting."

"No meeting if you've touched a hair on her head."

"No, no. No question. But we should have a very confidential talk. You understand?"

"Just make sure you understand—"

"No question, here, Mr. Lamp, you talk to her. . . ."

"Nick? I'm all right."

"Can you talk? Where are you?"

"Here. Shanghai. Yes, I can talk."

"What the hell are you doing there?"

"You know me. Traveling. Remember those puzzle

you used to do in the papers, join the dots and you make a face? Like that. One thing led to another."

"I want—"

"Mr. Lamp? Everything okay?"

"Not okay. Leave her alone, leave her out of it, or no meeting, no nothing."

"Sure, no problem. Nobody get hurt. Right? We both come to a reasonable arrangement, clean everything up. Tonight. You make tonight? Eight o'clock in Caofeng Park. Okay? By the pavilion, very private but safe, out in the open—everything out in the open."

I didn't want any mistakes, so I switched to Mandarin and made him say it over; and then I thought about it, because I wasn't sure . . . tonight. I'd have to come by plane, which was fine, except he'd know it, and he might try something at the airport. But I didn't want to stretch it out anymore, so I agreed and said, "Put her on again." She came on and I said, "You're sure you're okay? I don't like this. I don't understand."

"Nick, there's nothing to understand, believe me. Just be careful."

"Is he threatening you?"

"No . . . not like that."

"He's listening—Ito—"

"No, no, Mr. Lamp, no threats. She'll be there, in the park. Okay?"

"Where are you? What hotel?"

"No, no, we have a nice, mutual arrangement. Okay, I see you later."

The line went dead.

I felt sick. Ito had Laurie. I didn't see how it coul have happened, but he had her. For a moment I wa purely angry but then, like a flush of shame, cam doubt . . . all the old doubts. Could I be certain? Hov could she have fallen under his control? But it didn' make any difference. One way or another, I'd known a along that I'd be walking into a trap. Laurie was the bai or she was one of the jaws, but it didn't really chang what I had to do.

It took me a while, though, to figure out how to do it.

In fact, it was only after we'd bundled Du Shan off t the train station, and were waiting for a taxi to the airpor ourselves, that the notion came to me.

I was more relaxed; I liked Du Wing and she like me—I thought I could count on her. And as we hit th airport highway—a reasonable facsimile of an express way—I put it to her:

"Du Wing, do you think you could make me up?"

"What do you mean?"

"Well, could you make me look like a white? A Roun Eye? I mean, so people would really believe it? At lea in the dark . . ."

She smiled.

"Of course I could, it's what I do. And it's not hard anyway . . . it's not the skin, but the hair and the eye that's what makes the first impression." She laughed an cocked her head, eyeing me. "It wouldn't be hard at al You're so tall, Nick, for a Chinese."

19

PEOPLE ARE ALWAYS TELLING ME THAT I'M TORN between East and West, that my soul is divided by a fault line of race and culture, but I don't buy it. Maybe I'm even suspicious of people who think that way. I am who I am, and I'm loyal to that, not the color of my skin or the memory of my great-grandfather. If other people make an issue of it, then obviously I've got to deal with it, but it's not the first thing I think of when I wake up in the morning, not even the second. People—especially Americans—treat race as a terrible problem, something to agonize over, but I'm not sure that gets you very far. The world is full of reasons and excuses for failure, but I'd rather be a success. Is that immoral? Maybe. I don't mean, though, that you should accept the world as it is, it's just that when I was a kid, I couldn't wait around for the world to become a place of perfect racial harmony before I grew up. Racists are everywhere. I've met my share—in schools, bars, on trains, planes, beaches, in boardrooms, anyplace people rub up against each other. But racists are just another species of bastard, and when it comes to bastards, all you can do is ignore them, tell them to go to hell, or kick their teeth down their throat depending on how much trouble they're making.

Now, walking over to Nanjing Donglu, thinking like this, I let my glance linger on my reflection in a store front window—the extraordinary new reflection Du Wing had created. I was not *quite* blond. Was I attractive elegant, handsome? That was a question only a lady could answer, but I certainly looked Western. Without my yellow skin and black eyes and smooth black hair, realized how Western I was and what that meant, how you could see it in the way I stood, moved, the cant of my hips as I slipped one hand into my pocket. It was strange; I was a stranger . . . I was myself, of course— who else can you be?—but I was obviously someone entirely different. I could see it in the looks people gave me, the quick look and then the look away. As a Chinese in these crowds, I'd been invisible. Now everyone noticed me, and as I walked along I remembered that first hour in Taipei, after I'd found Cao, and the relief I'd felt on the street, knowing I was totally anonymous, and then the way I'd jumped when I'd seen a white American face, as if that face might recognize me when the truth was exactly the opposite, it wouldn't see me at all, and so I'd been led to a memory of sitting in the movies, hidden effaced, lost in the dark, projecting myself onto a screen where everyone lived in the same black-and-white world I kept walking . . . I felt a little funny, to tell the truth Starting out, I'd felt pretty good; I kind of liked the way looked. Sitting in the chair, watching Du Wing work on my face in the mirror, it had seemed a bit of a lark. Perhaps I hadn't realized her skill, how convincing I'd be; she'd told me (or herself, for she talked to herself the whole time) how she had to play everything down, that the stage wasn't fifty feet away, but five, how she had to be subtle. She'd worked a long time on my eyes—now they were blue—and my hair, fitting it, changing it; and then, as a last touch, she'd remembered a costume, a suit that she thought might fit me. I was wearing it under my raincoat, an elegant, light fawn suit, very English—some play in which English ladies and gentlemen spent the evening passing from the drawing room to the garden through the French doors; God knows why they would have had it. And she'd given me her black umbrella. I'd thought the suit was a good idea just because it was sufficiently different from what I'd normally wear to give me the sense of playing a part; I'd be reminded, on my toes. Now I wasn't so sure—it made me self-conscious. And that was driven home as I made my first test, spoke my first lines. I turned off, into a shop, to try myself out. I'd just buy a paper, I thought, and as I stood at the counter waiting for another customer, the old lady gave me one quick glance, defining me, noting me, dismissing me, not seeing me ... but then, when it came my turn and I opened my mouth and spoke, doubt crossed her face, she knew something was wrong. My white face and my yellow voice didn't match. Of course! Someone as white as me couldn't speak Chinese, not with the accent I learned as my mother rocked me in her arms and sang me lullabies or the edge to my tongue I picked up from my father's quick, muttered jokes, the deadly barbs he whispered under his breath. It was impossible—Round Eyes can't speak; when they try you must work so hard to be polite, not to laugh in their smelly faces!

That was a bit of a shock; it was, I realized, going to be fairly easy to give myself away. I felt suddenly nervous. But then I told myself this was perfectly natural; in fact what's more natural to someone in greasepaint than stage fright? It was ironic, really; now that my exterior self and interior self were in perfect harmony—I looked as Western as I'd always felt—I was apparently on the brink of discovery and embarrassment. I was Chinese, was white, but what did it mean to be Chinese or white? If I took off this makeup, resumed my yellow self, the ordinary workings of my mind would distance me utterly from these people even though they took me as one of themselves. In a way, got up as a Round Eye, turned inside out, I was almost more honest. Thinking of the look on the old woman's face as my white self had spoken in her own perfect tongue, I thought of my father, his insistence on English, his love of the language. To him, the language had been the heart of the matter, not skin color, and for the first time I now understood something that had always, in a small way, been baffling. My father, in a sense, had never emigrated; obstinately, he'd never assumed any particular citizenship. Though he never came out and said so, I realized that this was even part of the reason he'd ended up in Vancouver—though of course with my father, it was also a question of business. My eldest brother had been born in Shanghai,

Denise and Alistair in Hong Kong, and Barrington was
born in Canada; they'd gone up there, had him, then
come back to San Francisco and had me. One way or
another, we've all sorted out our status. But my father,
discreetly, had refused to become an American—that
would have represented an irrevocable choice he wasn't
prepared to make—and this created various small annoy-
ances in his travels, especially getting back into the
country. In Canada, on the other hand, no one bothered
him, and though he never took up citizenship there—
another choice he comfortably avoided—I know he
voted in elections. His loyalties were expressed and
defined in his own way; he refused to let the world
impose them upon him. Now I understood. Yellow or
white, either way, I was at home in my own skin—
yellow or white, either way, the world wasn't necessarily
at home with me. Everything important lies under the
skin, but most people only look at the surface. Du
Wing—in every way a very smart lady—was absolutely
correct, first impressions were everything. People, looking at me, would want to believe I was white, especially
the Chinese people I was now passing on the street. Only
a maniac would want to be a Round Eye. What could be
crazier? To want to be a black, I suppose . . . yes, in
every way, I could count on the racism of my fellow
man, certainly my fellow Orientals. Still . . . the problem
of speaking just hadn't occurred to me, and I had to work
it out. So I turned into the same place, that coffee shop,
where I'd followed Ke Ling, where he'd met Du Wing,
just to get used to it. And I played it through. I tried

English. I spoke louder and frowned. I pointed. I made funny gestures. I resisted the temptation to speak bad Chinese—to imitate the execrable accents of the average white when he has a go at one of the Yellow Emperor's tongues—and when I was finally brought coffee and had a sticky bun in front of me, I closed my eyes and tried to hear the talk all around me as a Round Eye would, a singsong of soy foo wok tan luck chop yung, and it worked, it must have, because from the far end of the room English floated out of all that yodeling.

". . . I'm not sure it's a problem, really, the Chinese give things a different name and that takes care of it for them. . . ."

"I know what you mean, names are everything aren't they, it's not the People's Republic of China, that's not what the words mean, Central Glorious People's United Country, something like that isn't it . . ."

"Yes, exactly, or take communism as Mao translated it, *tatung*, the word really means 'great harmony,' goes right back to Confucius or whoever, makes you think of one of those lovely paintings, not bloody Karl Marx or Birmingham, the good old dark satanic Mills. . . ."

"So what you're saying, really . . ."

"Well I mean now they call the old treaty ports the Special Economic Development Zones and really think they're something different, but of course they're exactly the same, and I don't think it's any different with capitalism, it's just a word, so they'll find another and be perfectly happy."

"Maybe you're right. Do you remember that little ditty

from the Great Leap Forward, how did it go, 'Great power is monopolized / Small power is dispersed / The Party committee takes decisions / All quarters carry them out?' If they just rejigged that a trifle it would pretty much describe the way Hewlett-Packard works . . ."

I listened, searching for them, but I didn't see them until they got up, two Brits a little older than myself—but not so old that their fathers, and my father, might not have walked down the Bund together, even done a little business—and when they came by my table, of course they nodded and of course, seeing me, my white face, they smiled—"Good afternoon . . . good afternoon . . ."— and absolutely believed my smile in return.

Yes, I could pass. As long as I kept my mouth shut, I could pass. I felt a sudden rush of confidence; I was out of the wings, on the stage, and it had gone all right. Besides, I wasn't trying to win an Oscar, just catch Ito by surprise. That shouldn't be hard, I thought; he'd only seen me once, briefly, and in that strange, dark room of his brother's. Did he have a photograph? I doubted it. Anyway, I had enough trust in Du Wing's art not to worry. . . . I wanted a little time, some doubt, uncertainty, that was all. *To have any chance, I had to make the first move.*

As I paid—as clumsily as I could—and left the coffee shop, that was about all the plan I had in my mind. And I didn't want any more than that, I didn't want my mind cluttered with preconceptions, notions of what I should and shouldn't do. I had to hit him before he hit me, and the best strategy would be my reflexes. I walked on. It was already getting dark now, and the crowds were less interested in the stores than home. I kept walking down toward the Bund. I had shifted my base of operations—another nice irony—to the Overseas Chinese Hotel, but I knew I could get a cab at the Peace; Christ, with my soft white skin and fat wallet, I could get a cab anywhere.

I got down there. I felt tired. But that street, one of the truly great streets in all the cities of the world, always does something to me. And didn't it have something to do with my new white skin? Because I opened my raincoat, it wasn't that cold, and let that fancy suit show, and using my umbrella as a walking stick I marched past the Peace, and crossed the road, and promenaded by the river. The Huangpu. Or, as Round Eyes like me used to call it, the Hangpoo or the Whangpoo. We used to come up here in our great liners, our *Stars, Presidents, Castles, Maurus*, and all the great *Empresses—Empress of Russia, Empress of Asia, Empress of Japan*. We landed with our Strand bags and Foot's trunks, and our letters of credit and introduction. We came out to cushy jobs and drank pink gins; we looked forward to our leaves and we made our piles. Those were the days, weren't they? Maybe they were back. But dirtier . . . Watching a tug on the river, I lengthened my stride, feeling the small knife against my ankle and the stiffness of the long knife inside my jacket. I hadn't brought that gun—I don't know anything about them, and I hadn't wanted to bring it through the airport security. . . . Was it dirtier? I doubted it. As my father always said, you only remember the good parts. Such as? Pretty girls, sunny days, being young, you'll see, just wait. Had I seen? Was I seeing? I could feel the adrenaline beginning to flow. I'd been walking pretty fast, I was way past the Peace now. In fact I was coming up to the pier the tour boats used. I made myself slow down, checking my watch. Did the park close? Probably, but you could always get in. Did I want to get there early or late? *Not too early, not too late, just come drifting in. . . .* By this time I was walking across the Waibaidu Bridge, and just the other side is the Shanghai Mansions, one of the old hotels. Not so grand really, though it has a grand past: after the war, the U.S. military mission to CKS stayed here, and before the war, when the Japanese took it over, they cut down the legs of the billiard tables so they could play. . . . There are lots of great stories about it, but really it's pretty plain, dirty red brick, fifteen or twenty stories, originally British, proper, dull, but now very expensive because of the incredible views it has of the river. A good place, though, to get a cab. I crossed the road. And then the doormen and the people around the entrance were like a challenge, and with the umbrella in the crook of my arm I breezed right past them—that tight little smile, You know me, I own you, this is my place—into the lobby. I had time for a drink. Something yellow, I thought. Bols. Or that French aperitif, Lillet. There had to be a bar here somewhere. . . .

That's when I saw her.

There was a subtle moment of confusion in my mind, when I both knew who she was and I didn't, or at least I simply found myself looking at a beautiful white woman in a hotel lobby in Shanghai, sitting in a leather chair, the leather so smooth and cool that she must feel it on her skin, smoking a cigarette, and then crossing her legs, crossing them so smoothly you could hear the nylon whispering between her thighs, and finally rising in a simple, easy motion, straight up from the hips, the beauty of her body disciplined in the perfection of that single moment's tension, then released, as her legs stretched forward in a long, reaching stride. She walked across the lobby. I stepped back, out of sight. But she wasn't looking my way. Her eyes were across the room, where Ito had appeared. My stomach turned. He was a short, hard, thick man. His eyes looked distracted. He'd made the mistake of trying to grow a mustache, a nasty sprout of black hair on his upper lip, and even from where I stood I could see the beads of perspiration clinging there. I thought he looked like a psychopath, but then I was prejudiced. Laurie went over to him. If she had kissed him, I would have been sick on the floor. In fact, she stood a little away from him. He looked around, looked around again. They said something. I was straining to hear, but all I was hearing was Suzy, Cao's actress wife, talking about Coralee, *Especially, she liked her Chinese men. My beautiful Chinks, she used to call them.* And then I remembered how she'd smiled and added, *So now tell me, does our little girl take after her mummy?* Trembling, I stepped back farther. Did I have the answer? Oh, and all my old doubts came back, the way she'd showed up that night, everything that happened. My body tensed—I thought she was about to take his arm. I began to turn away, but I had to look . . . and again, in fact, she didn't; but she walked beside him. Together they moved across the lobby, side by side, and for one instant, absolutely, in my heart, he could have been some rich fat Chink trying to get a white woman in the club, some private domain of my white skin. It was a violation. *It simply isn't done, old boy.* I felt a surge of disgust, sexual, but deeper—visceral—how dare he put his filthy hands on her, and what a horror that she let him. Only when they were out of sight—through the doors, outside—did I finally take a breath. Now I had to find the bar, that was a clear imperative, and I needed something primitive, with an edge, a double CC I was thinking, rye whiskey to cut the bile curdling in my gut, and—first time in years—I bought cigarettes, dragging the smoke down, the nicotine hitting my innocent lungs like opium, carrying me off in a filthy swoon.

I drank and smoked and waited . . . and it seemed to take forever to get my mind back. But I had to get it back. I looked at my watch. Was I going to go, or wasn't I? *Nothing had changed, not really. . . .* I laid cash on the bar and left.

I was in a killing mood. There was no point disguising it from myself, I was up for it, I was going to do it, I was going to do whatever I had to do. I had the film but that was only half the prize and I wanted all of it. If I felt horror, now I welcomed it. And the night matched it. Darkness had come down, and with it a sulfurous, misty rain, that nightly shower of pollution that falls all over China. Lights hung in the fog; shapes receded in the shadows. I had to wait for a cab. That was fine by me. I needed to cool down. But I was still jumped up, some circuit between my brains and guts had shorted out. I was a live wire, and the driver knew it—I broke my rule, I spoke Chinese, and I could see his eyes in the mirror looking back. But that was okay, too. Because I'd worked it out, no one was going to trace me, I gave him a place to drop me a fair way from the park. It was a long drive. He stayed north of the creek the whole way around, a quarter circuit of the city. It was a trip to end romance, destroy illusion, all diesel fumes, frustration, horns, vibration, engines, ugliness, stupidity, crowds— too much, too many. Come to China. You've never seen so many people: here were the yellow hordes the Round Eyes fear, trudging down Canal Street, Yonge Street, sifting into all the dirty alleys. Sitting back, looking past my milky reflection in the window, I thought of all the fornications, the wombs, the jism, you know what they say about a Chinese woman after she's borne children? It's like putting it in a gunnysack. Everything was as ugly as my mind. The car reeked of sweat, tobacco; I rolled down the window, and the gray miasma of the city, a distillate of its endless, exhausted possibilities, came rolling in. I took a breath, held it down like dope: this was the air I had to learn to breathe. And it worked. There was something in that air. My lungs burned but my metabolism kicked up another notch. I was off and running. Setting me down, the taxi disappeared in the foggy gloom, and I headed up toward the park, opening my umbrella against the rain. But I was a cunning dog. Rather than seeking the main entrance, I walked all the way around, to the northwest corner, and a cluster of vaguely Victorian, institutional buildings. They'd once been a university, but were now some sort of legal institute, vaguely academic or governmental. There was a gate, but it was open; the guard just gave a look and then ignored me. Lights were on in the buildings—the entrance was all lit up. People were still working. But I faded off into the darkness, crossed a little parking lot, and slipped around some bushes; this put me into a service area—trash cans, a tiny three-wheeled van, gardening tools—and here I picked up a gravel path. Bracing my steps against a slope, I followed this down to a line of trees and shrubs, which marked the edge of the park. But a fence was virtually woven into the shrubbery. I had to work along this until I came to a break, or at least a section where the old wrought iron had been replaced by wire. Tossing my umbrella over, I began to climb—the wire sagged and creaked but it wasn't very high—and dropped quickly down on the other side, crouching in dead, wet grass.

No one had seen me.

Though I had no particular plan, I was making a number of assumptions. The most important was that Ito would have a team. He liked giving orders; that requires people to give orders to. So there'd be several of them watching for me, presumably at the park's main entrances or the other easy places to get in. I wanted to find them, mark them. Scrambling to my feet, I retrieved my umbrella and headed across the grass toward a couple of dim pools of yellowish light. This signaled a path; in fact, the intersection of two paths. A number of people were hurrying along here, mainly coming toward me—the park was clearly open, at least in some capacity, and these people were probably using it as a shortcut to Zhongshan Lu, a major road on the park's west side. I put up my umbrella and joined them. Except for being white, I looked perfectly ordinary.

I strolled along. In a moment, however, one difficulty became apparent: it was hard to see. Because of the dark, because of the fog, but also because of the park's layout. It was flat enough, and not really that big, but there were too many trees and bushes. Even in a good light I wouldn't have been able to see very far. That changed my approach. They were looking for me; I'd let them find me. As though waiting for someone—and every few moments I checked my watch, to make it look convincing—I positioned myself beside a bench, which was near enough to a light to give anyone a good look at my face.

I waited. It took all my patience, but I waited. And eighteen minutes later, he came along.

He wasn't hard to recognize. The small-time Cantonese thug—I was learning this new Chinese type. But he was a universal type, in fact, a young punk, he had that look, and a cheap ski jacket with a nasty turquoise sheen. He gave me a glance and I shifted the umbrella so he could see my hair, my face—and since a white man in that park, at night, was worth a look, he gave me another one, but I wasn't what he was looking for. Already, though, I was certain he was what I was looking for; and then he removed all doubt, taking a walkie-talkie from one pocket of his jacket, holding it quickly to his ear, and putting it back in the other. Yes, that was the way Ito would do it; with a couple of thugs and a couple of tricks, a lot of gimmicks and gadgets.

He passed by me. I looked quickly up and down the path ... and I got a break because there was no one around, in fact there'd been fewer people passing all the time ... and at this particular point, once you were beyond the light I was standing in, trees and bushes grew right down to the path. I followed him. I made no attempt to hide this—I furled my umbrella, my shoes grated on the path—and he did glance back, but he immediately turned around again. He'd seen who I was; he'd seen me check my watch—now I was leaving in frustration. Or something of that sort must have passed through his mind, because as my steps came quickly up behind him, he never turned and with one hard thrust I drove the point of my umbrella straight into his spine—he gave a cry— and then I kept pushing, driving him forward into a sprawl on his belly in the grass. I was on top of him before he had a chance to turn around and I smashed the pommel of the knife into the back of his head; he gave a grunt, and he was out cold. I held the knife to his throat but he was out cold.

I dragged him off the path. He had a gun in his belt, and I took it, and of course the walkie-talkie. I felt his pulse—it was rough. I'd hit him with all my strength. But he was breathing. And why should I care? And why did the son of a bitch think that his particular power, the willingness to do anything, was his alone?

I got my breath back. I retraced my steps . . . I wanted to look at the walkie-talkie in the light. It was on "Standby" and I pushed the switch over to "Receive," then stuffed it in the pocket of my raincoat. I hesitated. Something had tightened in my throat; I worked my jaw. I looked back; I'd dragged Ito's flunky behind a bush, not quite out of sight, but you wouldn't notice him unless you deliberately looked that way. He hadn't moved yet, and even if he did move it wouldn't be very fast. I thought about the other one—there'd be another one, at least—but now I was moving ahead of my mind, and I started walking toward the pavilion; Du Wing had told me roughly where it was. I slid my umbrella up, and as I walked on I suddenly felt light and easy, self-possessed, full of confidence, satisfaction. I wasn't afraid. On the contrary, I was full of power. Was it the power of a kid accepting a dare? It must have been something like that, because, as I walked along, I took the gun and threw it off in a bush—I didn't need it; that's not where my power lay. I knew exactly what I had to do, didn't want any external distractions. I felt completely alone, but I didn't need anyone or anything. I walked ahead; a minute later, the radio hissed and crackled in my pocket, and a voice muttered something I couldn't catch, and then another voice, much clearer, said to stay exactly where he was. And then the same voice began squawking, and I realized it was Ito, trying to reach me—or at least this receiver—and I took it out of my pocket and put it on "Transmit," rubbing it up and down against my leg, then holding it away from me and muttering back. He swore

He squawked again, and I slapped it against my leg, dropped it, then dragged it along the path for a yard or two with my shoe. Then I picked it up, and I threw it away too; I didn't want it going off at an awkward moment. I slowed down. I was ready. But only now did the situation I was about to face begin to take shape in my mind. How was he going to play it? What did he want to do? He had to kill me, that was clear, but I wasn't sure if he wanted to talk to me first—why set this up here, if he didn't? The trouble was, I had absolutely nothing to say to him. Then I thought of Laurie, how she might come into it, how would he use her? And how would I . . . But now my steps slowed even more. Through trees I could see the peaked roof of the pavilion, the shade in summer for the babies who were perambulated here, the showcase for lovers who kissed among the bushes. It was dark. Trees cloaked it in deeper shadow. I stopped. . . . I took a breath of foul air. I didn't like what I was seeing, because there was so little light to see. I furled the umbrella; I wanted my fair hair to show. But the pavilion was a good fifty feet away from the nearest light, up a hill, into a deep lane of darkness created by the trees. Still, I had the cigarettes. . . . If I went up there, and paused, and lit one—that could be enough.

Starting forward, I came up to the last bright light. Here, the path I was on, and the path approaching from the opposite direction, joined to make a Y, the united paths continuing up a slope to the pavilion. I was approaching from the right, and so I turned left; and just as I did so—when I was able to look down the branching path—I saw Laurie, sitting on a bench, just beyond the point where the two paths came together. She was sitting with her legs crossed, an umbrella lay across her knees. She wasn't looking my way, but up the other path—was that how they expected me to come? Did Ito lie in ambush, waiting? Of course. I stood in the full light, looking in her direction. And now I knew it was all so close. I looked at her shining hair, I recalled the whiteness of her body. In my mind, I heard her voice, speaking white, God knows she did. I didn't move. I was remembering . . . what I remembered was one day as a child in school, the day they made me pay. The teacher had been late or sick, we'd been on our own, and some kid began to tease me, then another, and then they all joined in, circling around me, chanting, *Chinkie, chinkie Chinaman, chink, chink, chink . . .* , and, ever since, that memory has been fear to me, fear both of others and myself: of what others can do, but of what I can do in return, for I'd jumped one of those kids and left him bloody. If they hadn't hauled me off him I would have left him dead. Well, that's who I am. Isn't that what I am? A Chink, a Chinaman, a slant, a gook . . . but now I had my white skin, and I stepped forward, this movement precisely catching Laurie's eye, swinging her glance around; now she saw me. I stopped in my tracks. I was staring at her. And her eyes grew wide with incredulity and then her face changed to a look of recognition. She knew me instantly. She wasn't fooled a second. That was the truth. And at once she glanced to her left, a scattering of rocks and trees, and then with her hand she softly beckoned to me . . . *but beckoned to me as a Chinese does, a gesture that confuses Round Eyes for it seems exactly opposite, as if the hand is pressing them away.* She knew who I was; was this her way of telling me? I stepped ahead. She was rising now, up off her bench, that same elegant lifting of herself in space. She beckoned once again, more urgently. I took a step. She was right in front of me. Did I trust her? I took another step, faster now, past three scruffy pines. But did I have any reason not to trust her, beyond my own fears, my own imaginings, the strange questions my mind had found? Except for the evil which the world puts in your mind, what did I know against her? Nothing. Here was the truth and at last I faced it: I didn't trust her, because I didn't believe she loved me—because I was Chinese. That was the shameful, awful truth, and in shame I stepped ahead, and stepped ahead . . . and then I didn't move.

Because someone had moved in the rocks behind her. A man, half rising, tensed, not quite standing—tentative. *Who is this white man? What is this Round Eye doing here?*

And then a foot scraped, someone was behind me, someone who'd been standing in the pines. . . . "Sir? Sir? Private matter sir. Strictly private. Please. Go around the other way. Shorter that way . . ." Ito. *He'd seen my face, he thought . . .*

I looked at Laurie. I knew I was right between them, and as her hand came out of her raincoat pocket I saw the gun, and she looked right at me, shouting, "Get out of the way, get out of the way!" and I threw myself to the right, threw myself so far I went beyond the path, hitting the grass as a gun went off, rolling, and on the second roll seeing Ito fall back with a strange dumb look on his face, he was just barely smart enough to realize he was dead. And then I was up on one knee. I ripped the knife off my ankle as the man who'd stood up by the rocks lifted his gun. . . .

It all came back to me, in my muscles and my nerves, my father in Macau, and a few tricks I'd picked up from a Mexican, night after night in an oil camp, passing the time. Above all, throw from your shoulder and your elbow, not your wrist. . . . I could tell from the sound it caught the bone but I threw it so fucking hard it went right through. He made a funny noise, half a grunt and half a scream, and his hand flapped at this thing sticking in his flesh and then he went down, in a sort of bow, he was trying not to fall on it, but then he didn't care, he didn't have anything more to care about, and he went over on his face.

I got to my feet, but I felt a little faint and I had to bend over a moment to get the blood out of my guts and back to my brain. Then I looked back at Ito. He hadn't moved. Dead, he looked very soft, like a baby.

Laurie said, "He was going to kill you. As soon as he knew who you were."

I said. "You're a damn good shot."

"My father." Then she held out the gun; she held it away from her. I got up and went toward her; her hand began to sag as I reached her, and I caught her wrist and took the gun. She smiled, but she was trembling. "God, you look awful. No wonder he didn't recognize you."

"But you did."

"Of course I did."

"I'm sorry . . ."

"Why . . . ?"

For so much . . . I just said it again, "I'm sorry."

She put her arms around me. "No, no. At a certain point, you just couldn't trust anyone—I knew that. But I had to find you. I knew it—I just knew it—you were going to need me to help. That's why I followed him."

"You followed Ito?"

She nodded. She was looking beyond me, at his body. "He came to my place and ripped everything apart—he was looking for you. But then he phoned, right in front of me, and told someone he thought you were in Shanghai. So I came here . . . and then he saw me, but I thought, why not, just play along, let him arrange it—"

"Okay." So far, the shot hadn't drawn anyone. But I knew we didn't have much time. "You all right?"

"Yes. Just a little shaky. Yes."

"All right, then. Did Ito find the rock?"

"No—what rock?"

"That photograph . . . you know, the one Yuki took from Cao's apartment. I found out what it meant. It was taken in this park, those people were on a treasure hunt. A clue was hidden underneath a rock . . . here, you see, in the park . . . that's why he wanted to come here. Cao hid something here. Years later. He was frightened, he was carrying some very dangerous items, and he wanted to hide them. He remembered the treasure hunt, this park. And when he got back home—"

"He marked the photograph—he put that white mark on the spot."

"Exactly. That was the only difference between his copy of the photograph and my father's."

I had the photograph in my hand now. Laurie took it and said, "I guess Cao would have known exactly where to go, but it's really not that clear—"

"I know, but this is at least the general area. And it'll be big, it'll stand out somehow. And there's a crack in it, you know, like the sword in the stone."

We started looking.

Taking a lot of my thinking from Maclean in Hong Kong—and bearing in mind what I'd learned from Little Ying and his course in the history of the Chinese cinema—I'd already made some guesses about this. Cao, returning to Shanghai in 1971, had been attempting to alert Mao—through his wife—of the details of Lin Biao's plot to overthrow him. He'd had documents with him—or something—that would give him leverage, prove his bona fides, and he'd wanted to hide them. I wasn't exactly sure why. Perhaps he was keeping them in reserve, or it might have been safer not to have them on him. Maybe, in fact, it was something the Americans had given him, but which he'd decided to turn to his own uses. In any case, when it came to hiding places, Cao wouldn't have wanted anything too fancy, which was no doubt why he'd remembered the park and that long-ago treasure hunt. Unless they'd drastically changed the

ayout of the paths, I didn't think it would be too hard to
ind. Still, that's a park with a lot of rocks—it took about
ifteen minutes. The rock was huge, with a slope of grass
growing around most of its base, a mangy pine on the
other side; it would have been nice to lie in the sun, lean
back against it. It had a crack right down the center, but
scarcely thick enough for an envelope.

"You couldn't get very much down there," said
Laurie.

"No, but it should be hollow underneath, or there
should be some sort of cavity. We'll have to dig."

She'd already started, nails or no. As soon as she
pulled the grass away, you could see how the rock curved
in; she reached in and found a little hollow, pulling out
an oilskin packet, tied shut with a piece of twisted wire.
Inside was an envelope with a half a dozen photographs
of a very particular type; also a number of documents—
birth records—and a tin of movie film sealed around the
edge with wax.

"Who's that?"

She was looking at the photographs; specifically, at the
image of a tall, handsome Chinese man. He was entirely
naked. I said, "My father."

"My God, I thought so—you look just like him . . .
even with your clothes *on*. And who's that?"

"Cao, I'd guess."

"And the lady—?"

"Which one?" I asked. Because there were four very
naked ladies in the picture.

"This one, of course. The one who's with your father."

I held her hand. "I love you."

"Of course you do. And I love you. But . . . my God, that's not who I think it is?"

The lady in the photograph was very beautiful, and also a very accomplished fellatrice; my father's cock was halfway down her throat. "Yes. Jiang Qing," I said. "A couple of years after this was taken, she became the wife of Chairman Mao."

20

IN HONG KONG, THE SUN WAS OUT, THE SKY WAS BLUE, the air was clear. Clearer, anyway. I took a breath. An illusion? Maybe. Probably . . . But it was good being here all the same.

Looking down from the balcony of our hotel room, I watched ships moving around the harbor, white wakes blazoning chevrons on a navy sea. The Royal Navy, yet. But not for long. A ferry set out from Kowloon, a freighter left the lighthouse on Stonecutters Island well to starboard, and a tiny Shell oiler scurried about its business near the piers. . . . It all looked so normal—now. But everything was going to change, and I wondered—along with everyone else—what was going to happen. It wasn't simply a question for Hong Kong, but all of China; everything built up since Mao's revolution was giving way. I remembered Xian. Chin, buried with his great terra-cotta army, had been the first emperor to unite the country. When he died, his government—fearing rebellion and collapse—tried to hide his death, disguising the stench of the imperial corpse with rotting fish. This, pretty much, was the model they were following now, but eventually the stench would be overwhelming and then the great changes would begin. Hong Kong, I guessed, would suffer a relative decline. A lot of scores would be settled, it would be out of favor, and it would have rivals. But also great advantages—not least the port I was watching now. China's eastern rivers are full of silt, and most of the coastal towns are hopeless for deep-water ships. Shantou, Shanghai, Xiamen—the old Amoy, just across the strait from Taiwan, where Koxinga holed up to fight the Manchus—were Hong Kong's only true competitors. And I suspected there'd be room for all of them. This might still be a very good place to be. It was something to think about. . . .

Laurie stepped through the sliding door. "They're here. The Japanese contingent has insisted on Kirin, but the Caos are being abstemious—Evian water all around."

"They're not sitting together?"

"Of course not. It's almost empty down there, and that young man behind the bar was very helpful."

I smiled. For a long time yet, she was going to find young men in bars entirely helpful; how many women can look so sexy in a suit? She was very happy. I was happy too . . . if a certain degree of nervousness is not incompatible with happiness. She kissed me lightly, not to muss her lipstick. "Who first?" she asked.

I'd gone back and forth on this. Now I made up my mind for the last time. "Ushida."

"Okay. There may be a problem. There's three of them—"

"Young?"

"No sign of him. I guess we have to wait for *Marcus Welby* reruns. Just a translator and a bodyguard."

I nodded. "I expected that; he's vulnerable. An American, in Taiwan, operating as a Japanese agent. They're afraid I'll give him away."

"Anyway, Ushida wants to bring the translator."

"His translator? He speaks English . . . of a kind. Well, pretty good. And I'm sure he's got perfect—"

"No Chinese. Absolutely no Chinese. His face went very stern, like clouds over Mount Fuji, at the very thought."

"Interesting. All right . . . he can bring him. But not the other guy."

"I don't like it, Nick. You said only one—"

"No one's going to try anything."

"I don't care. Talk to them downstairs, in public, then you can be sure."

"I am sure. Don't worry about it. It's a ploy—just gives him a little more time to think. Go on. . . . Tell him to come up."

I went inside. It was a pleasant, even large, hotel room, typically bland; everything was beige except the reproduction watercolors on the walls, views of the colony in the nineteenth century painted by Brit army officers and surveyors. Pleasant, but a far cry from where this had all begun, Cao's extraordinary dragon room in Taipei. But then, in a sense, we'd moved from the past to the present, and Cao's old world was very different from the one we were living in now.

I waited. In a couple of minutes Laurie knocked
lightly, then opened the door for Ushida, who was
accompanied by a tall young man wearing glasses.
Ushida's arm was in a sling—he bowed. I shook hands
with the other fellow, who gave me a name I promptly
forgot.

Laurie departed, I invited the men to sit.

Ushida, taking the couch opposite me, looked uncomfortable. It was his arm, I thought; it wasn't physically
bothering him, but the neat white triangle of the sling,
laid across his immaculate charcoal-gray suit, didn't do
anything for his image. It looked like a truss; in fact, it
made me think of a diaper, and I smiled to myself. His
slightly earnest, stolid face didn't display any ani-
mosity—again, he reminded me of a very competent
manager, his private being completely subsumed in his
professional role. I had no intention of apologizing for
what had happened on the train, but obliquely I tried to
deal with it. "Let me begin, gentlemen, by saying that as
far as I'm concerned this is a completely amicable
meeting. I didn't ask you here to quarrel or recriminate,
and I don't see any fundamental conflict between your
interests and my own. If there have been misunderstand-
ings in the past, I'm perfectly content to overlook them.
thank you for coming."

I waited for the young man, and maybe he actually
was an interpreter, for he'd placed himself to Ushida's
right, his chair slightly withdrawn, and now he leaned
forward and quickly whispered; Ushida even seemed to
pay attention, though I was certain he'd understood me

perfectly. He muttered in Japanese, and the young man said: "We will be interested to hear what you have to say."

That was neutral enough. I nodded and went on.

"Let us agree on some basic assumptions. Everyone knows that Japan and China are the great powers in Asia, and everyone knows that for the last century their rivalry has taken the form of a long war, a war that has had various names, but has always been the same. I assume you learned the dates in school. Eighteen ninety-five, Japan takes Formosa; 1910, Korea is annexed; 1915, the Twenty-One Demands give Japan enormous concessions in China itself, special economic and political rights; and by the Treaty of Versailles, Japan gained all the old German concessions as well. By 1931, you had seized Manchuria, and soon afterward effective control over the northern Chinese provinces. In 1937, Japan finally invaded all of China, and by 1940 you had established a puppet government in Nanking. In many respects, 1945 was only an interruption. In fact—"

The young man held up a palm, and Ushida frowned as he heard everything again in Japanese. At the same time, he didn't seem displeased—I'd thought he might be impatient, but on the contrary, his expression settled into one of curiosity: clearly I was taking him by surprise.

The young man concluded with a small bow toward me, and I continued.

"So, 1945 was a calamity but only briefly. In many ways the American triumph in Asia was a blessing for Japan. Don't you think, Ushida-*san*, that there was an irony, when the surrender was signed on the decks of the *Missouri*? Because from that point on the American navy protected Japan, her trade routes, and the oil routes to the Middle East; in fact, the U.S. Navy was the shield of Japanese prosperity. Just as important, the navy isolated China; even the Chinese atomic bomb made little difference. Any challenge to Japan would have been a threat to America, and since China had no way of directly striking America, she was powerless—even with the atom bomb she couldn't take back Taiwan, let alone challenge Japan's resurgence."

Sitting back, I invited the young man to do his thing, but this time, though Ushida listened, his eyes never left my face. I realized I had him completely buffaloed.

I said, "All that, of course, is the past—most of it, we should probably remember, before any of us were born. But today—our day—everything is different. America is declining. She was defeated in Vietnam, she's financially weak, and now, as of course you know, she's pulling back from the Pacific. I was in the United States, Ushida *san*, when the navy left Subic Bay in 1992; people hardly noticed. As well, relations between America and Japan have changed, and are now dominated by great trade disputes. All that is on one side. But then think of the other side. China grows more powerful every day. Her economy is booming. And with foreign investment and technological help, this is bound to be translated into greater military strength. America pulls back, China grows more powerful, and Japan is faced with her ancient enemy—don't you think? What if the Americans no longer provide a shield? That is the point. For Japan, advanced military capabilities in China create many difficulties and anxieties, but the most important concern China's strategic capacity, her navy, her long-range air-strike ability, above all her ability to deliver strategic atomic weapons by ballistic missile. This last point—ballistic missiles—is what interests you, wouldn't you agree?"

The young man began translating, but Ushida cut him off. "Yes, I would agree. Is that what you want to talk about—China's missiles?"

"Yes. Do you want to hear?"

"You know I do, Mr. Lamp. Go on—go on about the rockets."

"I find it amusing, Ushida-*san*, because China invented gunpowder and rocketry but one has to say it—the first Chinese rockets were primitive. China, you know, had only one scientist, H. S. Tsien, who knew anything about modern rocketry, and that was because he'd been part of the American teams testing the V-2s captured at the end of the war from the Germans. As well, the Russians sold China some early versions of their missiles. Accordingly, the earliest Chinese weapons were very simple—really, based on the V-2—and all had Soviet origins; Chinese students at the Moscow Aviation Academy became adept at picking the Russians' brains. But in the late 1950s, China began development of a series of weapons that were more original: the *dongfeng* rockets—which means 'east wind,' from Mao's line 'the east wind will prevail over the West.' The first, the DF-1, was designed from the outset to threaten Japan—it

was given sufficient range to hit all of Japan from Eas
China with an atomic payload—and later development
of the same missile were used to launch the first Chines
earth satellites, and had the power to reach Guam and th
Philippines. By the late 1960s, without any Russia
help at all, China was developing rockets with soli
propellant motors, and learned how to launch from sut
marines. But of course you know all this. . . . Just as yo
know that the final development of these rockets will b
the DF-31, DF-41, and DF-25. When they become full
operational in the late 1990s, they will constitute a serie
of sophisticated, multiple-stage, solid-propellant rocke
with ranges up to seventeen thousand kilometers an
payloads of seven hundred to two thousand kilogram
Of course they will be a direct threat to Japan, but they"
be—more important—a true strategic threat to the Unite
States. They'll be able to attack America over the Sout
Pole, where she's virtually defenseless."

"You seem to know something about this, Mr. Lamp

"I've done a little research. And I have, as I think yo
know, access to some special information."

"I mean, as well, you understand the significance (
what you're saying, that the real problem is not the thre
to ourselves, but to the Americans."

I nodded. "Japan has always been able to count on th
American nuclear umbrella. But when China can tru
strike at America, will that still hold good? Will th
Americans be prepared to put Los Angeles, Houston, ar
Dallas on the line in order to protect Osaka and Tokyo"

"Exactly." He smiled. "For myself, Mr. Lamp, I have no doubt about the answer."

"Nor do I, Ushida-*san*. In any case, the Chinese are proceeding rapidly with the development and testing of these missiles, especially the motors. I have here photographs of papers and documents of various kinds—I often work with engineers, so I can grasp them generally—they include test results, specifications, possible design modifications, questions about propellant grains, different launching modes, and so forth." I laid a manila envelope on the coffee table between us. "I assume, all along, this is what you've wanted?"

"You know how important these are?"

"Yes . . . I've tried to make that clear."

"And, Mr. Lamp, I hope your understanding implies sympathy. In any case, I will pay you fifty million yen for this envelope. I can have that sum, in cash, in an hour."

I shook my head. I pushed the scientist's photographs closer to him and said, "That's not how I earn my living, Ushida-*san*. Take them. They're yours."

"What do you mean?"

"I mean what I said at the outset. This is an amicable meeting . . . a friendly meeting . . . a meeting of friends." I smiled. "Let us say that I'm a businessman, and I will take my payment in the form of goodwill. Hopefully, I will be able to amortize it over many years. . . . Besides, it doesn't hurt anyone to have a friend in the Boeucho."

"No, it doesn't. And I'm sure the Boeucho would be happy to have you as a friend."

"Of course, I'd be a more useful friend if I managed t
stay out of jail. It would be helpful if I could get a fev
points clear. For example . . . Yuki, Cao's girlfriend, wa
your agent and she killed him. I assume that's wha
happened."

"Yes."

I'd been pretty sure, since Shanghai, in Ke Ling'
shop. Yuki had lied, but not entirely. She heard tw
people come into Cao's room. One was me, of course
but the first person had given him that mock-up of th
magazine. As soon as I realized the connection betwee
Ke Ling's shop and Cao, and also saw that he wa
capable of some sort of desktop publishing, I was pretty
sure he'd been the first man with Cao. And since he wa
clearly shocked when I told him Cao was dead, it wa
obvious he hadn't killed him—and if he hadn't, and I
hadn't, who had? It had to be Yuki.

"Good," I said, "so it happened like this. A man, a Chinese from Shanghai, came to see Cao that night. He wa
telling him about these documents—these photographs—
and how he intended moving them. He was simply going
to print the text in a false copy of a real magazine. But I
think he also told Cao that someone near him, probably a
Japanese, was betraying him."

That had been a problem in my mind—why had Yuki
killed him?—until Du Shan had voiced her suspicions of
the Japanese. But now Ushida looked quizzical. He
shrugged. "I don't think so . . . anyway, that isn't what
she told me. She said she was trying to listen, to hear
what they were saying, and the old man caught her. They

had a struggle and she panicked. She killed him. . . . You understand, Mr. Lamp, she was exactly what she said she was, a prostitute—a singsong girl. Cao found her on his own—or one of his sons found her for him—and that gave us an opportunity. But she had no training. We intended to replace her. . . . When he grew tired of her, she would introduce him to a friend, another pretty Japanese girl, but she would be working for us."

Well . . . that made sense too. "All right. She killed Cao. She started to run away, but she heard me coming up the stairs and hid."

"Yes. She'd known someone was coming to visit him, but she thought it was the man—as you say—from Shanghai. She hadn't expected anyone else, so you took her by surprise."

"And after I left, she went home and called you—"

"I told her to go to work, as usual."

"Which gave you time to arrange killing her."

He didn't say anything—but he nodded. Killing her was utterly ruthless, but then, from his point of view, he would have had no choice. She had, after all, killed Cao. An investigation of his death would probably lead to her. And of course that would have revealed Ushida. He had to get rid of her. Another question . . . Did he have sex with her first? It was a question, after so much, which I suddenly didn't want answered. But then it occurred to me that I only had Robert Young's word that she'd had sex with anyone . . . perhaps there was no mystery, only a lie.

I said, "But you missed the photograph."

"She never told me that she had it. I suppose, tha
night, Cao had it in his hand, or nearby—he wa
intending to show it to you for some reason? All I knew
from what she told me, was that a very important docu
ment had been involved in Cao's discussions with th
man—you tell me now—from Shanghai. This fals
magazine, obviously, but I didn't know. Whatever it was
I thought you had it."

"So you came after me. . . . How did you know I'd lef
Taipei?"

He smiled. "I expect you don't think much of us, Mr
Lamp, after all this. But you'll admit that we Japanes
are good at electronics. We wired the room at your hotel
and the young woman's room. Unfortunately, Youn
wasn't able to find out which of the villas in that valle
belonged to your lady friend's family. He was actuall
watching the wrong one. But he saw the police arrive
and saw you run out. He guessed where you were going
Up. The only place you could go, really."

I nodded. And I gave my mind a moment, but it didn'
come up with any more questions. Finally. At last. I ha
all the answers, or at least the ones I needed. An
Ushida—with a little difficulty, on account of the sling—
leaned forward and said very earnestly:

"Mr. Lamp, do not have any worries at all in you
mind about the Taipei police. If you have any problem
we could . . . arrange things. Fix things?"

I nodded. "Fix things."

He smiled. "You trust me?"

I said, "Of course I do. But also, you have an incer

ive. Cao, for many years, ran a network of agents in
China, and I made contact with them. It operated for the
Americans. The Cao family—I promise you—has no
interest in it anymore. On the contrary they see it only as
a source of embarrassment. You might like to take it
over."

"And you would help?"

"We'll see."

He nodded, and sat back. It seemed a natural conclusion. Surely he'd received more than he could have
hoped for. I rose. He stood and bowed, and the young
man bowed. But then, just as they were about to go, I
made up my mind about something. "Tell Robert Young
he has nothing to fear from me. Tell him that. He has my
goodwill too." And then—one last detail—I held out his
passport to him.

He took it—using his left hand—and smiled. "You
used it, getting out of Taiwan?"

"We look a lot alike, Ushida-*san*."

As soon as they were gone, I called down to the bar.
Laurie picked up before the first ring had finished.
"Nick?"

"Uh-huh. Everything went okay. But I turned down a
lot of money . . . it always makes me anxious to be so
virtuous."

"You see, I should have been there."

"No, no. We did a lot of bonding, Ushida-*san* and me.
Give me ten minutes before you send up Cao. I want to
order tea."

"I don't know, he's champing at the bit."

"You're a girl in a bar. Entertain him."

I wanted a breather. But I thought Ushida had gone okay. I'd established relations, sketched a common future; no matter what happened, that couldn't hurt, not in this part of the world—the Rising Sun wasn't going to set anytime soon. I ordered the tea. They brought it; I set everything out a little fussily and then called down to Laurie.

Cao arrived by himself. This time, there was no long robe, but a light gray suit and a fedora in his hand. Yet he looked more the patriarch; he wasn't dressed up, this was him. No bows: he offered his hand at once. And since this was Hong Kong, we were speaking Cantonese. Very businesslike: he had taken over the business, that was clear. I was glad of the tea; it slowed things down a trifle. In comparison with Ushida, this was going to be a touch delicate.

I tried to indicate this at once.

"I asked you to come because of a difficult matter. It concerns our fathers, and our families. Both our families." Cao nodded, then he made a quick gesture with his hand—this was a man who had subordinates—telling me to go on. I said, "Your father, I think you know, wanted me to do something for him. He wished me to retrieve a great prize, which he had buried, documents and materials of great value as your family moved back to the mainland. He did not, I think, wish to involve or endanger members of his own family—and he knew he could trust me. But he wasn't able to give me that commission. I never spoke to him—because he was mur-

dered. He was murdered by his mistress, a Japanese girl
named . . . but her name doesn't make any difference,
especially because the murder was more complicated
than a crime of passion. If you'll permit me—it might be
better to put those details to one side."

"I'll respect your judgment about such details, Mr.
Lamp, but I'd prefer to reserve my own, at least for the
moment."

"Of course. In any case, through a peculiar set of circumstances, the Japanese girl was herself murdered and I
became briefly involved in the police investigation. At
the time, that upset me, but it actually proved to be fortu-
nate. Because I was shown a photograph the police had
taken from the apartment of the Japanese girl, a photograph she had almost certainly taken from your father. I
recognized it instantly—because my father had a copy of
the same photograph. In fact, he was in it."

"I know. It is a photograph of a group of people in
Jessfield Park in Shanghai. Taken in the 1930s."

"That's correct. It was taken at a time when your
father and mine were friends, I think friends in business,
but also as young men who . . . enjoyed life together?
You understand. This photograph, I was sure, was the
key to what your father wished me to do. I went to
Shanghai. I tried to discover its meaning. This led me to
uncover long-standing activities of your father connected
to the Americans, again details it might be better to set
aside—they are only details. I finally understood the
photograph. It marked a hiding place, and this is what I
discovered there."

I had everything in a Lane Crawford shopping bag. I pulled out my bits and pieces, one by one, and set them on the coffee table: the oilskin packet, the sealed can of film, the photographs, the envelope of documents. He picked up the photographs at once.

"This is my father," he said.

"Yes. The other man is my father. And the woman is Jiang Qing, eventually the wife of Mao Tse-tung."

"Yes, I see. She was an actress, wasn't she? Quite pretty . . . except her legs."

He inspected the photographs carefully, angling them to the light; and then he put them down in a neat pile on the table. "Those were incredible times, Mr. Lamp. Extraordinary times."

He couldn't have been more discreet. I nodded. "They were."

"And this . . . it's movie film? What's on it?"

"Your father financed films, possibly mine did as well. Accordingly, they knew many actresses, beautiful women. So I expect the film is just a more animated version of the stills. You'll have to be careful, though. That's old nitrate film—obviously someone has tried to preserve it, but it's probably not in good shape."

He hefted the can. "During the Cultural Revolution, people said that Jiang Qing was ransacking Shanghai, searching for embarrassing reminders of her past. These must have been high on the list. . . ."

"Yes. And the Chinese government would still find them valuable—anything that could discredit Jiang Qing, even Mao, would still be important to them."

He made no comment, though he certainly knew it was true. Presenting this material to the Chinese government could considerably ease the family's transition back to the mainland. He nodded at the envelope. "What about that?"

"That's different. I don't want to give it to you—it was in the packet, so I want you to know it was there, I wanted to show you everything, I wanted you to know I've held nothing back—but it concerns my father, not yours. That envelope contains the birth records and other documents of a child my father had with . . . one of the ladies."

"I see. But my father had it . . . for a reason I expect."

"Yes, of course. You know the circumstances of your father's visit to China in 1971?"

"Perhaps . . . but then some things are best forgotten."

"This would only be a reminder, then. And it has no direct connection to Cao Dai at all—but to my father, yes."

He sat still, and thought; his stillness and his thinking were, ever so slightly, uncanny, for they were absolutely unembarrassed, and his face betrayed absolutely nothing. He was just sitting very still, absorbed in himself, and I might not have been there at all. Perhaps he was being inscrutable, one of our Chinese traits so beloved by Round Eyes. But finally he said, "You have been exceptionally discreet, Mr. Lamp—in every way—and in this conversation. Several times you have passed over details, concentrating on essentials. But some details are essential. You've learned a great deal about my father's activities in China. They have a long history and a great potential for embarrassment. To a degree, as long as my father was alive, not a great deal could be done about this—he was susceptible to pressures. But I'm not. When he died, I sent my younger brother to China to see what could be done, and I think he might also have been looking for you. He was killed. Do you know anything about that?"

I looked him right in the eye. "No."

I watched his face.

He knew I was lying.

He looked at me long enough, and with exactly the expression in his eyes to leave no doubt that he knew exactly what had happened. But then he said, "It's all very regrettable, but I expect it will only become another mystery—all we have heard is that he was killed by a Westerner and perhaps that is what actually happened." He shrugged. I said nothing. If that was the fiction we were going to accept, he had to write it. He went on: "In any case, Mr. Nick Lamp, I'm still worried about that potential embarrassment."

I shook my head. "There's no reason to be. I can assure you of that. If you like, I can go even further. I have contacts in the defense department in Japan, their military intelligence, the Boeucho. What your father was doing, the remains of it, could be turned over to them. After that, everything would be their responsibility." And for Du Shan, I was sure, ignorance would be bliss.

He thought again, then gave a tight, quick smile. Was he satisfied? Had I bested him? No, it was just an acknowledgment of the world passing on. He said, "You've been very resourceful, Mr. Lamp. Resourceful, daring, intelligent, discreet. Those are great qualities. You've done a great deal for my family . . . not least, you have reminded us of an old family friendship. I hope you will not be offended if I wish to reward you."

"I only did what was necessary."

"Now let me thank you for doing it so well."

"But I expected no compensation."

"Of course, so now you must let me make you a gift."

I am Chinese. He was Chinese. It could have gone on all day. Desperately, I wanted to speak English. Finally I said, "Originally, I came to your father with a business proposition. I would like it to be given thoughtful consideration."

At once, Cao shook his head. "Oh no, that won't do, Mr. Lamp. I've already looked at your project, and of course we will do it—and I'm sure profit handsomely. That's almost a gift from you to me, and it's certainly not proper thanks to a man who has helped our family so much, who knows so many of our family secrets, whose relationship with us goes back so far. No—that is quite unacceptable."

Quite unacceptable . . . I looked at him. His voice had gone hard; now his face was hard. He too, in his way, was his father's son. And he was telling me that I knew too much, or, knowing so much, I must now be bound to his family in the most substantial way.

Well, I thought, he was probably right. He needed insurance. Those photos and that can of film would buy a lot of forgiveness with the Chinese, but I knew too much about his father, too much about the spying, too much about everything. He had to be absolutely certain of my loyalty. But for insurance, especially that kind of insurance, you have to pay a premium price. I looked at him as cool as I could and said, "Give me ten percent of your Shanghai project."

For just a second, his eyes went a trifle blank. I'd probably pitched it high—five percent was more likely the figure he'd had in mind. But having set it up like he had, what did he expect? His expression remained a little fixed, but he finally nodded. And then, after a bit of a struggle, he managed, "That's better. That is more in keeping with your efforts on my family's behalf." That's right, that was better, I'd been working for him all along, I was just one of the minions—overpaid, but everyone knew he had a generous heart. Still, having paid such a steep price, he wanted to be sure of value for money. "You will be marrying Mrs. Stadler's daughter?"

"Yes . . ." You hope.

"The young lady's mother is in San Diego, I think. You're curious, Mr. Lamp, a son of the Yellow Emperor, but you've led such a wandering life, your family's so scattered. Perhaps it would be simpler if everyone came to Taipei and you let me give your wedding. It would be a great honor."

"Sir, the honor would be ours, as you surely know."

He'd paid for that "sir," I thought, and my skillfully feigned humility. And I think he enjoyed it, even though he knew exactly how feigned it was. In any case, he had

turned the tables on me, ever so slightly. This was Asia.
Whether you're white or yellow, all relationships—
of love, passion, friendship, interest—are strategic alliances. They begin at birth, those alliances you can't
avoid: with your ancestors, whom we worship and ceaselessly placate, and with our families, whose loyalty and
interest become everything. And marriage is part of it
too. Which is why the "oppressed" women of countries
like Pakistan, India, Sri Lanka, and even China have produced great national leaders long before the "liberated"
West. Sirimavo Bandaranaike was wife to her husband,
Benazir Bhutto was her father's daughter, even Jiang
Qing was ... whatever she was. Cao Feng wasn't so
much reminding me of the color of my skin as the world
I was living in—and now he drove it home. "If it is an
honor, it would please me to have you accept it, Lam
Yau-kan."

I didn't exactly drop off my chair, but it was interesting. It's not the name on my passport, it's a name I
never use, even with Chinese people—sometimes,
maybe, with my mother. But he'd found it out. A neat
way of telling me I was joining quite a family. And he'd
waited a long time to become head of it; it was a part he
clearly relished playing. As I loaded his Lane Crawford bag with all his new goodies, he was beaming. We
shook hands. And, beginning to laugh and joke a little—
wasn't he almost my father-in-law?—I walked him to the
elevator.

Five minutes later, I headed downstairs.

Laurie was in the bar.

I suppose I was wearing a pretty big grin. She began laughing as soon as she saw me. "What *did* you do?"

"Do you want it in yen, Hong Kong dollars, or green-backs?"

"Yen. It's always the most exciting."

Besides, it's how we count our money in this part of the world. I worked it out, very roughly, and whispered a figure, very low.

"Sweet Jesus," she said.

"Let's go outside. . . . It'll be okay in the sun."

They had a deck; you could see the city and the harbor, even hear the piping whistle of a ferry, though, up this high, you missed the smell of it all—the gasoline, the people, the perfume of the money.

"You've got a nerve," she said.

"I do."

"Something else you get from your father? I just hope you're not that *bad*."

"Oh, I don't know," I said. She was looking at two of the photographs I had discreetly slipped into the envelope along with my half sister's birth documents—I'm not quite as honest as I look. "They were chorus girls starlets, bimbos I guess we'd say now . . . my father was a rich playboy. That's the way it was."

"Except he got her pregnant. Jiang Qing. Mao's future wife."

"But he looked after the baby. . . . Give him that much credit. I wonder, does that make Madame Mao closer to being my stepmother or my aunt?"

"I think it's very Chinese of you even to wonder." She

looked at me. "I do have it right now—Jiang Qing, later
to marry Mao, got pregnant by your father, gave up her
baby to that other woman, the mother of your film
buff. . . ."

"Jin Shi. Who named her Yunnan, and brought her up.
I expect my father arranged all that, or Maclean. Or even
Cao."

"Both of whom—*all of whom*—were playing around
with these actress ladies, share and share alike. But then
one of the ladies became very famous and was afraid it
was all going to come back to haunt her . . . Chairman
Mao's wife in dirty pictures."

"Not just that. It was the relationship itself, that close a
connection to a man like my father. I think she later pre-
tended that at least part of her pregnancy was spent in a
Nationalist jail cell, because that might have been prefer-
able to the truth. My father was KMT of course—anyone
with money was—but he was worse, he was a com-
prador, he was one of those Chinese who did business
with the Round Eyes, profited from them, spoke their
language, had their manners. . . . It's crazy. He represented, in fact, what everyone claimed they wanted, a
modern China. But they couldn't accept that a modern
China had to be, in many ways, a Western China, not like
the old China at all. The attempt to be modern without
being Western almost drove them out of their minds.
Like Islamic Fundamentalism. That's what Maoism
was, and the Cultural Revolution. Jiang Qing was the
ayatollah."

Laurie turned my father's naked countenance firmly over. "What will you tell your mother?"

"Everything of course. She'll be fascinated."

"Nick, you'll hurt her feelings."

"Oh, no. It all happened before she met him. Besides, this woman—Yunnan—in effect becomes a daughter. I'm sure Mother will have the poor woman in Vancouver by the end of the month." I smiled. "You do understand—you're going to have to meet this lady—my mother, that is?"

"What do you mean by *that*?"

"You know perfectly well what I mean. There's no getting around it. There's no escape. It's time. I am now going to pop the question."

"You don't have the guts."

"Will you marry me?"

There was now a pause. She sat back in her chair ever so slightly, and her face assumed an expression which was certainly aloof—indeed, for an American, almost regal. She said, "We have to get a few things straight."

"Of course."

"Well, first . . . I'm an American, but I don't think I can live there. Not all the time, anyway. I've been too long out here. This is my world. This is where I want to be. At the same time, I have to go back there sometimes, just to hear the voices. So it has to be like that for me. Back and forth."

"No problem. Back and forth. And around. Lots of around, too, for me."

"Second, I like to be comfortable, but I don't like

things. I like money so I don't have to think about money. You know? I mean, I want to live well but I don't really want to be rich."

"I can make money. You can give it away."

"All right. Remember that. Also ... you're very strong. You're tough. And I don't like bullies—"

"I'm not a bully."

"Okay, but I don't like them anyway. I don't like fascists, I don't like feminists, I don't like fundamentalists."

"No question."

Her face was looking funny. I was pretty sure she was about to cry. She said, "And I don't want you fucking other women."

"Absolutely. Look, you're just putting off the evil moment. Or are you relishing your last wretched seconds of freedom?"

She looked at me, and then she began to smile and cry at the same time, "Don't be an idiot, I knew I wanted to marry you five minutes after I met you, and you damn well will."

With her sort of girl, you're unlikely to get any better answer, and I wasn't going to quibble. I went around and kissed her, kissed her again, then gave her my handkerchief. I watched her. It was quite something. She had to blow her nose.

I said, "I'm very happy."

"So am I."

She looked away, her hand trying to hold her chin firm. I didn't say anything, but followed her eyes, down to the harbor, Kowloonside, beyond. Then, as she seemed to settle down, I let myself look at her face. I was very sure of her, after all my doubts, and I knew she was far better than I deserved. All at once, I smiled to myself. She hadn't mentioned children, and I wondered what she thought about that . . . but of course she was already miles ahead of me. She shook a cigarette out of her pack, but said, "You know, this is going to be my last one."

"All right."

She lit it. She said, "I know everything's going to change, and I want that, but right now I want to be the person I am, the person I've been right up to this moment."

I thought I understood what she meant, and didn't say anything, letting her keep her thoughts to herself as she looked down at this ancient world that was changing so rapidly too. And I had my own thoughts to think. I thought of my brothers and my sister, and what this might mean to them, and how I should tell them. And I thought of my father, wishing he could know what had happened, that the family was back in Shanghai, making money again. . . . The yellow Shell boat was still puttering around, the ferries were running, and overhead Air France was circling. . . . Laurie stubbed out her cigarette.

"It's getting cold," I said, "we should get going."

"Where to?"

I gave her a look. "How about home?"

For just a second, her eyes looked very quizzical and then they crinkled up with happiness as she laughed, that clear direct laugh of a happy American girl. And I thought of Father again. He was right; don't marry a girl unless she laughs at your jokes.

"Robert...Robert, thank God it's you."

"I'm sorry. I only got back this minute. Western Union just called."

"I've been phoning you....I phoned every other day last week. I sent another telegram Wednesday—"

"I was in New York. What's the matter?"

She took a breath. "I'm sorry—I'm all right. It's my father. He's disappeared....I know it sounds insane, but he's vanished. He just went off—no one's seen him."

I'd never met her father, but I knew he was important to her. In fact, I'd sometimes suspected that her refusing me had some connection with him, for her change of mind had taken place after she'd flown up to Toronto to see him—to tell him the happy news, as I'd thought at the time.

"When did this happen?"

"Ten days ago. A week ago Saturday."

"You've told the police?"

"Yes. They...they were worried he might have been kidnapped, but there hasn't been a ransom note and now they say he's just gone off on his own and will turn up when he feels like it."

"Well...they're probably right. It's upsetting—"

"*No*. They're not right. He'd never go off without telling me."

338

Her voice had exploded with anger—the intensity of it was startling—but then she caught herself and added, "Robert, I'm sorry to trouble you with this—"

"No, no. Of course not."

"Maybe I shouldn't have called."

"Of course you should have called. I'm just trying to think. What can I do?"

She hesitated. "There's one thing. I'm afraid—I'm afraid he's killed himself. I know all the reasons why you'll say he hasn't—the police have already given them to me—but I'm still afraid...."

Suicide. On this day, of all days, it wasn't a question I could easily dismiss. "Why do you think that?"

"I'd rather not say. Not on the phone."

"But you do have a reason? Something specific?"

"Yes."

"Have you told the police about it?"

"They don't think it means anything. That's why I called you. I need someone who can find things out for me. Someone who knows how to ask questions..."

"May, I'm not a policeman. I want—"

"But you're a journalist, Robert. You can get things out of bureaucrats."

I paused. Once upon a time I'd been a journalist, but I'm not any longer. And I hate getting things out of bureaucrats. "What sort of things?"

"It's personal. I'd rather not say. Not till you get here."

"So you want me to come to Toronto?"

"Yes. I know you must be busy...but it won't take very long. I'm sure it won't take very long."

She was right; I was busy. The past two weeks had been a holiday, more or less, and I was anxious to get back to work. She said, "And of course I'll pay your way—you—"

"Don't be silly." I thought for a moment longer, but

there really wasn't much choice. She was clearly upset and even if I couldn't help her—and I wasn't certain I couldn't—I could at least hold her hand till her father showed up. "You're sure you can't tell me anything more?"

I heard her sigh. "You know I'm adopted?"

"Yes. I remember."

Remember: I could sense her falter as I said the word, as if she was uncertain about how much she could rely on the past we hadn't quite shared. But then she went on, "It has something to do with that. That's what I'd want you to find out about."

"All right."

"You'll come?"

"Of course. I can probably be there tomorrow."

A breath, all relief, fluttered down the line. "Thank you, Robert. Bless you. I'll meet you at the airport."

"No, no. That'll only get complicated. Just give me your address and I'll try to make it by early afternoon. And you try to relax."

So she told me where she lived, we said goodbye and hung up...and right away I knew something was wrong.

It was an odd sensation. Strong. Definite. And yet unaccountable. For a moment, I thought it was the call itself—a strange summons, under strange circumstances: fears about the suicide of a father on precisely *this* day. And given our past connection, any conversation was bound to be awkward.

But such feelings could hardly be the cause of the intense unease that now swept across me. May's request, by any standards, had been unusual, and if I'd had the faintest idea of where it was going to take me, I would have felt foreboding. But in fact that wasn't at all what I felt. It was a more particular sensation—as if I was being watched, as if someone else was with me in the house...and then—thinking this—I knew what it was.

340

On the phone, May had said she'd sent me two telegrams: the one I'd received today, but another last Wednesday when I'd been in New York. It hadn't been in my mail, I was certain, and now I checked again to be sure. It wasn't. Carefully I played my arrival back through my mind. As I'd come in, I had a bag of groceries in each hand. To work the lock, I balanced one on my knee. And then I'd kicked the door shut behind me and gone straight through to the kitchen. From there—the sequence was perfectly clear—I'd carried my coffee into the living room, tidied up for a moment, and slumped down on the sofa. *And that's when I'd discovered my mail:* a great pile, two weeks' worth, scattered all over the coffee table...instead of lying in the hall, under the mail slot, where it ought to have been.

THE RED FOX
by Anthony Hyde
Published by Ballantine Books.
Available in your local bookstore.

By

ANTHONY HYDE

Published by Ballantine Books.